PUFFIN BOOKS

The Tiggie Tompson Show

Tessa Duder began to write for young people when the youngest of her four daughters went to school. Seven novels, including *Night Race to Kawau*, *Jellybean*, *Mercury Beach* and the four award-winning books of the *Alex* quartet, have established her as one of New Zealand's leading writers.

She has also written short stories, plays, non-fiction books and educational readers, and was script consultant for the feature film *Alex*. In recent years she has also revived an interest in acting, including a guest spot on 'Shortland Street' in 1997.

Three times winner of the Children's Book of the Year award and Esther Glen medal, Tessa has won several Arts Council writing bursaries and was the University of Waikato's first Writer-in-residence in 1991. She visits schools all over New Zealand under the Writers in Schools scheme and has been a featured speaker at literary and educational conferences in New Zealand and overseas.

Tessa Duder was the 1996 recipient of the Margaret Mahy award given by the New Zealand Children's Book Foundation.

Also by Tessa Duder

THE
TIGGIE TOMPSON
SHOW

Tessa Duder

PUFFIN BOOKS

PUFFIN BOOKS

Penguin Books (NZ) Ltd, cnr Rosedale and Airborne Roads, Albany,
Auckland 1310, New Zealand
Penguin Books Ltd, 27 Wrights Lane, London W8 5TZ, England
Penguin USA, 375 Hudson Street, New York, NY 10014, United States
Penguin Books Australia Ltd, 487 Maroondah Highway, Ringwood, Australia 3134
Penguin Books Canada Ltd, 10 Alcorn Avenue, Toronto, Ontario, Canada M4V 3B2
Penguin Books (South Africa) Pty Ltd, 4 Pallinghurst Road, Parktown,
Johannesburg 2193, South Africa

Penguin Books Ltd, Registered Offices: Harmondsworth, Middlesex, England

First published by Puffin Books (NZ) Ltd, 1999
10 9 8 7 6 5 4 3 2 1

Copyright (c) Tessa Duder, 1999

Designed by Mary Egan
Typeset by Egan-Reid Ltd

Printed in Australia by Australian Print Group, Maryborough

Acknowledgements

Thanks are due to Creative New Zealand for their assistance of a Writing Grant, and to editor Bernice Beachman, Shirley Duke and Tro Rowarth for their considerable and invaluable help.

The author also wishes to thank Peggy Claude-Pierre for her acclaimed book *The Secret Language of Eating Disorders*, Susie Orbach for her 1978 classic *Fat is a feminist issue*, and the thousands of unknown young women whose heart-breaking stories are available to anyone searching 'eating disorders' on the Internet.

One

'Last but certainly not least . . .' says the teacher, giving me my cue. The late-morning sun is beginning to bite at my cheeks. That's my sweat I can smell. Surely she will rescue me?

'I'm . . . um . . . Tiggie.' And when the silence becomes unbearable, I sigh and straighten my back. 'It's short for Antigone.'

'Can you speak up, dear?'

'Antigone. I get called Tiggie. I'm fourteen. We've just moved here.'

Again there's silence, except for the constant traffic out on the road and an embarrassed shuffling around on the prickly grass. Everyone else has mentioned brothers, sisters, pets, dads, hobbies, achievements. I see eyes rolling sideways to take in a neighbour's glance – who's *this*?

Some of the girls are studiously cleaning their nails, the boys doing exercises to stretch their hamstrings, all bored to death.

'Are you related to Cassandra Tompson, by any chance?' asks the teacher, checking her list. It's not only teenagers who go silly about my connection with the glamorous person who's my mum. 'Tompson without the "h". It's a most unusual spelling.'

I've had to listen to the good talkers and the clever dicks and hated their easy confidence; I've shoved them all (in my mind) around a little. Right at this minute, with Mrs Tariq, her silver earrings swinging like wind chimes, her lime-green Pakistani outfit and her perfect singing English, I would gladly go all the way. Boiling oil, bolt of lightning, an earthquake or a circular saw. Seriously denying your own mother in public is a pretty hard call but I try yet again.

'I'm here as me. Just me.'

'She *is* related,' accuses a voice from across the circle. 'I know someone from her last school, and Cassandra Tompson is her mother.'

I glare at the girl, thin as a stick of fettuccini. She's already told the group that to be a champion rhythmic gymnast, she trains four hours a day.

Why do people like her talk about me as though I'm not here, like I'm a loony?

'Do you mean the one on "60 Minutes"?' adds a toughie with braids who'd said that she does karate and her father's in jail.

Well, you wanted a really different sort of school, Tiggie, and you've got it. This is a school of the global village. Around this circle of thirty-seven are South Africans, Bosnians, mainland Chinese, Korean, Thai, Canadian, Maori, Tongan, Aussie, half-Turkish, English and Pakeha. Because Eastern College has its home rooms arranged by vertical grouping, we're all ages from thirteen to nineteen.

'Must be exciting, mum who's a big TV star,' says the Canadian, a cool customer.

Oh yeah, it's exciting. Go into a post office with her and everyone stares. You can't go anywhere without people nudging each other. They barge up asking for autographs. I hate it.

I mumble, 'It's okay.'

'Do you go to the TV place?' Female, Maori, gorgeous, a junior rep netballer whose dream is to be a Silver Fern. 'Watch her filming and that?'

'No.'

'I think she's getting a bit old for the job,' says a male voice. I look up from examining the withered blades of grass and find the smooth smile of the boy directly opposite who earlier informed us he wanted to be a film actor. He looks like New Zealand's answer to Brad Pitt. 'Has she had a face-lift?'

'No she hasn't, course not!' I burst out. Fool! I shouldn't have even answered that. And Brad Pitt, when you're thirty-nine like Mum and worrying you're getting wrinkles and too old for television, remember you said that.

'I have a very great admiration for your mother,' says Mrs Tariq hastily. She throws the long filmy loop of scarf back over her shoulders for about the two hundredth irritating time. 'She's very, very good at what she does, a most excellent interviewer.'

'Thank you,' I say politely. Why doesn't the bloody bell ring? But Mrs Tariq is not finished yet.

'Antigone is absolutely correct, class, to insist that she herself is here at this school in her own right and on her own terms. Her mother is just doing her job.'

'She lets politicians and bosses off the hook, every time,' says the actor. 'I watch her. Pulls her punches.'

Don't rise to it, Tiggie, don't answer.

'She never asks the really hard questions. The guys on that show are better. They make the tough calls.'

'It's all prerecorded,' I say. Don't you know, sonny, about producers? Directors? Editors? Mum has no control at all over what goes to air. She's just the person who asks the questions and looks good. Then she gets the blame.

'Television has become a very structured, very controlled medium,' says Mrs Tariq. 'The advertisers exert a great deal of pressure . . .'

The bell goes for lunch. At my old school we had to wait at least until the teacher had stopped talking before we even moved. Here, people pick up their bags and are off and away across the dried-out grass at the speed of light without even a nod in the teacher's direction. Mrs Tariq gives me an uncertain smile as she stands, adjusts her lime-green scarf and heads off for the staff room. Down her back are the two ends of scarf and an impossibly thick plait, for such a tiny woman, of heavy black hair.

I stay sitting for a while, alone, wondering about the thirty-seven enemies I've just undoubtedly made. I asked, bargained and fought for this. I knew the first week would be hideous, but after that, surely I can get lost in the crowd?

I go back into the nearest building trying to find a toilet.

* * *

The corridors are long, dark, scruffy, and panelled in cheap wood. They all look exactly the same, leading everywhere and nowhere at once.

Why aren't there any signs? Where's the front office gone, the main entrance? Where's the main road? The situation is becoming desperate when I hear, as I walk past a group of grinning boys, a whispering chant:

Who ate the pies?
Who ate the pies?
She did, she did,
She ate the pies.

And when I do find a toilet, it's locked.

Who in their right mind locks a toilet in a school? Or the nearby outside door, also locked? What happens when girls get floods or one of the sneaky smokers starts a fire or they have one of their famous bomb scares?

I have to go back past them. They're all in their basketball gear — relaxed, laughing and infuriatingly smug as only boys who've just been doing sport can be. They are singing again, soft and sneaky:

Who ate the pies . . .

How do I get out of here? Before anyone points, or laughs, or sings, or talks about my mother again.

It's the story of my life, really.

Two

There, at my old school, I was Tiggie — the dumpy girl who got pneumonia after a school camp and caused all sorts of grief.

At Eastern College on day one I am already tagged the Pie Girl.

Where to from here?

You know, no one chooses to get pneumonia. I didn't say to myself, right, now what's the best revenge on classmates who swiped all my clothes out of the shower and made me walk down a bush track stark naked and freezing my tits off in the middle of winter. Hey, let's get pneu-mon-ia! Stand clear — Girl Power at work! Let's develop a fever and a nagging cough. Let's continue with the bush walks and the games (though I absolutely drew the line at the last-night concert) and continue to take lots of photographs as the unofficial camp photographer even though I could hardly hold the camera still.

Let's arrive home on Friday afternoon looking so awful, with the shakes and such glittering eyes and hacking cough, that Mum cancels an important appointment and marches me straight off to the emergency doctor.

Oh wow, it's pneumonia! Oh dear me, says the doc during a long listen with his stethoscope to the weird workings of my lungs. Consolidation in the right lower lobe! Herpes around the lower lip! Bedrest and antibiotics! Ointment for the cold sores. X-ray, plenty of water, light meals! Two weeks off school!

Anyone for a guilt trip?

They knew, of course, that I would never tell, and I didn't. But gradually, when they heard I'd gone down with nothing less than pneumonia, out it came. Just one with a slightly guilty conscience must have told her mother or an older sister. I can just imagine the sincere, regretful tears and the mothers ringing round each other on the phone. Poor Tiggie – what a terrible thing. How *cruel* girls can be. Of course *my* daughter wasn't involved.

Like hell. They were all in it, up to their size ten armpits.

Inquiries were made. My parents were summoned. Girls were interviewed, but not me. I refused all requests to be interviewed or put anything in writing. I refused to talk about it at home or at school. I neither confirmed nor denied. They got nothing out of me.

I got better. Some other scandal was talked about. I went back to school, to finish the year. Somehow I was made to feel that the fuss about the camp was all my fault. Excuse me for breathing. I left without telling anyone I was going. At prize-giving I won no prizes or certificates for excellence or even for endeavour.

Something positive did come out of it, though. First, I did lose four kilos even if I put it all back on over Christmas. Second, it was the lethal weapon I needed to persuade my parents I had to leave that school or die. It wasn't, however, without a fight.

'You'll be fifteen thousand dollars a year richer,' I said desperately, an hour after I first told them.

Here I was, a student at Auckland's most prestigious fee-paying school, where you've got to have the right address and rich parents and a certain number of brains even to get an interview. Then you do a written test and finally, if you're lucky, you get offered a place.

I was quite cute, a bright little five-year-old when I was interviewed and tested and offered a place. What a disappointment little Antigone Tompson has been since then!

But celebrity Mum compensated for dumpy boring daughter. They were always asking Cassandra Tompson to present the prizes at prize-giving or come to black-tie fund-raising dinners, or take part in a debate. Mum did them for free, even though she gets a thousand dollars a night for speaking at corporate dinners. Dad went along for the ride and got out his gold credit card every now and again. They said it was their way of supporting the school.

We'd already been over the many advantages of staying on there. I would make influential, life-long friends. The school had gifted staff, rooms full of computers. Huge grounds, lovely buildings, rose beds. A wonderful music and drama department. Great productions. It had national champions galore – in debating, problem-solving and chess, as well as netball, hockey, water polo, sailing, rowing, skiing, and orienteering.

'What does any of that mean to me?' I asked acidly.

I was told to think carefully about the dubious reputation of the school I was proposing to go to. Poor pass rates, high ethnic mix, undoubtedly drugs.

There were no grounds as such, few trees and no roses. And you only had to look at the students as they surged in and out of the school twice daily! They openly smoked and swung their backpacks at each other. They jammed up the footpaths, the buses and the traffic. A scruffy lot, in the main, except for some of the Asians, who drove in and out in their brand-new uniforms and smart cars, always managing to upset at least one bus driver.

'If I go there,' I said, 'I won't need to catch a bus. I can walk. Exercise.'

'A twenty-minute bus ride,' said Dad, sipping his gin, 'is a small price to pay for a decent school.'

'Think of the *money*,' I said again. 'We can go to Disneyland again. Another gold chain for Mum.'

'The money's not the issue,' Dad said.

'You think because you pay mega-bucks for something, it's got to be better. I don't believe that. I've got no friends there . . .'

'Some friends came to see you only yesterday!' said Mum brightly. She drinks triple Pernod on the rocks and was onto her third.

Oh, Mum, grow up! If she was exasperated with this conversation, so was I. And I was only drinking orange juice. I said, 'They'd just driven up from Whitford and wanted somewhere close to change.'

'Are you sure you're . . .'

'Let's go to Tiggie's famous mum's highrise with the fantastic view. All with their little flat tummies and straw hats and German sunglasses. They didn't give a flying fuck about seeing me.'

'Unnecessarily crude, and harsh,' said Dad.

'It's *true*. And when we went down on the beach, they couldn't get far enough away.'

'Tiggie, they're your *friends*,' said Mum, looking at her watch.

'And you've got a short memory. Those girls have got all the answers including how to get honours in grade six violin and stay size eight for ever, or eight and a half on a bad day.'

'Dawn French and Roseanne . . .' said Mum, holding out her glass to Dad to refill.

'Bad choices, Mum. They made a career of it. Just like the Spice Girls made a career of being size eight bimbos.'

Dad got up and deliberately filled Mum's glass with plain soda water. She took it, sighing.

'Genes come into this,' said Mum. 'Your dear departed grandmother, Dad's mother . . .'

'That is irrelevant,' said Dad, who'd not spoken to his parents since he lost all their money in the stock-market crash when I was one. Even so, he wasn't going to have Mum blame his mum for my shape. 'We're talking about something far more important . . .'

'Nothing's more important when you are fat. Of course, you wouldn't know, either of you. There's no pool at Eastern College.'

'What's that got to do with it?' said Dad, puzzled and irritated.

Let's see. Swimming togs? Why did I untruthfully plead my period yesterday and sit on the beach dying of heat while my smart friends frolicked in the water? If my parents can't work that out, they're stupider than I thought.

All three of us looked at each other, exhausted by arguing.

'Twenty thousand,' I said, 'if you include all the books and uniforms. Trips to Germany if I start German, a new laptop every year, a designer dress for the school ball . . .'

'Tiggie,' said Dad angrily, picking up the television remote, 'enough!

I can't take any more of this crap.'

'It's status, isn't it?' I can't stop myself now. 'Celebrities can't just let their dumpy daughter take her chances in the local school . . .'

'Unfair to accuse me of snobbery, Tiggie,' said Mum, genuinely hurt.

I played my last, so far hidden, card. 'I got pneumonia, remember. I don't want to see any of them ever again.'

They hate to be reminded of my pneumonia.

Dad eventually breaks the silence. 'Your mother wants to watch the news.'

I look at my parents. On the apricot leather couch, the celebrity relaxing in designer tights and white linen shirt, slightly pissed. Just as slim and beautiful as when she first needed to work after Dad lost all his money and his job. Then he had a bad car accident which his horrible old mother (according to Mum) relished saying was really a failed suicide attempt. Couldn't even get that right.

Mum's never slow, when she's interviewed herself, to remind the world she knows what it's like to look after an injured husband in bed for months and be so poor that you can't take your toddler to the doctor and have to sell things to buy groceries. Even though her picture's up there on the '60 Minutes' billboards all round the city, she's been there, done that. Is that why she's such a good, tough reporter? Probably, says Cassandra Tompson.

I suppose that's the reason she wants the 'best' school for me.

But as a workaholic she's the reason we're not on holiday now, like everyone else in the first week of January. The year coming up to the Millennium. Yawn. Yacht races and parades and Maori cultural events and fireworks and people getting drunk in the sun.

And sipping his gin next to her, supportive and handsome husband Murray who works partly from home as a consultant and earns more than he ever did before the crash. I don't know what he consults. He has contracts, something financial with big corporations.

They will talk about it in bed, later, but I think I've won.

This is the third great life-changing decision I've made.

'Dad and I have been talking,' said Mum. She was doing a black coffee breakfast in her power suit, ready to dash. Dad had already gone, an hour at the gym before work. 'Muesli?'

'Yes, please.' I had the choice of Mr Hubbard's toasted or untoasted, orange and lemon flavoured or berry flavoured, with lite yoghurt. Mum wasn't the sort of mother who set pretty breakfast tables. I clattered open the cutlery drawer.

'It could be argued that one of the disadvantages of your school is that you're all female, pretty much white, and from the same socio-economic grouping.'

She meant filthy rich as opposed to downtrodden poor, but journalists on TV these days have to say *elitist* and *underprivileged*.

'Yep.'

'There's a lot of emphasis on how you look. Clothes, hair.'

'Sure is.' I noticed she didn't say figure.

'Nevertheless, Tiggie, it's a great school. It has pride, tradition, and the best pass rates in the country. Middle of the middle class is no bad place to be.'

I shrugged.

'Your teachers care very much, you know. They want every pupil to achieve, according to their abilities.'

'So they say.' What abilities? They never found what mine were.

She suddenly looked a bit sad. 'Haven't you been happy?'

Where could I start? Always last to be picked for teams. My costume the last to be made for the nativity play, when they'd run out of material? The camp.

'You won't find it easy, Tiggie. There'll be distractions – tough, unruly boys demanding the teacher's attention.'

'I know that.'

'They say Eastern College is great for motivated students, not so good for those who don't want to work or come from homes where they get absolutely no support. You might get lost in the crowd.'

Didn't she know by now, that was exactly what I wanted?

THREE

SO HERE I AM ON MY VERY FIRST DAY AT EASTERN COLLEGE, THE PIE GIRL in her horrible new blue uniform, running away down a slippery endless corridor looking for a loo. Under less desperate circumstances I would ask directions from another girl about my age, or failing that an older girl or a female teacher, a male teacher, a younger male student, or as a last resort, an older male student.

Now, I don't care. The very real prospect of the Pie Girl dumping in her pants on the first day at school has removed all shame.

I whizz, slide, skid around another sharp corner.

'Excuse me,' I say to the first human being I see. 'I want a girls' loo. The nearest girls' loo.'

'It's miles away, but you're in luck. Come with me. I just happen to have the keys.'

It could be a very young teacher or an older male student. He's carrying a huge untidy bunch of keys and shouldering a heavy burden of what looks like video gear. 'If you're new,' he says unlocking a nearby door, 'then you need to know this is the drama and video production suite. The House of Pain. There's a loo in here.'

The drama suite. This was a place at my old school I had always deliberately avoided. First, because kindly English and drama teachers assumed that because her mother was a 'performer', then jolly Tiggie had to be, too. Second, only size eights went in there, as normally screwed-up females. They came out moodier than ever, talking loudly because they were ac-tors and therefore superior to everybody. They had scary fun 'finding their inner truth'. They did improvisation and sexy physical exercises, with lots of shouting and rolling round the floor. They took risks. I would have given anything to take a risk or two myself, but the risk felt like open-heart surgery without an anaesthetic and the drama suite at that school was no place for me.

Except that, my urgent visit to the loo accomplished in the nick of time, I am now inside a drama and video production suite with a strange male. There's no sign of him so I will tiptoe quietly out of this big carpeted area. There's no need to fuss around with thanks.

Then my training in niceness kicks in. Boy, am I well trained! A door to a small office is open and a light is on inside. I poke my head in.

'Um – thanks.'

'How good are your eyes?'

'What?'

'Sophia swore the book was on these shelves. I love her dearly, and she's a great and creative director but Jesus, this office is something else. Can you see something called *Directing for Community Theatre* in this mess?'

I decide he's definitely an older male student and begin looking in shelves crammed with torn photocopied playscripts, books on acting, old books of plays, magazines, boxes of photos and yellowed newspaper clippings. There's no order at all, just a horrible clutter and dust which looks as though it's been there for ever.

'What's community theatre?' I ask.

'It's what I've just been told I'm going to be co-directing. With Sophia. At the end of term three.'

I can feel a sneeze coming on.

'You use whatever resources are available. Dance, song, music, poetry, mime, puppets, stilt walkers, physical theatre, you name it.'

'Sounds fun.' *A-tish-shoo!* 'The dust.'

'Sorry about that. Do you get hay fever?'

'No. What do you do for a script?'

'We write it. It's multimedia, multicultural, multitalent, multi-everything. Shit, I'm almost beginning to convince myself it's a good idea. Are you into drama?'

18

I look at him sideways to check if he's taking the piss, but he's squinting at the titles on an upper shelf.

'Um – no.'

'New here?'

'Yep.'

'Hating it?'

'Yep.' And then I can't help myself. 'How can *anyone* operate in this *shambles*? Is that what you want?' I hold out the book, which has been there, right in front of our noses, all the time.

I am rewarded by a smile of pure, heart-warming gold. He has one of those mouths which is quite stern and thin until it smiles and then the ends tip up like a pixie and you're instantly knocked off your perch.

'Champion! Name of . . .?'

'Tiggie. Short for Antigone. Year Nine.'

'I'm Gareth. Twelve.' He holds out his hand and we shake formally. I've registered the smile, now I register the brown eyes, the black ponytail, the plain black T-shirt, black jeans and bare feet. He could be part-something – Samoan, Italian, West Indian, even Asian – or maybe he's just got global exotic good looks. Whatever, he's a knockout. So Year Twelves can wear mufti. Amongst the theatrical clutter of this tiny office I suddenly feel very pathetic and schoolgirlish. My old school uniform had been a designer label, costing megabucks. It looked great on all those up to size 12. What I'm wearing now looks ghastly on absolutely everyone – a drab blue check skirt, white polyester shirt (not tucked in), roman sandals and, because I forgot the deodorant this morning and it's been a long, hot day, I'm stinking.

Time to go, Tiggie.

'You don't like messes,' he smiles.

'No.'

'And you're not into drama?'

'Nope.'

'What about the production side? If you don't like mess, you might have good organisational skills. I'm going to need those. Interested?'

When every bone in my body wants to say *Thank you!* for even thinking of me and Y*es! I'd love to help*, I mumble instead as I always do, 'I . . . sorry, don't think so.'

'Ah well,' he says, indicating we are leaving, 'if you change your mind . . . no, wait!' He's staring at the pile of video gear he's dropped in the middle of the carpeted space. 'Tiggie, there's something you can do for me. Could you stay ten minutes?'

I hear myself saying okay, and I feel myself going hot and cold when he says what he wants is to test drive a video camera that is supposed to have been fixed over the holidays. He could just shoot some solid object like say, that upright piano, but a real body's better, to check close-up focus and sound.

Just sit over there by the window, and perhaps just sight-read something out of a book. Would I mind? He could go and get one of the drama people, but frankly, that means the whole lunchtime gone and he has a double maths lesson with a new teacher straight after lunch.

How could I refuse? Perched on a stool, watching him setting up the tripod and the camera, his unhurried, deliberate, absolutely controlled way of moving around, I couldn't believe I was doing this.

I've had practically no pictures of me taken, of any kind, for over three years.

Here's me aged eleven at a birthday party. It's a very expensive little party in a very expensive mansion. There's a medieval fairy storyteller with glitter on her face, and an ancient old man magician also wearing make-up who slices right through someone's wrist with a little guillotine thing and there's no blood. There's smart food brought in by a caterer, and endless drinks like V and Blue Jeans.

But the food is good.

Then it's time for photos and the birthday girl's mama wants the twenty of us grouped for posterity. She's waving round one of the newest digital cameras bought, of course, in Hong Kong.

I may be only eleven but I know my place in life and it's not in the front row of this photo with all the others in their Double Bay designer gear and skinny as rakes. I sidle towards the door but the camera operator is too quick for me. 'Tiggie?' she shrieks. 'Tiggie! Photo time, dear. Come along.'

She's about to say where to go, but I'm too quick for her. I head straight for the back of the group and slot my head, the only bit of me now visible, in between two others. We smirk at each other, grateful birthday girl's mama and me, sharing our little secret. Everything about this house is perfection. She is perfection; the children are perfection; the enlarged photo of her little girl's birthday to go silver-framed on the wall will be perfection, and she doesn't want me buggering it up.

'Big smiles now! Say cheese!'

'Sex,' we all say, and giggle.

At that moment, unsmiling and ungiggling, I decide that in future I'll be the one who makes the images, the one who clicks the shutter, who's behind the camera. I'll not be in front of it, no way.

I get a camera for my own birthday. I take it everywhere, as an almost foolproof device. I take pictures all the time, rolls and rolls of them, and have reprints done at a dollar a time for people who say thanks Tiggie but never offer to pay. When there's a group photo to be taken it's jolly Tiggie who's up there with the professionals, talking lenses, or Tiggie who offers first and loudest to work her way through a pile of everyone's cute little point-and-shoot cameras. No one else offers. I won't be in their pictures and they won't even notice.

Someone famous once said, 'I am a camera.' Was it that girl Sally from the film of *Cabaret*?

I'm not a camera – I'm the operator. I compose the picture and I push the button, in charge here if nowhere else.

That was the second great life-changing decision I made.

So what the hell am I doing perched here on a stool, breaking all my rules, while this tall gentle skinny person in black, whom I've never seen until ten minutes ago, trains a video camera on me?

He is, though, looking at something else.

Outside the window, in a small enclosed courtyard, a boy is being bullied. At least I suppose that's what is happening. I'm new to this scene. Girls do it under hedges and behind trees and in secretive little groups.

It's a dumpy little Asian boy with spiky hair and round glasses, probably a Year Eight, who's being used for target practice. Apples, clumps of earth, small stones, empty tinnies, a dart.

'Excuse me,' Gareth says. 'Back in a minute.'

Then he's out into the blazing midday sun and has yanked the Asian boy to his feet. His uniform shirt is so crisply new it still has square crease marks across it. Gareth picks up the dart, eyeballs the leader, puts the dart in his pocket, takes the second dart from an astonished hand and then picks up the rest of the missiles and chucks them in a rubbish container. Then he hauls the little Asian across the courtyard and back inside. Yelping slightly in some Asian language, he twists his plump arm out of Gareth's grasp and takes off. Ungrateful little sod.

Gareth bends over the camera, fiddling with the controls, breathing only a little more heavily than usual.

'Sorry about that,' he says.

But it is not over yet. The bully boys have spotted me on my perch and are dancing round on the other side of the window, pulling faces, waddling round like pregnant women, hurling abuse through the glass.

Gareth straightens up and looks over at the window just as the leader is poised to hurl a sizeable clump of earth my way, glass or not. There's a moment of silent eye-contacting challenge. The leader looks away and throws the clod well below the window as the others slink off and he's left looking stupid.

'Are you a prefect?' I say.

'We don't have those here.' He's looking at me through the viewfinder. 'Now, can you just stay quite still for a moment.'

'What do you have then?'

'Student councillors, and no, I'm not one.'

'You should be.'

'Directing a play's quite enough for my authoritarian urges.'

I suppose the camera is running; there's no noise, only a tiny red light. I feel myself going redder and redder, wishing I'd sat up straighter 'cause I know my two spare tyres will be bulging like I'm wearing swimming tubes, wishing my face was less fat, my skin clearer, my hair less boring, my neck longer, my arms skinnier, my bust smaller, my thighs undimpled and my whole self anywhere else on the planet other than sitting here being used for target practice using film instead of stones.

In some countries, India, China, Iran, I'm not sure exactly, they won't let foreign tourists take their pictures. It's stealing their souls, and not allowed unless you want to risk getting rocks thrown at you and your camera smashed. I'm temporarily Indian or Chinese. My essence is being sucked out of me into a machine. I'm off, outta here.

'That's great,' says Gareth, straightening up. 'Stay there.' Like a dog, I stay. He glides into the office and comes out with a book. 'Can you just read something from this. It's the first thing I put my hand on, Shakespeare, who else?'

'I can't read Shakespeare.'

'It's only for sound levels . . .'

'Sorry!' I am starting to tremble. Maybe it's delayed reaction from having a clod of earth threatened at me.

'That's cool. Just tell me about yourself, then.' Which is worse.

'You're new here,' he prompts. 'New to Auckland?'

'No. You'll have to get someone else for this. I have to go . . .'

A scream from the doorway. 'Gareth, darling!'

'Like her. She'll be perfect,' I say, impressed by my own newfound ability to get a word in edgeways. 'Absolutely, fabulously perfect.'

There she stands in the doorway, the all-purpose Year Twelve size eight *ac-tor*. Black leggings, skimpy crop-top, black boots even though it's over thirty degrees outside, arms outstretched. True to type, she clomps across the carpet for a massive and noisy hug. Do I detect a wink my way as he is embraced, an amused look that says, see what directors have to put up with?

'Absolutely fab to see you, Gareth,' she burbles. 'Gorgeous and talented and enigmatic as ever. What's the production this year, then? Part for me? Oooh, sorry, you're doing an audition. So sorry.'

'No he's not,' I say. 'I'm just casual target practice and I'm leaving.' This girl might be a fishing rod, but she's not got much going for her face.

'Tiggie's joining the production team,' he says, putting his hand lightly on my shoulder. Is he a friend, a control freak, a sleaze? Is this sexual harassment? I don't know what I think. I get the full pixie smile. 'Yes?'

'No. You don't want me.' My niceness training kicks in and I add, 'Excuse me. Gotta go. Thanks for your help, before.'

'Thank you for yours,' he calls at my departing fat bum. 'Think about it.'

I have, mate, for all of ten seconds and the answer's still no.

FOUR

HOME FROM MY FIRST DAY AT THE NEW SCHOOL, REASSURING MUM THAT it was fine, nothing much happened, yes it was fine, truly. I guess now's the time to show you where I live.

Click.

You thought I'd start with my bedroom, didn't you? Well, this is the most unusual room in our house. The bathroom. All Italian fittings. Cool, eh. I used a wide-angle lens for all these pictures. Mum and Dad spend hours in the spa bath, often together, hence all the hanging plants, the soft lighting, the magazine rack, the expensive sound system playing Celine Dion, the black candles and the aromatherapy oils. Behind that huge mirror is a chemist's shop. Mum reads the glossies in the bath and Dad meditates, or says he does. I think he just goes to sleep.

I shower. That way I don't have to look down at myself.

Click.

Their bedroom. Pretty, eh? I took this picture on a day the cleaning ladies had been, when it was tidy. Mum's hopeless and when Dad's home he's usually shut in his office, so he doesn't really care. They changed to single beds when Mum got famous and said she needed her beauty sleep. Mum has to have lots of clothes for her job, so she had a walk-in wardrobe built, and a special make-up area with about twelve lights around a mirror, like a theatre dressing room.

But Dad's no slouch when it comes to power dressing, either. He's got nine suits hanging in here. The most expensive one he bought in Melbourne and it cost thousands. I don't know how many ties, I think they breed. Mum likes the teddy bear one and the buzzy bee one best, but I think they're just a rather pathetic conversation starter.

Click.

Kitchen, third millennium. All Italian fittings again, everything stainless steel, even the cupboard and fridge doors. So it's a bit like those mirrors at a fun fair where you go all wavy and distorted. Not good at breakfast time. Not good ever. We don't eat much together anyway. We rush in at odd hours and heat things in the microwave.

Through there's the formal dining room, where occasionally they have dinner parties. Mum trained me to set the table with all the silver and coasters and Irish damask napkins and Austrian crystal wine glasses and flowers delivered by courier. How's that for perfection? Twelve place settings, all the cutlery lined up, the glasses exactly in place, everything shining and spotless, nothing crooked. I like doing that. I like order, and beautiful things.

Click.

Several different shots of the living area, French doors out onto the patio, glass-enclosed because of the wind and to stop people jumping off. Terracotta tiles throughout, apricot leather sofas, original paintings, Turkish carpets. Visitors always look at the terracotta tiles and the turquoise-washed walls and say, 'It's gorgeous, Cassie. So Mediterranean.'

Click, click.

Two bedrooms used for his 'n' her offices. His has his computer, files, books, tartan curtains and a male smoker's smell. Hers has her computer, all the TV and video equipment that '60 Minutes' reporters apparently need and a female smell.

Click.

At last. You might think this picture of my bedroom was also taken after the cleaning ladies had been, but they're not allowed in my room, By Order of Me.

This picture could go in a house and garden magazine, truly. The Perfect Unreal Teenager's Bedroom. I chose the colours, and I water all the pot plants. I make my bed every day, smoothing down every wrinkle, and pile up all the teddies on the pillow, just so. I hang my clothes up. I used to brush my school uniform blazer that was dark green and showed every speck of dandruff. The new one I wouldn't bother to iron but Mum goes on about it, so I do. I have a rubbish basket that I empty regularly. I vacuum. I even dust.

Now this might seem like really oddball behaviour because all the teens I know are totally disorganised and live in absolute pits. The few girls who've seen my room raved about the view but absolutely hated everything else. It made them feel nervous. 'Tiggie, how could you! Boring! So retro! Get a life!'

But this is my life. I know where everything is and it's clean and I like it. That's not boring, that's sensible. They're the ones who are totally boring predictable about their disgusting rooms and always losing things, and about having no clothes to wear that aren't torn or dirty or lost after some party, and about their parents banging on about health hazards and bomb sites – only they're just too stupid to know it.

In my room, with the curtains open, I may feel like a goldfish on the top of a very tall pole, but I'm in control.

We haven't lived here long. About three years ago, Dad's consultancy stuff took off and Mum got her job at '60 Minutes', and suddenly they had more money and wanted something a bit special. They certainly found it, top floor of a twelve-storey highrise towering over the waterfront road and the harbour.

Dad said no way, the price was over the top. I said no way too. I didn't want to move from the nice old bungalow where we had no view at all but an enclosed garden where I had a dog. She was a Labrador cross, Brunhilde, and I loved her to bits. But Mum had set her heart on the view and living where everything was so clean and new and efficient. She wasn't much of a gardener and she'd only need the cleaning ladies once a week.

So Dad did some sums, he's good at that, and they both took a deep breath and made an offer. This sleazy land agent who wore a bow-tie and had bad breath just about lived with us for a week, and suddenly we had a deal and we moved in a month later.

Brunhilde had to go.

I think views are overrated, don't you?

I showed you my photos because I think they're rather good – I'm not totally a fraud. Maybe I'll go to polytech or art school and study photography. I might take it in Year Eleven, I can at my new school. I might be a fashion photographer who wears mad hats and clicks away at the stick insects who are the models. I might be a sports photographer or a war photographer, wearing baggy green combat gear and getting shot at. Or one of the paparazzi with a huge white telescopic lens on a tripod outside the Oscar awards or Buckingham Palace, one of the boys.

Don't know what else I'll do. Can do.

The other reason I showed you the photos was that when people come to my house they don't see the rooms themselves. They don't really appreciate Mum's clever interior designer's expensive tastes. All they see is The View.

Come around with me again and just look out the windows! It's a 360-degree view – first, north from the living and dining rooms, across the harbour to the North Shore, Rangitoto of course, the islands and all-day sun. East from the kitchen, across the gulf to the purple Coromandel ranges. South from the two studies, across the isthmus to One Tree Hill and right down to the airport. Can you see the jets, two of them lining up to land?

West from my room out to the Titirangi hills. I get the setting sun, but I also get, if I stand in the left-hand corner and look out diagonally, the bridge, the city skyscrapers and the Sky Tower, blinking red at night. I like it when they light it up deep blue.

And northwest, from the master bedroom, we have the bridge, the central city, Sky Tower again, wharves, the inner harbour, ships, yachts, America's Cup village, the yacht race hopefuls now arriving from all over the world. A grandstand, helicopter view of everything.

Yeah, yeah, yeah, great views, stunning, fantastic. But getting all the furniture up here was a mission and the real trouble living in a highrise is that when your famous mother picks you up after school you have to help cart the groceries twelve floors up.

The reason she did this after school today has nothing to do with maternal love for her daughter, first day at new school, or the hot February weather. It's Tiggie as bag carrier, Tiggie as slave.

Excuse *me*, I hear you say. There's underground carparks with self-opening doors, air-conditioned lifts with pink carpet walls and a 24-hour telephone in case there's a famous Auckland power cut.

Excuse me, but I've just walked up eleven flights of stairs, twice, for the following reasons.

One, I know people will make a connection between Mum's silly great wagon at the school gate and the size I take in knickers.

Two, I hate four-wheel drives and Mum perched up there on those ridiculous tyres, peering down to earth like someone driving a crane.

Three, I hate Mum for being there at all, flaunting her famous nearly-forty face to two thousand goggling high school students pouring out the gates, and then for arguing in public with me when I say I want to walk home thanks.

'Oh get *in*, Tiggie,' she says impatiently, not listening. 'I've got two network bosses, three print journalists and their partners for dinner tonight and I'm running late. I need some help.'

Why didn't she go to the supermarket earlier in the day? Why does she leave everything to the last moment?

She reads my mind. 'I've been working. Getting my hair cut, writing up interview notes for tomorrow's shoot, stressing out, okay?'

Four, I hate myself for not just giving her the mental fingers (I'm too nice for the physical ones) and walking off.

And five, I hate Mrs Sparrow.

'Let's try a little experiment,' Mrs Sparrow said in our first Health class this afternoon, looking up at the stairwell of the only three-storeyed building in the school as mountaineers look up at the summit of Mount Cook. 'Darryl, Jo, Tiggie, off you go. Take these bags. Up and down, please.'

'To the top?' squeaked Darryl. His body shape can be described in one word: square. 'We've just had lunch, Miss.'

'I know that.' She clearly eats like a bird but has a face crinkled like a hundred-year-old boot and she was enjoying this. How old is she? Forty-five? Seventy? 'To the very top, please. I know it's hot, but that's no excuse. And Fiona and Wayne, please, to follow on as a control group. Come along. Chop chop.'

The three of us, who well knew why we'd been chosen, set off each carrying two extremely heavy leather balls from the gym in plastic bags, one in each hand, watched by the rest of the class slouching around the bottom. Up three floors, down three floors, all three of us soon breathing hard and shiny red with rage. At the bottom, Fiona, the rhythmic gymnast, and Wayne, a nerd who plays schoolboy hockey for Auckland, eagerly seized the bags from our sticky hands. They bounded up and down three flights of stairs like mountain goats, two steps at a time and no doubt a world record.

Back in the classroom the rest of the class were invited to test the weight of the bags.

'If that was your body weight, Fiona,' said Mrs Sparrow, 'how would it feel?'

'Gross,' said Fiona right on cue, and grinned further as Mrs Sparrow pointed out to the class Darryl, Jo and Tiggie's slow recovery rates and likelihood of heart disease later on.

'Where are you going, Tiggie?'

'Home.' Could I take a case against her for cruelty to dumb animals to the Human Rights Commission? The bell was about to go anyway. 'Migraine,' I muttered.

'Did you know the first thing to get fat is the tongue,' she cried enthusiastically to my back. 'You'll need a note.'

'Get stuffed,' I said quietly to the seagulls in the empty courtyard outside. I'd rather my tongue looked like a salami than a snake's.

Mum, early for about the first time in her life, was sitting there in the carpark.

So that is why I have just carried four heavy supermarket bags of tonight's dinner for twelve up eleven flights of stairs instead of catching the lift. This self-imposed challenge reminds me of what I want more than anything in the world. It reminds me that at times my mother is a self-centred and social-climbing middle-aged bimbo and my Phys. Ed. teacher is a self-righteous and insensitive prig. So Mum wants her bags carried up? So I'll do it my way. So she and Dad want to live in a snobby highrise? So where's Brunhilde now? So Dad's got . . . a new job . . . so Mum will probably . . . have a . . . nervous breakdown . . . so I just . . . had to . . . change . . . schools and . . . this one is . . . worse . . . I know . . . and I know I . . . need . . . exercise . . . so I'm . . . bloody well . . . getting it, aren't I?

And when I delivered those four bags, I turned straight around and went down the two hundred and eighty steps for the next four. 'Don't you *dare* go down in the lift,' I said to my bewildered mother waiting in the kitchen for the soy sauce to arrive so that she could marinate the chicken.

I know their secret, you see. The likes of Mrs Sparrow and all my classmates and even my bloody mother, they know they can always get away with their lecturing. Unlike people with asthma or diabetes, tubbiness is not an act of God, but all our own fault and thins are always right. I've always known that, long as I've lived.

'Tiggie,' said Mum, when I staggered boobs heaving and dry-mouthed into the kitchen with the second load of bags. She had a large tinkling glass of iced water waiting and was probably standing by the phone so she could ring 111 for an ambulance. 'Thank you, but . . .'

'Don't . . . say . . .'

'Sit down and tell me about your first day. And when you're ready, could you set the table?'

'. . . *anything.*'

Sitting on my bed staring out at the Sky Tower at dusk, remembering those bullies with the darts, I shiver. There are nearly two thousand students, zillions of classrooms, a million miles of corridors, two sports fields and over a hundred staff. A dart is only one degree worse than words; in one way, a dart is preferable. It's sharp and deliberate and you can pull it out and throw it away and scars heal. Words, however, burn their way in, whether deliberate or careless the effect is the same, and they stay there, like branding marks, festering.

The dinner party is in full swing in the dining room. If it was a weekend, I'd be doing the cleaning up in the morning, for a fee. Tomorrow, Mum has the cleaning ladies coming in. She just walks out on the mess.

'You don't like messes.' I can feel the touch of Gareth's hand on my shoulder. *'Tiggie's joining the production team?'* No, I am not. *'Are you into drama?'*

No one's ever seriously asked me before, for all they went on about providing opportunities at my old school. They had brighter, pushier, slimmer types who didn't wait to be asked. All I ever got offered in a patronising sort of way were the fat old women parts, someone's grandmother or mother. Or the cleaning lady. The servant. The nurse. The beggar woman. The frumpy witch. The teachers offered and I kept on saying no, and some time in my Year Seven or Eight they decided Tiggie wasn't interested and stopped making the effort.

That was the first great life-changing decision I made. I must have been about eleven.

Are you into drama, Tiggie?

Dare I? Here, where it's not all so precious and serious. Dare I?

'What's the production this year? Part for me?' She of the boots didn't even have to ask herself the question.

'If you change your mind . . .'

I am not going to change my mind.

Five

'Tell me,' says Gareth, all amused, 'what made you change your mind?'

It had taken me just five school days. On the sixth day, I knew that I was going under and no one was going to throw me a lifebelt. Except Gareth, who for reasons beyond me, already had.

'It's the . . . mess.'

'What mess?' He looks around the drama suite. I'd found out from the school notices that here, after school, he was interviewing people interested in the production. I'd read a book under a tree for an hour until the school was empty and all the others had gone home.

'Muddle,' I say, but he hasn't understood.

'This is quite normal,' he says, 'one Coke tin, some KFC wrappings, bits of Xeroxed music. I know Sophia's office is over the top but . . .'

'It's not just her office, Gareth. It's everything.'

'Life's messy.'

'I know that, but . . .' Get it out of the way, Tiggie, with about the only person in the world you feel you can currently trust. You certainly can't tell your parents, who think you're blissfully happy being co-educational and multicultural. I mumble on, 'You probably know I've come from a private girls' school. I chose to come.'

'I didn't know that. Good for you.'

'We had new tidy classrooms where everyone was the same age. The same teachers, school assemblies three times a week. No one would have *dared* arrive with orange hair or a nose-ring or something through your

33

tongue. There was no rubbish, no pushing and shoving, no people turning up late.'

'Are you glad you chose something different?'

'Nothing's been the same here two days in a row. My home room's got everything from stupid little Year Eights to a mature student trying to get into med. school doing bursary science. He's twenty-four. I've had three different teachers for English and two for maths. In six days? There's no principal, just three managers, and every day the person in the office is different. They lock up the toilets. They lock up the library at lunchtime, so I can't even go there. There's been no school assemblies . . .'

'There's nowhere big enough. You have your dean groups.'

'I know, but even there it's all about stolen bikes and sports teams and who wants tickets to things. No one seems to know what's going on! I get myself to a lesson and we're in the wrong room or the teacher's different or hasn't got the key or half the students don't turn up, or wander in late with lost books and nothing to write with and no one seems to care.'

'It's messy,' he says gently.

'Yep. So I reckon if I join the production team at least there'll be one thing in my life I can count on.'

'That seems as good a reason as any.'

'You don't just want me for my mother?'

'Excuse me, but who's your mother?'

'Don't you know?'

'Should I know?'

'Forget it then.'

'Okay. Done.' He flips over pages on a clipboard. 'Do you want to be one of Tara's team?'

'Who's Tara?'

'Sorry, she's the producer. I direct, which means I make the performers unhappy. Producers organise everybody, bring it all together. That's where we need good people.'

Having bared a fraction of my soul, why can't I go a bit further? *Gareth, I'd really like to be one of your team.*

'Tiggie? Okay?' he prods. 'Tara's team?'

34

'Okay,' I say, settling for less as I always do. 'What happens now?'

'Arrange a meeting with Tara. She was supposed to be here this afternoon . . .' He sees the look on my face. 'Okay, Tiggie Tompson who likes things tidy and punctual.'

'Gareth.'

'Yes?'

'If you say that again, I will be out of here so fast that . . .'

'I won't say it again. Promise.' He gets up from the table he's been behind and goes and stands on his head against a wall, his arms stretched out for balance. 'Headstand. Normally one of a whole sequence of asanas, but it's been a long day. I need a rush of blood to the head.' His black T-shirt falls down, exposing bare flesh, outlines of ribs, not an ounce of spare.

'I've got to go,' I mutter, turning away.

'Before you do, one thing.'

'What?'

'You haven't been involved in a production before?'

'No.'

'It's a messy process. Fact. Bad enough with a published script. A thousand times worse without one. There'll be a time, about two weeks before opening, when no one will believe it can possibly happen. Count on technical problems, flu, nervous breakdowns, panic, tantrums, bickering and open warfare.'

It can't be so easy to talk upside down. I feel obscurely flattered by all this. Why, indeed, is he bothering so much with a fat Year Nine?

'Can you cope with that?' he asks. 'Producers get caught in the crossfire. I need to warn you.'

'Sounds like a challenge. Do you tell this to all the others?'

'No.'

'Why not?'

'Ever done any yoga?'

'No.' As always, I am checking for a piss-take. *Yoga, me? Come on!* But even upside down, I can see that he's looking at me.

'When I was fifteen I was wearing a striped blazer, cap, tailored shorts and my grey socks were pulled up. I probably still would be, but my old man died. He left all his money to his fucking mistress. Pun intended. Mum's still contesting the will. If and when she gets anything, it'll be too late. For school, anyway.'

'I'm sorry.'

'Don't be. He did me a favour. I like this better, multi-mess and all. You will too, when you've got over the culture shock.'

'My mother's Cassandra Tompson.'

'I know, Tiggie Tompson.' His voice is quieter still, almost as though the rush of blood downwards is calming him. 'Welcome on board. Cheers.'

I leave him upside down against the wall, eyes closed. It would have made a good picture.

The first meeting has been called for a lunchtime, in the huge indoor stadium which is part of the school but also used for outside sports, basketball, gymnastics and that. It's vast and it echoes, not the best place for a meeting. I arrive to find Gareth and an older woman right out there in the middle, pulling up some benches into a circle. They are laughing together. They like each other.

Gareth spots me about to lurk off behind a pillar until I can come in with a crowd. 'Tiggie my friend, give us a hand?'

'Sure,' I say, setting off gingerly across the polished wood. Within a metre of reaching safety, my feet shoot out and I fall bang smack on my tailbone. My camera, filled chicken roll and drink bottle fly out in all directions. They talk about shooting pain – well, one shoots itself red-hot right up my spine and into my brain. A combination yelp and swear word escape from my lips, so that the first time I meet the famously untidy Sophia I am untidily scraping myself, swearing, off the floor.

'Bugger!' Then, pulling off my leather sandals in a laughing fury, to Gareth, '*Don't* come near. I'm fine. Lucky I've got padding, eh?'

Sophia is not a small woman either. The bum under her dark green velvet culottes is a substantial one. The culottes look odd with a white T-shirt. 'Hi, Tiggie,' she coos. 'I did that once, on the opening night of the Scottish play. I told them my nightgown was too long. Broke my coccyx and couldn't sit down for a month. Are you all right?'

'Fine.' I'm on my feet and picking up my camera and chicken roll and hauling over the last bench to complete the circle, all the time in agony.

'Shouldn't you . . .?' begins Gareth, until he gets a closer look at my face. 'Well, take it easy. Lie down, stand, whatever. Here come the troops.'

For the next ten minutes they drift in, until finally about fifty people are sitting round the circle. I decide it's safe to sit down and Sophia decides it's time to make a start. We all introduce ourselves. This time all I say is, 'Tiggie, Year Nine, helping with production.'

Or need to say. At my old school, sure we would have had jazz dancers, ballet dancers, gymnasts, choir people, school orchestra, string trio, jazz band, rock group, barbershop quartet, drama students, even a very small Maori cultural group. All these were either represented here or their names read out by Sophia as being interested but not able to be present. What's really new to me is the thought of a Maori cultural group which apparently has eighty members and wins awards at cultural festivals; likewise the various Pacific Island groups.

Then there are the Korean and Indian dancers, the Irish tappers and two blonde girls who already earn good money weekends in Turkish restaurants as belly dancers. There's a couple of guys who are stiltwalkers, a whole group who do theatresports and one who's into juggling. Not all of them are oozing confidence, or look like performers. The Pacific Islanders and the Koreans especially talk so softly they can barely be heard. They look at the floor while they are speaking, or drop their eyes when they sense me looking at them. Several leave; others arrive. No one cares about this. Gareth makes notes and checks that everyone has put their home phone numbers on a clipboard that's gone round.

Towards the end of this, producer Tara makes a grand and noisy entrance. Sophia and Gareth, sitting together, welcome her warmly into their group. They are comfortable with each other, these three, I can tell. We all shuffle round to make room on the benches. She's tall, curly dark hair, only slightly on the big side, and like Gareth dressed entirely in black. Leggings, and boots, of course, and bumbag, and a bunch of keys hanging from her belt. Large water bottle in her left hand.

She's late, she tells us all, because she's just come from a meeting of the school magazine committee; this year will be a bumper Millennium souvenir issue. She's the editor and had to be there.

I dislike her on sight. She's the producer and she should have been here. I notice that the stitching on the hem of her black singlet top is unravelling and things are falling out of her backpack. She's got a rainbow tattoo on her upper arm. Her voice is low-pitched, husky but loud. She's my boss.

My butt is sore and I don't have to do this.

We have only twenty minutes left before the bell. Sophia, who after all is the producer of whatever grand event we are going to put on, tells us that she's called the meeting in this space because this is where the event is going to take place. I take a few pictures of her and of the rapt faces round her for what I've decided will be a photo record of the production.

We do a bit of visualising. All the stands up there around us full to bursting, giving us a possible audience of 2500. A buzz of excitement greets this. Three performances, with static displays in the foyers and over at school by the photography, art and craft students, a food festival beforehand provided by the cooking and catering students. The audience can come late afternoon, enjoy all this and then go straight in to the evening's entertainment. What a way to bring in the third millennium! Wow.

She's got people to sponsor and erect and run the lights, which will need to be spectacular, and someone else who's a sound engineer, and a third who's into large-scale videos. Someone is going to design a simple but spectacular set. Most of us will provide our own costumes, but advice and help will be available. We will need make-up people, and ushers, and front-of-house and publicists. The graphics students will design and do all the tickets, the fliers, the posters, dream up the image that will brand-mark the event and attract the audience.

She's still looking for a stage manager, the person responsible for calling the show – that means, making it all happen on the night. Gareth? He's already got one job, he protests, smiling. For one horrible minute I fantasise that he might suggest me, but who am I, just a new Year Nine. All he really knows about me is that I don't like messes and was the only person to arrive on time for this meeting so of course it doesn't even cross his mind.

It's only fifteen minutes from the bell that the meeting ignites. Sophia has been impressive, I'll give her that, but so far it's been a one-woman show.

'A theme,' she says. 'This is where you folks decide.'

There's a silence while we all think.

'This is the school's salute to the Millennium,' she prompts. 'I want it to be the sort of show you tell your grandchildren about.'

We are all spellbound, even Tara who considers herself a tough nut. Her face is worth a picture. Click.

'"But best of all, my school had this show. It was so good we had to do two extra performances and people came from all over Auckland to try and get in. I was in it. I was part of it." That's what I want you to be able to say to your mokopuna.' It's still Sophia's one-woman show.

'Let's do the spacey thing,' says one boy, Maori. 'Everyone in silver, eh? *X-Files.*'

A Korean girl says quietly that she is wearing her national costume or not at all. Then the dam bursts.

Suggestions fly so thick and fast that when the bell goes no one takes any notice: a space opera, a history of the twentieth century. No history, people interject, it's boring. Just the major events like Hiroshima and the Pill and when they discovered AIDS and the death of Lady Di. But how do you fit cultural groups into that?

Well then, just a fantastic concert without a theme. Or let's do a far-out musical version of *Romeo and Juliet,* like the film, or *Phantom of the Opera* or *Les Mis* set in New Zealand. Dream on, you'd never get the rights for those. You don't need rights for *Romeo and Juliet!* Let's do it as a circus. A space-age circus.

Twenty-five minutes into the first period Sophia looks at her watch and calls a halt. We must all apologise to our class teachers. We'll have another meeting in two days. A notice will be posted on the foyer board. We haven't got much time to make a decision about the theme and structure of the event – four months, in effect, to write and mount a show.

Tara, who has drunk a litre of water through all this, says her bit. Production team, meeting tomorrow after school, drama suite, be there.

Will I?

Gareth is still busy writing. He has made no special acknowledgement of my presence. Neither, indeed, has anyone else past the first curious stare.

This time I walk out with the crowds, careful, in my bare feet and a pain in my tailbone. Do I have a bad feeling about this? A good feeling? I can't decide. Sophia has a reputation for pulling these things off at the last moment. She's also had her disasters, or so I've heard.

Tell my mokopuna? Ha!

Six

Tara's team. It sounds great. Have you noticed, whenever people want to give something an impressive name that sticks in your head, it's often got alliteration? Sounds like you know what you're doing. Especially in advertising. Just Jeans. The zit zone. Ponsonby Pies. Millennium madness. 'Shortland Street', sort of.

Tara rushed in, clutching her drink bottle and an armful of papers, late again. This time it was a student council which had gone on a bit. Sixteen strangers were hanging round the drama suite, embarrassed and bored and not too keen to start talking to each other. My tailbone was still sore to sit on. It kept me awake last night. No one even looked twice when I lay down on the carpet on my tummy.

As a meeting it was worse than useless and I decided early on not to take any pictures at all. Tara wrote down our names and asked what each of us had done in the past and would like to do this time. Some of the others had helped with school productions before, so they tried hard to look as if they'd been there and done that and might even do it again, given a bit of a push. Others, like me, had just come along to see what it was all about, or make up the numbers.

The first thing we learned was that some people were too grand to come to meetings. She read out some names of people who couldn't be there but who had told her they'd be helping with the lighting, sound engineering, props, wardrobe. The designer would be giving her and Gareth some ideas to look at next week.

'Anyone into publicity, promotion, stuff like that?' she asked. No one was. We needed people, she said, to design posters and fliers, come up with an amazing logo which would feature on all the printed material. She had one of the Year Twelve graphic design students in mind. Any suggestions, let her know. Had to get on with this, like *now,* once the writers had come up with a theme and a title.

'Front-of-house?' Yes, there was one taker, a Year Eleven girl.

'You, Tiggie, would you like to help there?'

'What's front-of-house?'

'Um, taking tickets at the door, selling programmes. Arranging ushers, the foyer displays. Getting the bums on the seats, basically.'

That meant being very visible in the foyer of the stadium. 'I'd rather do something more backstage,' I mumbled.

'Okay. Gofer for me, interested?'

That sounded suitably lowly. I nodded. I saw some ominous smiles creep onto the faces of several others propped up against the walls.

'Great. Gareth says you're a good organiser.'

How would he know, when I had no idea myself?

'Can you type? Got access to a computer?'

'Yes.'

'Ex-cellent.'

Why am I so damn honest? Why haven't I backed out of this? Stupid me.

I am lying at home, though, like a flatfish. Every night, every breakfast of those first few awful days.

'How's it going at school, Tiggie?' says Dad heartily, gin in hand and his face still slightly flushed from a session at the gym. 'Not feeling too overwhelmed?'

'No. It's good.'

'Someone was telling me today that Eastern College has students with fifty-three mother tongues. I suppose that's all the different languages from places like India. I'd be hard pressed to come up with fifty-three languages.'

So he talks about me with his friends. Well, I know that. Parents talk about their children's schools, how they're getting on, about their teachers and their love lives. They boast to each other about their children's achievements, which would leave mine right out in the cold.

'Happy with your teachers?' he asks.

'Yeah.'

'Made any friends yet?'

'A few.'

'Are you doing Phys. Ed.?'

'Yes.'

'Like what?'

'Bit of volleyball. We can do aerobics if we want. Don't you want to watch the news?'

He grunts and points the remote at the screen, probably grateful that I've given him an excuse to switch me off and the six o'clock news on. Full marks for trying, Dad. No marks for telling me yet again, in code, that I'm too fat.

The problem is I hate exercise because I'm too fat and I wobble and people laugh, and I'm too fat because I don't do any, except walk to school each day.

Lying to Mum is even easier because she's doing big documentaries about the America's Cup and I hardly ever see her. Me settling into a new school is about the last thing on her mind.

'How's it going, Tiggie?' she says, shovelling in the muesli because she believes in staunch breakfasts.

'Fine.'

'Good. That uniform doesn't do much for you, does it? Jesus, must go. The traffic round this city is a nightmare.'

She looks, for her, terrible. Her skin's bad, she's got big rings under her eyes and she's scrawny through working so hard. On Sunday nights I see her on '60 Minutes' and she's a different person. It's spooky how different.

She must be slightly unconvinced, though, or have a prick of conscience about me.

'You're coping? No regrets, Tiggie?'

'Course not. It's great. Love it, Mum.'

'Well, I suppose there'll be a parent evening soon, I'll get to meet your teachers . . . sorry, Tiggie, must dash.'

'I need some lunch money.'

'What? Oh, here. Don't go buying pies, darling. Filled rolls are better.'

Code again. Happens all the time. But I'm Tiggie, the Pie Girl, don't you know?

My first job for Tara was to take all her scribbled notes, names, phone numbers and jobs so far, plus the sheet that was handed round for signing at the big meeting in the stadium, plus some more scribbled notes from Sophia, and put them on the computer. Print out hard copy for delivery to her the next day. Her to check, Gareth to check, Sophia to check. When okayed and amended, top copy for photocopying on the school machine. Do a hundred, she said, that'd be brilliant.

I spent hours on it. I've seen Mum's call sheets for her television work, and I've seen the sort of reports that Dad produces for his clients, so I know when things look okay. This production 'who's who' list was four pages long and it looked good. In fact it looked bloody marvellous. It was formatted with names in bold and different font sizes and spell-checked and saved on a floppy for later amendments.

I crept in and gave the heavy box of paper to Tara at the writers' meeting after school, mainly because I'd been trying to find her for two days and I knew she'd be there at least.

Bad, bad timing.

'Ta,' she said, and put it without looking on the floor beside her. Gareth, involved in the same noisy brainstorming with about five Year Twelves, got up from his place around the circle to come and take a copy from the box, give it one swift appraisal and touch me briefly on the shoulder as he returned. He looked through the pages and gave me a thumbs-up. Then he gestured at me to sit down.

I plumped down, astounded. This was the holy of holies. I had no place here among the creative geniuses of the school, not even as Tara's gofer.

That Year Eleven male bimbo over there was a singer-songwriter and had been on 'Shortland Street' for six weeks last year as someone's younger brother. The Maori girl next to me did performance poetry and stand-up comedy at the Laugh Festival. The blind guy had won a national short story competition and was writing a novel. The guy with the completely bald head had won a young playwright's competition. I knew all this because I'd read the school's 1998 yearbook, full of these and hundreds of other laughing students achieving things.

Right now, though, the creative geniuses were being very sarcastic and rude to each other, with not much to show for it. They didn't even seem to notice when I got out my camera and clicked off a few shots. After a few more minutes of this there was an uneasy silence. I saw Gareth and Tara look at each other with a 'where do we go from here?' expression.

Now if I had got up and quietly left at this point, gone home to The View and life in a highrise with Cassandra Tompson, my life would have been totally, totally different. I should have gone. These were all Year Elevens and Twelves, geniuses who had known each other since for ever. I was a lowly Year Nine outsider and this was not, and never would be, my scene.

Get out, Tiggie, before it's too late.

The bald playwright has a play. He's been working on it over the holidays and he wants the group to take a break from farting around with Sophia's mad and grandiose project and do a quick reading of the first couple of scenes. Okay, guys?

He's handing it out. He's handing one copy out to me.

I say I'm only the gofer and I have to go and he says he needs three females 'cause it doesn't sound right read by males. 'It'll take only twenty minutes. Sorry no one's told me your name.'

'That's Tiggie,' interrupts Gareth. 'More correctly, Antigone.'

'My gofer,' puts in Tara, swigging away at her bottle.

'Okay, Tiggie,' says the playwright, 'you read Fran, you're about the right age. Kiri, read Beryl, she's the older sister. Tara, read Josie.'

I open my mouth to protest and I see Gareth looking at me. The

45

message couldn't have been any clearer. I look down at the script. 'Fran, aged 16, an unemployed actor who's dying of AIDS.' Good one.

The playwright, James, suddenly feels the need to set the scene in some detail. In one way it sounds awful, just way over the top. But then I realise that the shaven-headed playwright can actually write, and what happens is that we get really into it and there's this sudden weird tension in the air.

Two things seem to be simultaneously happening to me. One is that I get really interested in Fran, who's the younger sister and constantly put down by Beryl. I could play this part for real, a little voice keeps saying.

The other, louder voice keeps saying, you're just a fat gofer, Tiggie, don't you dare show any emotion about this. Don't show anything, do anything risky, just read it like you've always read a play in class, unemotional and dead boring.

The scene ends with Fran telling the other girls that she's just been told she's only got a year or so to live.

'Cut,' says James. 'Thanks, guys.'

'Great,' says Gareth. 'Powerful sister play up and running there, mate. Dialogue's spot on, comes off the page dancing.'

James goes into self-criticising mode and I can see Tara very quickly get bored with this. She interrupts, saying same time same place tomorrow after school and *please*, guys, *this* time come with some genuine *ideas*? She asks if I'll carry my box out to her car. This is what gofers do, I realise. I pick it up and follow her down the endless corridors like a porter through the jungle.

Tara drives off and I go back into school for my bag. I'm hungry and it's hot, and yes, I've been quite stirred up by Fran. For a wild moment I see myself playing the part, the violent scene ending with Fran falling, her coming round and her realisation that her own sister . . .

Get a grip, Antigone Tompson. *Get a grip.*

I say this out loud and too late see Gareth by the main gate, obscured by a bush. He probably heard. I do not want to walk even part of the way home with Gareth. I do not even want to talk to him.

46

'Tiggie Tompson,' he says, making it quite clear he has something to say.

'What?'

'Thanks for doing all that typing. It was great. You must have spent hours on it.'

'Not really. About all I can do, type fast.'

'Where did you learn to sightread?'

'What?'

'Sightread. That OTT melodrama of James. Your sightreading's brilliant.'

'Is it? We read lots in class, at my old school. I always thought I was hopeless.'

'Most people haven't got a clue. A bad first read-through can kill a play stone dead and send the playwright screaming into the night. You did James proud.'

'Kiri's good. Lots of experience, I suppose.'

'I'm talking about you.'

I turn away. 'Have to go.'

'Tiggie? You've got a natural feel for language.'

'There are never any parts for me.' He knows what I mean, all right.

'There will be. Join the drama group. Get some acting lessons . . .'

This time I do walk off. I half-turn and call back angrily, 'What for?'

Then I decide I've had enough of this. I whip my camera out of my backpack, walk back and indicate I want to take his photograph.

'Why?' It's his turn to be surprised.

'You're the director, aren't you?' I say, zooming in on his puzzled face. 'They'll need publicity pictures. That background's as good as any.'

'Okay,' he says, 'on condition that you think about it.'

Click.

This is getting to be a habit. I have thought about it, and once again, the answer's no.

Seven

My turn coming, to leap into the abyss. Off the cliff. Bungey jump. Sky dive and other forms of attempted suicide.

This time I have to stand up, walk to the end of the room and turn around. Face and forget the nine other people in the room looking at me, waiting for the fat lady to sing. Remember what I have spent hours learning. Start, struggle through it, finish. Walk back to my place, be judged, hear the verdict – which will of course be patronising and critical. Die.

The big bare room, with late afternoon sunlight coming in broad dusty beams through the open windows, is reminding me of something.

'Always remember,' the teacher had said in his amazing fruity voice forty-five minutes ago. 'Criticism is not personal. Any criticism you might hear is of your work, of the choices you've made within the creative process, not of you. We learn mostly from our mistakes, from repeated and committed attempts to do something better. So.'

He crossed his legs, settled himself into the black director's chair, and smiled around at us with kindly relish, like the big bad wolf about to be delivered a feed.

The three others who do the monologue before me are all word perfect and brilliant. They are torn to shreds, by the teacher and each other. They smile and nod and take notes, all good, clean fun.

'Tiggie.'

Decision. To make a fool of myself by a) doing it, or b) not doing it. If b), I could run for the door and never be seen again. Cassandra Tompson's daughter?

I walk out and sit down as nimbly as I'm capable of, which isn't very, on the carpeted floor. My mouth opens and, almost as though I'm on automatic pilot, I hear myself speaking the words from some play of a confused and depressed girl trying to make up her mind if her boyfriend loves her. She decides he doesn't.

Well, never having had anything remotely resembling a boyfriend, that's not a problem I've ever known. I substitute father for boyfriend. Father who's never home and when he is, is always going on about my weight. He would love me more if I was normal. Does he love me at all? But at least I don't forget the words.

Towards the end something inside me shrivels, my mind goes blank. I feel tears in my eyes. I decide I've exposed and tortured myself enough. I haul myself to my feet and return to my seat.

The teacher is staring at me. Does he know my shameful secret? Does he know that ever since we started reading and doing plays at my old school, ever since I knew I couldn't be part of that scene, I've been a closet actor dying dramatically in my bedroom?

'You didn't finish,' he accuses. 'Tiggie?'

'No.'

'You can ask for a line.'

'Sorry.'

'Pity. Great pity. You were going rather well for your first class. Want to have another go?'

He stares at me until I can feel my cheeks burst on fire and I have to look away. 'Thank you very much anyway, Tiggie. Comments, anyone?'

By now I am so spooked that I don't really hear what they say. Bit more volume – more pace – need to see your eyes – hold head up – if you sit, you lose energy, so you need to compensate – always play out. Something like that. When they all run out of comments, the next victim gets up to do her thing. She obviously hasn't learnt it properly and gets torn to shreds by the teacher. 'This is the second lesson of the series, Angela, for fuck's sake! Where's your *passion*?'

Gareth was wrong. Any commitment or talent I might have imagined or dreamed I had, has gone right out the window. This firing range is not my scene.

There is another class waiting in the dark corridor outside. We have been given next week's script to learn, paired off, told to come back with the New Ideas marked on our scripts. I'm surprised it's not a scene from a famous play, just little pieces which Rowan writes himself for acting technique. We have had a discussion about new ideas. You mark every place in the script where the character has a new idea. A new idea is always accompanied by a breath, by a physical movement, even if it's only a slight movement of the head. The bigger the idea, the bigger the breath. Since I'm not coming back, I've not listened too closely.

Out the window I can see the wharf cranes and yachts on the harbour. 'Tiggie,' he is saying. 'Stay behind. Just a word?'

The others are laughing and joking, being very familiar with this famous man. Then he tells them to move along, darling ones, and I'm the subject of his attention.

'I see from your application form that you're a pupil at Eastern College. Sophia Banks, whom I admire greatly, runs a very good drama department there. Have you enrolled?'

I'm hopeless and being fired. He doesn't want me. Go back to school. I am close to tears again.

'No, I haven't.'

'You should think about it.'

'I'm new there, and I don't want to.'

'Too much too soon? So you want a little anonymity?'

Am I so transparent? I am about to say why don't you be honest and say out straight I'm wasting my, yours and everyone else's time, when he gets in first.

'You'll be here next week.' It's not a question, nor a challenge, nor even a command, but a Truth. I will be here. 'I don't make it easy for new chums,' he says softly. 'I'm interested in people's bravery. Acting is hard. It's hard! It requires great courage and passion. We have to practise our craft regularly and constantly. I am very interested to see what you will bring to class next week.'

The next class of twenty-somethings in black is lined up on the semicircle of director's chairs, waiting for him.

Interested? Him, in me, acting? This is such a ridiculous idea that while I'm waiting for the bus home I get quite angry with what is obviously a patronising lie and want to kick something. I actually tear the script in half, an action which leaves me feeling vaguely guilty, even cowardly. If I will be there, I will need my script.

It was such a cruel joke. Gareth had wound me up and he seemed like he was being honest with me. By chance or fate, I'd noticed an ad pinned up on the drama suite noticeboard for acting lessons in the city. I remembered the name and phone number and wrote them down while no one was looking. I casually asked Mum who Rowan Hughes was. Only New Zealand's most famous stage actor and director, that's all, she said. Huge international reputation, originally trained in London. Doesn't do so much acting now, mostly directing and teaching. She'd met him over the years, around the traps. Any play he was in almost guaranteed a sell-out season.

On the phone this famous man was charm itself. An actory voice, warm and brisk. Asked my age. Sixteen, I said. Come next Monday: I'd be in excellent company, ranging from seventeen to about twenty-three. I'd missed the first class, but he had typed notes to cover most of that. He'd send me those and the script for lesson number two by fastpost. Please learn it. A monologue, not long, quite simple. He asked if I'd ever done any voice or stage work, any school productions. To my mumbled no, he said good, good. Clean slate. He couldn't abide cute child actors, he said.

I was there at that second class, and for reasons I don't quite understand I will probably be there for the third.

A week later I was just starting to feel less like a stranger at school. The writers had finally agreed on a theme for the production, and I'd done another whole bundle of typing and phone calls for Tara. Gareth had vanished off the face of the earth. I went back to the New Ideas class, and that was when I met Vita.

EIGHT

THE SEMICIRCLE HAD ALREADY FORMED BY THE TIME I ARRIVED AND ROWAN was explaining the difference between a new idea and a new thought. A new idea is a complete change of direction; a thought, an extension of the idea. I crept into the edge of the semicircle and sank down onto the floor, flushed and panting, trying to look invisible. Only when he had finished speaking did his eyes turn in my direction. They were questioning eyes, but warm, not angry even though his class one notes said that a proper actor is, among other things, never late!

'I'm pleased to see you, Tiggie. Are you well and happy to be here?'

'I'm sorry. I missed my bus. Sorry.' Because of Tara, I'd also missed out on time to change out of my revolting school uniform. Everyone else, including Rowan, was wearing black jeans and skimpy tops. Great start, Tiggie.

'Well. Since your partner hasn't yet showed up, you can do this exercise with Vita.'

There's only one Vita and that's the girl I've watched play someone's daughter then trainee nurse Nerida on 'Shortland Street'. Her recent departure from 'Shortland Street' as her storyline finished with a fiery car crash was a news item. Her gorgeous face has appeared on every women's magazine cover you can think of. Is the girl he's smiling at, next to me, above me – *that* Vita?

'Vita is brushing up her technique. I'm pleased to see her here, too. This difficult and maddening craft we practise requires us to be humble and rethink the basics from time to time.'

Vita is offering me her director's chair.

'No, it's all right. I'm okay.' Stars don't run around after beginners. Stop. Please. I'm not like some cripple, some old lady needing a chair. You're only making it worse.

But she's already dashed off to the far side of the room and brought over another chair, watched by the rest of the class who are clearly quite as impressed as me. The tiny body is dressed in boots, of course, pale grey leggings, black crop top so skimpy it's like a bra showing a lot of tanned midriff, and black beret revealing only some of her famous blonde bob. Everything looks new, expensive, a bit French. 'Shortland Street' stars are supposed to earn good money and she's had two years of it. Yes, she's the all-purpose fishing rod actor-person like that female who slobbered all over Gareth at school, but there's something about her. Something intense, fierce, fragile.

She's getting me a chair, for starters.

'Now off you go, my darlings,' says Rowan briskly. 'Fifteen minutes to rehearse and then we'll see what you've got.'

By the time I've climbed, dazed, to my feet, Vita has already taken both chairs to the sunniest corner of the room and got her script out of her slim leather briefcase. She's waiting for me.

'Thanks,' I say too quickly.

'You're welcome. You're Tiggie and I'm Vita.'

'I know. I watch every night and . . .' Tiggie, shut up — you're doing to her exactly what you see people doing to Mum. 'I was sorry you went.'

'I'm not. I asked to be written out. Time to move on. There's a new soap being cast. I'm down to the last two for a part. That's secret, by the way. I haven't told Rowan yet. He thinks I should be doing live theatre, getting back in touch with an audience. And with myself.'

Despite that fragile air, she looks very much in touch with herself. I've been watching the famous face. Her skin's not all that good in real life, but she's got all the right small things — nose, chin, ears, bones, waist, bum, ankles — and all the right big things — eyes, mouth, eyelashes, hair.

I say, 'I'm a beginner at this.' I'll be hopeless, please be patient, don't laugh.

'And I haven't even learnt the lines. We'll discover them together.' She looks down at the two pages. 'Who are these people? What's going on?'

'Flatmates? Or could be a mum and daughter.' I am so stupid. If she buys that, guess who'll be the mother?

She reads, quickly. 'Flatmates. Which lines have you learnt?'

'A.'

'Okay, I'm B. A is trying to tell B that she's moving to Australia, but every time she gets up courage B starts talking about the boyfriend who hasn't rung. So A is getting pissed off, but it's not resolved. Right?'

'Right.'

By the time we have read it three times, she knows the two pages better than I do. I must have looked amazed, because she made some comment about doing this five days a week for the past two years. Sometimes twelve scenes a day. The lines went in one side of her brain and came out the other as soon as they said 'Cut'. She suggests that A might be nervously drinking coffee, so we get a mug from Rowan's office. I cling on to it like a tiny liferaft. B could be taking out her anger at her boyfriend by smoking furiously. She gets a packet of cigarettes and a lighter from her briefcase.

'Sorry, but I do. Not for this, though. Rowan's so anti-smoking it's boring. "Preserve the Voice!" Just because he's given up himself.' She puts the cigarette in her mouth and blows out an elegant imaginary puff.

Slowly we add movements (on the new ideas) and pauses, which Vita tells me are called beats, until we've done it about ten times and Rowan is looking at his watch. But still that voice is talking to me: don't try anything interesting or risky. Play safe.

'Know something?' she says, as we pick up our chairs. 'You're good. You've got amazing eyes. You give heaps.'

I have no idea what she's talking about. I'm giving nothing that I'm aware of. Compared with her, who can say lines so naturally you think she's actually talking to you, I must sound boring as hell. All I know is what it's like to try and tell somebody something they don't want to hear.

Even as I get through it and some nice things get said (mostly about Vita) by the class, that little voice is still saying, acting with Vita Rogers, don't be daft. You're a fraud, Tiggie, a pathetic wannabee. Just get through it and go home. Back to being a gofer.

But I take the script Rowan hands me for the third session and Vita wants to be my partner again.

I haven't seen my mother for four days, except when she grunts at me from her bed as I leave for school. She's working nights and can't even blink until eleven. On the fifth day I make an appointment. For Saturday morning, before she goes to work.

'Sorry, darling. This time of the year is always bad for those suckers who have to work. All these public holidays, one after another. No one's at their desks, or they're in yachting mode.' She yawns and picks some mascara out of her eyes. 'Away skiing in Colorado, lucky buggers, or glued to the cricket.'

'What are you doing at the moment?' I am sitting on her bed in the morning sun. It must have been some party last night, because her clothes are all over the floor and she didn't take her make-up off. 'Where's Dad?'

'Out running. What am I doing? Routine piece on corruption in high places. A very respected charity this time.'

'Which one?'

'Sorry. Best you don't know.' I've always understood that investigative reporters have certain ways they protect their children. There are some real crazies out there. 'Tiggie, could you get me a very large glass of water? With ice?'

She's got a hangover. She always drinks a swimming pool when she's got a hangover.

'Bring a whole jug of it.'

And when I've brought a jug of it, with ice, she asks me about school. 'How's everything going?'

'It's all right.'

'No regrets? Not missing the other place?'

'No.'

'That's good. I liked the principal when I met her.'

'Senior management, Mum.' I hadn't liked anything much, that day. I'd nearly changed my mind when I saw a notice outside the front lobby. *No Students past this point. Use side doors.* What sort of school won't allow its own students into its own front door? The lobby, unlike the rest of the school, was all glitz and glamour to impress parents. Nice carpet, sofas, huge bowls of flowers, silver cups behind glass, pictures in silver frames, a receptionist to match. The senior management lady gushed all over her famous parent as much as they ever did at my old school and it was sickening.

'Ah yes. Mustn't forget, senior management,' says Mum. 'In my day she'd have been a head mistress. Well, I liked her anyway. Have you enrolled for any of those amazing courses they offer?'

'No.'

'What about the photography? You like that.'

'Only at Year Ten.'

'Well, surely there's a camera club.'

'I don't know.' We've had these conversations before, Mum getting increasingly exasperated. I know what she's thinking. Why doesn't she *do* something? Get *involved*. Get off her fat butt. She looks so miserable that I decide to throw her a crumb. 'There's the production.'

'Yes?'

'It's end of July. I'm sort of running round after the producer. Gofer.'

'That's great, Tiggie.' She's so pleased that's sickening too, although I can see it's a big effort to stretch her face into a smile. 'God, that light's bright. What are you doing? *Cats*? *Les Mis*?'

'Can't get the rights for those.' I see her eyebrows go up. 'A sort of big pageant. Community Theatre. All the cultural groups and that.'

'Great. Fantastic. You'll meet lots of people.'

'Suppose. Mum, do you know anything about a new soap that's being . . .' I nearly said 'cast' but I stop myself in time. Mum has the sharpest ear in the business. 'Planned?'

'Well, yes, I've heard a few rumours. Why?'

'Oh, just wondered.'

'It's supposed to be absolutely top secret, but you know what this place is. There's talk about it being set in a city gym.'

That would figure. Oh clever Tiggie, a wee pun! They'll only have girls' bodies like Vita's and all the boys will be hunks. No wonder Vita was so excited. Off with the dowdy peach-coloured nurses' uniform and the flat white shoes, and on with the stretch lycra bodysuits and matching headbands.

'Truly vile idea, if you ask me,' Mum is saying. 'Exactly the same as "Shortland Street" except that instead of nurses you'll have gym staff, instead of doctors there'll be personal trainers dispensing wisdom, and patients will be clients coming to get their bodies and self-esteem knocked into shape with pump classes and weights. Still, it might get a few more people going to a gym who need to.'

She's not looking at me as she says this. 'Christ, is that the time?' She crawls out of bed and points herself at the en suite.

Tara runs up behind me in the corridor on Monday afternoon. 'Tiggie, I've caught you! Another couple of lists. Can you have them done by the morning?'

'Sorry, but . . .' Say no.

'I need it tomorrow.'

'I've got something on after school and then a whole heap of homework. I can by Wednesday.' Say *no*. There's still four months to opening night.

'That's too late. Sophia's got a meeting with a sponsor tomorrow. She wants to be able to put a proposal package in front of them.'

'Why doesn't she ask the office?' Say no. What's that phrase I've heard Mum use – your incompetence does not justify me getting in a panic, something like that?

'They're run off their feet in there,' says Tara. 'Don't want to know. Look, this meeting might be the one that gives us the sponsorship we're looking for. The big one, enough to give us real money and them naming rights. It's not very much. Here.'

She thrusts a little pile of handwritten notes at me and smiles down on me for all she's worth. 'See what you can do, Tiggie. Good one.'

'I'll try.' And yes, I'll probably sit up till midnight to do your stupid lists.

That drink bottle is getting right up my nose and I'm going to miss my bus again.

'Ex-cellent.'

As I sit on the bus taking me towards Rowan's third class, I practise saying no. Can you type this list, Tiggie, *now*? No, I can't. Can you ring these people for me, Tiggie, *today*? No, can't you hear me, no! Can you deliver this message, Tiggie, *yesterday*? No, go away, get stuffed!

I also practise saying yes. Have you learnt these lines, Tiggie? Do you really want to go to this class? Has Rowan been soft on you because really, deep down he's sorry for you?

Are you looking forward to meeting Vita again? And if so, why?

Nine

The third class, at which I arrive in the nick of time, is to be about conflict. I don't do conflict. I do clowning and I do backing off and I do walking away but I don't do conflict.

Most problems go away if you forget them, or wait long enough, or put your head in the sand. I don't like conflict.

'Conflict is beautiful,' Rowan is saying as I stare at Vita across the semicircle. She's wearing even less clothing than last time: brief black shorts, which look a bit odd with the black boots and beret, and what looks like a white sports bra. Her arms and legs are the smoothest imaginable brown. Perhaps, unlike ordinary mortals, she doesn't get hairs growing on her limbs, only on her head. It's the circles under her eyes, though, that I notice most.

'Conflict is not necessarily something ugly or destructive,' he is saying, looking hard and straight at me. 'It's profitable and essential and it is the very stuff from which drama is made. All stories, even fairytales, are about conflict. Two wills in disharmony, or an individual in inner turmoil with him or her self – these are the playwright's raw materials. And the novelist's, no less. Now, tell me some situations that give rise to conflict.'

They're a bright bunch, these gals and guys in their black jeans. Suggestions come thick and fast.

'Okay,' says Rowan finally. 'Those all involve two or more people, and yes, I would agree that some of your examples are not beautiful at all, but ugly, violent and destructive. Often they rely on the notion that the end justifies the means. What about inner conflict?'

This time there's a pause before anyone starts speaking, and the answers come more slowly.

'For actors, it is imperative you understand fully what is the conflict for your character, and why. The "why" is even more important. As an actor, you must hang in there until the last possible moment, the last line of the scene, before you concede defeat. Therein lies the energy of a scene. Now, actors, enough chat. To work.'

Vita, who's not said a word so far, is not so quick this time with her chair to the sunniest corner. We settle for an open window where there's a tiny view of the harbour and a cool breeze coming off the sea. I say tentatively, 'Have you heard about your part?'

'Any day now.'

'Must be hard, waiting.'

'It's agony. Torture. It means two years' work if I get it.'

'Are you working at the moment?'

'Resting. See lots of films. Drink *lots* of latte. The gym. I run a bit. Voice classes, and this one. Auditions. Amazing how the days go. How's school?'

'Foul.'

'I loathed mine. My parents couldn't afford it and I wish they hadn't bothered. And then I had private tutoring when I started TV work. Lessons in between scenes. Speaking of which,' she sees Rowan's beady eyes upon us, 'what's this scene about? Who was I again?'

How can she be so laid back? Or perhaps it's just an act? 'You're B and you're funny!'

We rehearse and perform the scene, two people (again in a flat) bitching at each other. To my surprise, although I'm no less trembling and sweaty than last time, once I get going I rather enjoy it, since I don't bitch at people in real life and I do know the lines every which way. And this time it's me, rather than Vita, who gets the nod from the class. Not that I believe them. We must make a strange couple. Two of Vita could fit into the baggy trackpants and dull blue XXL T-shirt that I'm wearing.

At one point in the scene I'd noticed her eyes glaze over, almost as though she was going to faint. She sat down earlier than the place we rehearsed and began unlacing her boots. Everyone else thought it was just one of the actions her character would do.

Not that I knew any better, then.

Outside the shabby inner-city building where we have our classes, Vita says goodbye to me, turns away and collapses.

Just goes limp, and falls on the concrete. Her head makes a faint cracking noise, hollow, like when you hit a coconut.

I look at her stupidly for a moment, then around for the others from the class, but we were the last to leave and they've all gone. The new class is already in. There's no one walking around, no cars in the alley.

I don't know what to do. I bend down and a sensible voice tells me she's not dead because I can see a pulse beating in her thin neck. Another voice says to loosen off clothing especially round neck but that's silly when she's wearing next to nothing on her top half anyway. Raise legs? Head between legs? Which?

I get under her shoulders and fold her in half, like a rag doll. Under the smooth brown skin, I can feel rib bones, shoulder bones. Lots of bones.

'Vita?'

It's like a scene out of a cop movie – the star (beautiful blonde, of course) discovered unconscious in deserted back alley by helpless, innocent (and plain) bystander. I look around, my heart racing. There's even a cat mewing at me, and rubbish bins. I half expect to get ambushed by a guy with a gun. I want to put some protection round her bare shoulders but she has no extra clothes with her and only in a really dire emergency, like blood spurting out of an artery, would I take off my T-shirt. The school uniform crushed up in my backpack stinks. She's only fainted, I think, but I have no idea what to do next.

'Vita?'

She starts to twitch and then I see her eyelids flutter and her arm goes up to rub at her face and the back of her head where she hit the deck.

'Vita? Just don't . . . I'm going to get Rowan.'

She tightens. 'No you're not.'

'Yes I am.'

'Don't you dare.'

'What? You need help. I'm going to get help.'

'Tiggie, this is conflict class for real. I just blacked out. It's nothing. I don't want you to get Rowan, *okay*?'

'Just get you a drink of water?'

'No.' She is glaring at me with such ferocity that I back off. 'There's a cellphone in my bumbag. Call a cab.'

'Haven't you got your car?'

'I'll get it tomorrow.' She's already fumbling for her cigarettes.

When I've found the tiny yellow cellphone I don't know how to use that either, so she takes it from me and makes the call. The taxi must have been cruising close by, because it comes round the corner almost immediately. The driver looks at us sideways as I help her up and into the cab. Stoned, boozed, or both? But I'm almost certain he recognises her when he looks in the rear mirror.

She gives a Mt Eden address and lights a disgusting cigarette, even though there's a Thank You For Not Smoking sign in the taxi. The driver doesn't protest; famous people can break the rules. I wonder if she's fallen asleep. Her cellphone goes off. She blinks, swears, fishes it out again and turns it off. After twenty minutes of skilful, silent driving through the rush-hour traffic we pull up outside an old villa with great clouds of lavender bushes below the verandah and a drooping willow over the front gate. What now, I think. How do I get home from here?

'Your parents' place?' I say.

'Yeah,' she says, handing over a credit card. 'No one's there. Come on in. I'll pay for your cab home.' She wants a receipt from the taxi driver.

Well, I wasn't going to drive off in the taxi and just leave her, was I? We climb the steep wooden steps up to the front door, me behind in case she topples back again.

The house is a surprise. It's a bit arty-crafty and chaotic and looks as though no one quite runs it. No one goes around picking up newspapers, magazines, coffee cups, bits of knitting, men's running shoes, bills and the torn envelopes they came in. Maybe they never do, until someone decides they can't stand it.

'What do you want me to do?'

'Make me a very strong coffee,' she says. 'Coffee stuff is in the fridge. It's a plunger thing. No milk.' I leave her sitting on a sofa.

The kitchen is untidy but upmarket, all wood, and judging by the Italian cookbooks and garlic presses, her mum's interested in food. I guess from all the dirty dishes and marmalade jars and half-eaten salads that someone's had breakfast, and then lunch. I can't help picking at a chicken carcass and some fancy bread, which is not quite what you do in other people's houses, but who's to know. I'm an expert at rearranging leftovers on a plate.

There's a note on the table – *Vita, ring your agent. Urgent. Pissed off – rung six times, says your frigging cellphone's been off. Fergus.* When I've put the kettle on and washed the coffee plunger, she's disappeared from the living room. She doesn't answer my call outside the bathroom, nor any of the closed bedroom doors. I'm not a panicky sort of person, but I'm panicking now. Fallen down the steps? 'Shortland Street' star dies after faint, friend fails as caregiver.

'Vita!'

I know which is her bedroom because she's got a huge photo of herself as trainee nurse Nerida on the outside. Tiny noises are coming from inside, but I don't barge into people's bedrooms.

'Vita. Are you all right?'

In between grunts she tells me to make the coffee. Grunts could mean asthma (though I've not seen her with an inhaler), or someone in trouble. Grunts require action.

She's on the floor doing sit-ups, fast and furious, concentrating intensely.

'Go away.'

Strangely, she doesn't sound angry, or even as though she means it. I stare at this little body, hands behind her head, going up and down, up, down, up, down, like clockwork. About thirty minutes ago she was fainting in a back alley.

'Circu . . . lation . . . going. Best for . . . shitty . . . heads,' she explains when I don't move. 'It's true. It's working. Best thing.'

I would have thought it was the worst thing, but who am I, what do I know? I've only known this famous star and cover girl for two acting classes, a faint and a taxi ride. Perhaps a bit of mild exercise *is* good after a faint, gets the blood moving. But then this isn't mild exercise.

Clothes on the floor, mostly boring black. Lots of film posters, postcards of 'Shortland Street' stars, a thousand lipsticks and French perfumes on the dressing table. Black satin sheets and duvet on an unmade double bed. By the bed a tray of pills. I've never seen so many pills — Women's Multi, Berocca, other vitamins and minerals I've never heard of, odourless garlic, pills for stress and migraines and insomnia, to lift you up and calm you down. Just about enough to stock the homoeopathic shelves in a chemist. I'm exaggerating, but there are at least twenty bottles and packets.

A set of digital scales are under the bed, not quite obscured by the black sheets.

An unfortunate thought goes through my head. I know some of these people and they're scary, but not Vita. Impossible. Not Vita Rogers, rich and famous and gorgeous and absolutely everything going for her. Nah.

'There's a message for you,' I say. 'Someone called Fergus.'

'Ring Fergus? He's my lazy brother. Why would I . . . ring Fergus?'

'No, that's who signed it. Ring your agent. She's called six times. Urgent.'

She's into that bumbag and onto her little yellow cellphone before I can blink. I can tell she's about to ask me to leave, so I go back to the kitchen leaving her desperately keying in numbers and muttering, 'Emily! Answer the phone!' As I pour the water onto the coffee, I hear a great scream, then lots of talk, so she's not dead or anything. Laughter, so it was good news?

Then silence. So what the hell's going on now?

'Vita? Coffee?' I say cautiously outside the bedroom door.

She's crying, sobbing her heart out. What do I do *now*? 'Vita? Are you all right?'

'I've got the part,' she sobs. 'I've got it.' Another great scream. 'Yeah!!! Yes!! I've got it, Tiggie.' She leaps up and hugs the only person who's available, that's me holding her coffee. She has a sweaty body smell. But then it is hot and muggy, and fainting makes you sweaty.

'Do you want this? Or what's left of it?'

Still crying, laughing, snivelling, almost incoherent at times, she sits on the bed and tells me that the contract's for two years, two years' good money 'cause she's keeping the family in this house, really. She pays the rates and a lot of the bills. Her mother slaves sixty hours a week at a pittance for a kids' charity, and her father got restructured from Telecom four years ago and her brother, who's twenty-six and a plumber, just treats the place like a motel and sponges on all of them.

But apart from that, it's her first big role in her own right. Not someone's daughter and bimbo trainee nurse. Her character's one of the receptionists, but she also gets to do gym work, seeing everyone who works at the gym does classes and that.

Wow, I keep saying. Wow I say to someone who knows she's got no spare tyres and the tightest little butt in the world, no reason to worry about how she's being photographed in a bodysuit doing gym. I can't imagine what that's like.

'Tiggie, my agent has sworn me to secrecy. It's being announced in a week. Promise? Absolutely promise?'

'Can I take your picture?' I say. 'For your book — Vita, the day she heard about . . . what are they calling it?'

' "Shapers". Have you got a camera with you?'

'Always do. I want to be a photographer.'

I am such a liar.

When I see the pictures a few days later, there's Vita with cup of coffee, posing as a star on her bed. Though smiling, you can tell she's been crying and her hair, the bob that on television is always as smooth as corn-yellow velvet, curved under to her tiny neck, is all rumpled. But I took it in portrait format, that's up and down, so I could get in all her legs, and in the bottom corner of the picture you can see the digital scales peeping out from under the black sheets.

I get some copies made and send them to Mt Eden.

Ten

I'VE BEEN PROMOTED.

Gofer (over-worked), actor (secret), now editor (reluctant).

Yep, that's me. Antigone Tompson, editor of the programme for the production. It's a pig of a job and no one else wants to do it, and once again Tara used her inescapable logic to say, 'Well you've got a big home computer with desktop publishing for sure. You know how to use it, don't you? Set up databases and stuff like that? You're it, mate.'

I didn't tell her that Dad thinks he's a computer nerd and would most likely jump at the chance to teach me desktop publishing if I asked him. Father and daughter togetherness, for a change.

'I'm not all that good on computers. And I don't know anything about design.'

'We'll find a graphics student to do the design. You just have to get the material together, names and pictures, biogs, etcetera. All on a disk, no sweat.'

She threw in a bit of flattery, in between swigs at her pump bottle. 'Sophia's really, really impressed with your organisational abilities. You're so great on detail.'

She's lying, of course.

'And you can take the mugshots too. Excellent! You'll need pix of Sophia, Gareth. The musical director. And little ol' me, your friendly producer.'

Once again, I was unable to say no, no and no.

I said yes, just so she'd take her pushy self and her drink bottle out of my face.

What it actually means, Gareth tells me later that day, is that I have to go round all the groups taking part and get the names of all the performers. All of them. Sophia believes it's important that every single person involved, on stage and off, is right there in the programme. It'll be sizeable, but she's finding a sponsor.

'You mean all the Samoans in the Samoan group?' I ask. 'All the Koreans? The orchestra and the bands? There'll be *hundreds*.'

'Just get lists of names from the teachers in charge. Or the student organiser. It's a collating job, really.'

'For a sucker.'

'No way. Someone with an eye for detail and words. You'll be fine.' As he often does, he reaches out for a friendly pat on the arm. From anyone else I'd find this creepy and patronising. I get the full-on pixie smile. 'Give yourself permission to enjoy it, my friend. We'll be starting workshop rehearsals next week. The acting group.'

'That's only for Sophia's course.'

'Not exclusively. I'll give you a buzz. Okay?'

Programme compiled by Antigone Tompson. Assistant to the producer, Antigone Tompson.

If that thought might give Tiggie Tompson, who's never seen her name on anything, quite a buzz, what must Vita feel when she sees her name in cast lists and all over the newspapers and on the front cover of the glossy magazines. *Vita's new role in* 'Shapers' shouting at you from the racks in every bookshop and supermarket and corner grocery in the country. Yep, folks, 'Shapers', the long-awaited new Kiwi soap, is all over the place. They had a huge champagne launch this week, to which Mum goes of course, bringing home a media kit which includes interviews with the producers and the writer whose concept it was, pictures of the twelve core cast and designer's sketches of the sets.

There's Dr Ruth Bray, the owner of the gym, and her assistant, Mike Henare. There are two receptionists, Holly (that's Vita's character) and a spunk called Lloyd. There's the head of gym staff, Joe, and two personal trainers, Rata and Brody. The boss of the cafeteria is Pene, and the physiotherapist, David. And then there are two aerobics instructors, Mandy and Brent, and the facilitator of the cultural arena, Moana.

But wait, for those of you who, like Mum, thought it would just be a pseudo-medical drama set in a gym rather than an emergency clinic, there's much, much more. We get long interviews with the designer, whose brief is to create an updated version of an ancient Greek gymnasium. The set for the 'Shapers' gym, to be built somewhere on Auckland's North Shore, will be stunning Greek architecture, all pillars and statues and hot and cold spa pools of white marble. Obviously it will be a place for beautiful people, though of course a gymnasium for the third millennium would be for women as much as men and for all ages. Greek gyms were only for men.

But wait, there's more again. The twentieth century revival of the gym has been almost entirely focused on fitness, health and the body beautiful. People go to a gym to work out and coincidentally, to meet people.

'Shapers' gym will revert to the Greek model. Often the most beautiful building in a Greek city, it was a youth centre for both physical and intellectual activities. Part of the complex was also what we would today call a cultural centre. Here philosophers, poets, musicians and artists had debates about the meaning of life and art and listened to music and poetry. So 'Shapers' storylines will be able to include characters coming to the gym who are writers, musicians, dancers, artists . . .

'All wonderful televisual stuff,' snorts Mum when she comes home from the very long launch party (at lunchtime so they could be filmed to catch the 6 pm news) and throws the thick, glossy media kit onto the glass table. She smells strongly of cigarettes and she's in a dangerous mood.

'The point is, will we care a fig about these self-absorbed people in orange neon lycra, pumping away at their little weights?' she says, throwing herself on the couch. She's got red wine down the front of her silk shirt. 'Or their misguided, misshapen clients, each bringing their own sad little saga of doom and gloom to boost up the storylines and the ratings? I don't think so.'

My mother can be such a bitch when she's had too much.

'Did you get a taxi home?' says Dad, pouring her a soda water.

'Yes, I did,' she replies aggressively.

'Where's the wagon then?'

'Where it usually is, in the carpark. Quite safe till morning. Get off my back.'

I am looking at a picture of Vita in the brochure. It's the full star treatment and she looks stunning.

'Jobs for actors,' I say quietly, remembering the tiny weeping sixteen-year-old who pays most of her family's bills.

'Oh sure, jobs,' says Mum. 'Provided they're under twenty-three.' She looks over suddenly, her eyes not quite seeing me, gets up and goes and pours some whisky into her soda water. 'Since when have you worried about actors getting work? Have you got some new friends at school who foolishly want to be actors?'

'No.'

'No new friends?'

'Not much.'

'Why not?'

'I just haven't met any.'

'Antigone, my pet, I am getting just a tad tired of hearing that you have no friends and no hobbies and no ambitions and nothing that makes you feel glad to be alive.'

'Cassie,' warns Dad. 'Lay off.'

'No, let's have a little honesty here. I would very much like to see my daughter do something as well as walk to school, do homework and surf the Net. I would like to see her have a social life. I would like to see her do some sport. I would like to see her lose a little weight.'

'Don't you mean a lot?' I mumble.

'Well yes, since you ask, I do mean quite a lot. I would actually like my daughter to look healthy and fit.'

'I am healthy. I never get sick.' I can't resist adding, 'I didn't ask to get pneumonia.'

'*Cassie*,' says Dad again, stronger. This time Mum is obviously not going to be stopped by the unmentionable camp.

'I would like to see her father stop complaining to me . . .'

'. . . and me,' I say.

'. . . about her weight. I'd like to see him, as a self-confessed fitness freak, *do* something.'

'Like what?' he says. 'Take her on bike rides? Pump iron together?'

'Why not? I would like to see her name on a programme for something. Something – anything – that required a bit of oomph, get up and go. Enthusiasm. Commitment. What are you smiling about, Tiggie?'

'Nothing.'

'"Nothing" does not make people smile. There's always "something" behind a smile. A thought. A connection. An incongruity.' She has trouble with that word. 'Always. So tell.'

I suppose it's natural – when you're being bullied you want to do exactly the opposite. I can't tell her.

'Didn't you say you were gofering for a production?' says Dad.

'Yes.'

'Why, tell me – *why* doesn't this child ever volunteer any information?' cries Mum.

'I do.'

'You do not! You've told us practically nothing about your new school, your teachers – which reminds me, when's the parent teacher evening? There must be one soon.'

'It was Monday night. You were working.'

'You took the decision out of my hands?'

'I gave you the bit of paper.'

'No you did not!'

'In the kitchen. You put it by the phone.'

'You should have reminded me.'

'Cassie, calm down!'

'How was I to know that was why they were setting up tables and stuff in the hall,' I shouted. 'I'm sorry I'm such a disappointment to you and can't be your gofer and minder and secretary and desktop publisher as well as everyone else's.'

'So you are doing things at school you're not telling us about!' she says with a snarky victorious grin. 'Secretarial things. Desktop publishing!'

'Maybe. I'm going.'

'What is *so hard* about tossing your own parents a few crumbs, a little pleasure? When you're a mother, you'll understand.'

'I'm not going to have children. Anyway, who'd want me?'

'Tiggie, please don't walk off,' begs Dad. 'We can talk this through.'

'Conflict is not beautiful,' I state, halfway down the hall.

'Who said it was?'

'Someone.' Someone who paired me up with a gay guy with a huge Adam's apple at my class yesterday. Vita had rung with apologies; she was rehearsing. Someone who told me that I wasn't committing myself fully to the scene, that I lacked energy and focus – the first real criticism to come from him. The scene was two lovers working out whose job was more important. Would *she* follow *him* to his new job in Australia?

'Some dickhead,' I say sourly as I shut my door.

Down in the street below I could see a florist's van pull up, a delivery boy getting out with a bunch of flowers that was vast even from twelve floors up. Someone's in luck, I thought.

A minute later I hear the doorbell go and a voice through the intercom. If the flowers are for anyone in this apartment block they'll be for my mother. She gets presents like flowers and perfume and bottles of champagne all the time, from admirers and from people she's championed on her stories. 'Grateful patients,' she calls them. I see the van drive off. Then Dad is knocking on my door.

'Tiggie?'

'Go away.'

'Urgent delivery for you. Flowers.'

'Can't be.'

'So there are two Antigone Tompsons? There's a note with them.'

Crazy possibilities run through my head. My old school saying sorry? Rowan telling me not to waste his time, don't come back to his classes? A secret admirer? *Gareth*? When it's rumoured he's got girls after him in droves, nah. It's not my birthday. It's not St Valentine's Day. My three grandparents were last heard of on the Gold Coast and in Guernsey. I have a cousin somewhere down Gisborne way. Who else do I know?

'Don't you want to see them?' says Dad. 'Can I come in?'

'Okay.'

I can hardly see him for sunflowers, roses, carnations, greenery, ribbons, bows, and the basket they all come in. No one has ever sent me, just me, magnificent flowers like this.

'Where do you want them?'

'Oh. Just . . .' I take the envelope from among the yellow roses and turn it over. He stands the basket on my desk and says, although he must be dying of curiosity, 'Do you want me to leave you alone?'

'Yes.'

'Mum's sorry about the scene she made. She's worried about holding down her job.'

'Why?'

'A chance remark at the launch today, from someone very senior and powerful, concerning her fortieth. She thinks the writing's on the wall.'

'But her birthday is months away yet.'

'True, but . . . it's made her very upset and she's sorry.'

'That's okay,' I say resignedly. 'She's pissed.'

The flowers, by urgent courier, are from Vita. The note was obviously faxed through to the florist. The writing is neat and so tiny that I have to strain to read it.

Hi Tiggie – I couldn't get to class yesterday because I've started rehearsals for 'Shapers' and I was BUSHED. But it's fun because lots of the actors have been on 'Shortland Street'. These are to say thanks for taking me home last week, also the pictures. Now, if you get a phone call from a strange woman with an English accent called Emily, don't flip. She's my agent and she wants to meet you and probably arrange an audition for a guest spot on 'Shapers' coming up soon. I told her I knew just the person!!!! You may want to thank me or kill me, but I really liked those two scenes we did together and you have got <u>fantastic</u> eyes just made for tele work. Emily will ring around 4.30 and tell you more.

LOTS of love and good luck – Vita

I spend the rest of the evening staring out at the sun setting behind the western hills, watching the sky turn from scarlet to peach to pale pink. Then an apricot layer and all the blues, and a new crescent moon with one big bright planet beside it. Venus, I think. They say it's bad luck to see a new moon through glass, but up here where the windows don't actually open, I don't have any choice unless I go down to the garden around the highrise. The nights are, as Mum keeps saying, setting in, getting shorter. The leaves on the oak trees lining the street are turning brown, falling.

Emily. An audition. As if acting classes and programme editor weren't already enough. I feel like a rider on a runaway horse approaching a cliff-edged valley so wide you can't see the other side. In cartoons they grow wings and soar across the gap to music, or else drop like stones and end up swinging, snagged on a handy life-saving bush or splatt!! on the riverbed.

I try to do some homework but can't. Several times I pick up the phone to ring Vita and ask her isn't she really pulling my leg? What about Gareth? I've got his home number. Am I being silly . . . but what's the point, when I know he'll just say fantastic and go for it, girl.

Ring Sophia? I've only spoken about ten words to Sophia. She's too busy to get to know anyone much other than her drama students, and Tara's in fantasy land, too busy-busy being Tara, and she hates me.

Ring Rowan? Well, I'm ringing you 'cause I've been offered an audition for this new soap and I want to know if you think I'm just wasting everyone's time and surely Vita's just being silly even to suggest it? And there must be one fat girl floating about who's done lots of speech training and school plays (as nurses and grumpy old women). Rowan, tell me it's not really a good idea for a beginner and I'll forget Vita even mentioned it. When she rings I'll tell the agent that my parents say I can't take time off school. Sorry to trouble you. End of call, end of story.

Don't I *really* want him to tell me he thinks I've got a lot of hidden talent just waiting to be discovered?

Can I ask my mother out there, who's gone out for a meal with Dad 'cause she's too tired (and too pissed) to cook and they want to have some quality time together? What would she, when she's sober, say?

'I would like to see my daughter try for a soap. Yes, definitely. Go for it, Tiggie. Have fun!'

But she'd probably add quietly to Dad, later, 'It'll be the making of that girl, bring her out of herself. But . . . I just wish it was for a different sort of part. More, let's say, normal. Where she won't be laughed at.'

Well, I'm not stupid! I know I'm not in the same category as Vita and the other girls in Rowan's class, and the other girls in Sophia's classes, who all want to play Juliet and Ophelia and be core cast on 'Shapers'. I've already worked out that there's only one sort of part I'd be going for on 'Shapers'. What did Mum say: misguided and misshapen?

In the end, I don't ring anyone. I've got till 4.30 tomorrow to make up my mind.

Eleven

I MEANT TO SAY NO. HONESTLY, I DID. AT TWO IN THE MORNING, SO FAR sleepless, I'd made my fourth great life-changing decision. I will be proactive about this. I will ring this Emily person from school and tell her that Vita's very sweet to have suggested me, and thanks but no thanks. If she's not there, I will leave a message on her voice mail. I will not be home at 4.30 if she still rings despite the message. If and when I next see Vita at class, or she rings me, I'll say my parents said no. End of story.

Well, at morning break Tara was waiting for me outside my class. She took the whole twenty minutes to find and pass over scruffy bits of paper with the contact names of all the groups involved in the production.

At lunchtime, going past the hall where the Samoan group was rehearsing, and the gym where the rock band was rehearsing, and the music suite where a choir was doing its thing, I popped in and bravely introduced myself to the teachers. I told them what I wanted for the programme. I listened for a while, fascinated and envious. The bell went. Lunchtime was over. I didn't make the call.

After school I wandered home, practising saying no. At 4.30 the phone went.

'Emily Chatwin here. When can you come in and see me?'

'Well, I've . . .'

'You're at school until 3.30. What about after school tomorrow, Thursday?'

'Vita's got it all . . .'

75

'Would 3.45 pm suit you? I'm in Parnell, actually not too far from your school. Walking distance, if you don't mind a little walk.'

'My parents . . .'

'Oh yes, they'll need to be involved, in due course. Have you got a fax? The same number?'

'Yes, but . . .'

'I'll send a fax through now, something about myself and the agency. Best to know who you're dealing with. Confirm the time and place. Ciao for now.'

Another sleepless night, tossing and turning, staring out at the moon which is a little bigger than last night. I'm going to turn up with big black rings under my fantastic eyes. My eyes may be all I've got going for me. If I turn up.

'Emily Chatwin.' The person who stands at the front door and grasps my sweaty hand firmly is small, plain and brisk and she's already run her eyes up and down all of me. There is some sort of terrier dog at her heels, also small, plain and brisk.

'This is Jessie. She's getting on a bit. One of the advantages of working from home. Come in, do. I like people who are punctual.'

It may look like an ordinary restored villa from the outside, but it's a proper office she leads me into, with all the phones, faxes, scanners, computers and printers that Dad has in his. Theatre posters on the walls. She indicates that I should sit on the sofa and that the orange drink on the square table in front is for me.

'Please, Antigone, go ahead. It's still warm out there. Looks like another Indian summer. You got my fax?'

'Yes. Thank you.' I had stood by Dad's machine and grabbed it off in the nick of time.

'So you know a little about my chequered past in theatre, and my present work which I adore. What I offer and what I expect? Now, I know nothing about you, other than you're bravely doing Rowan's classes with Vita. Fill me in.'

'I am . . . well, Year Nine at Eastern College.'

'Age what, fourteen? Enjoying it?'

'Um . . . sort of.'

'Involved in drama?'

'Not really. Just helping the producer for some big production in July.'

'Aren't you doing Sophia Banks' famous drama course?'

'No.'

'Why not?' When I hesitate, she presses, 'But you've taken on Rowan, whose students either worship or hate him?'

'Do they?'

'Assuredly. On balance, it's worship. Quite rightly. He's the finest teacher in the country. But he can be very tough. Some can't take it.'

'I know. I've found out.'

'And you can?'

Jessie jumps up onto my lap.

'Jessie, off!'

'No, it's all right. I like dogs.'

'Do you have one?'

'I used to. He got given away when we moved.'

'Do you miss him?'

I can't trust myself to answer that. Jess is soft and old and warm.

'I've been Vita's agent for two years now. She's a very special, very astute young woman whose talent and interests I have carefully nurtured. From soaps, she could go a long way.'

'I guess.'

'She has a very clear idea of what she likes and what she wants. So when she tells me that she really liked acting with you, and I'm looking for a young actor specially suited for a particular part – so far without success – I'm inclined to listen. I would like to take you on as a client, if you agree? The first step will be an audition.'

I nod, and concentrate hard on not spilling my orange juice in one hand and stroking Jessie with the other. This is the jump off the cliff edge, Tiggie. From here there is no turning back. Are you ready?

'Yes?' she prompts. And I nod.

'Splendid!' The phone goes. 'Excuse me.' It's some actor complaining about a fax not arriving. She will send it again, give her ten minutes.

When she sits down she has a script and all the glossy stuff about 'Shapers' in her hands.

'I've seen that,' I say without thinking.

'Really? How?'

Curses! But we had to get it out of the way sometime. 'My mother went to the launch on Tuesday. She's Cassandra Tompson.'

'Aha. I wondered. Unusual spelling. That's very good.'

She says it with such enthusiasm that I blurt out, 'Why?'

'I know your mother's a reporter, not an actor, but she works in front of a camera. Presumably you know something about television culture. You would have watched her filming, I imagine?'

'She's never offered to take me. So I haven't.'

'Oh. Well, the publicists will be happy when the time comes.'

'I haven't got the part yet.'

'Ah, silly me, yes, the part.' Again the phone goes, but she lets it ring until her answerphone kicks in. 'The part, Antigone, is in "Shapers", as you know. It's one of the first major guest storylines they're introducing. Faith is a fourteen-year-old who comes to the gym as winner of a prize organised by a magazine . . . let me see, where did I put that bit of paper . . . to . . . ah . . .'

She's faltering. This prim lady in the navy skirt, white blouse and pearl earrings, whom I quite like, is embarrassed.

'To lose some weight,' I say, stroking Jessie's white throat.

'Precisely. Now that's about all I know at this stage. They've only sent the character breakdown and one audition scene. Oh, and . . .' Again she hesitates. 'They say the actor must be prepared not to lose weight during the shoot. You can cope with that?'

'Yes. Won't happen anyway.'

'Here's the audition time and the script,' she says, quickly, letting that pass. 'Ring and confirm you're coming. Just wear something comfortable. It's a nice scene.'

'Do I have to learn it?' In my hand are three pages of dialogue.

'Yes. Get the lines down. I always used to use a tape recorder. The casting director's an old friend of mine. She's very gentle and will give you some direction. If you're offered the part, your parents will have to give their permission and be involved on the contractual side. And it will mean getting over to the North Shore at some pretty odd hours. Do they know you've come today?'

'Not really.' She looks at me questioningly. 'No.'

'I have a problem with this, Tiggie. Legally and morally, they should know. If you got the part, or even if I take you on as a client for the future, my contract is with them, not you. So is the contract with the production company.'

'Why?'

'Because you're a minor.'

'I . . . can I do the audition and then tell them only if I get it?'

'It's certainly irregular.' Her hand goes to the telephone and my dream starts to feel like a cruel trick. 'What say I give one of them a ring right now?'

'No. I . . . it'll . . . they wouldn't say, good on you for trying. They'd say . . . or they'd make me feel . .'

'What?' Her hand rests on the phone, a sinister claw. 'Are you telling me you won't do the audition if they have to be told?'

'Yes. I guess I am. I'm sorry, wasting your time . .' I suddenly want out of here, before she sees my eyes are wet with disappointment.

'Tiggie, just . .' she says, taking her hand away from the phone. 'As I said, Edwina, the casting director, is an old friend. Just this once, I'm prepared to bend a little. On condition that you tell them immediately.'

'If I get the part,' I say for the second time, breathing again.

I'm rescued by a knock at the front door. It's her next appointment. I recognise the face of about the most famous 'Shortland Street' actor as I go out. The spunky ambulance driver. It's really odd – as with Vita, I feel I know him. But I don't know him, do I?

'Good luck,' calls Emily, holding Jessie in her arms. 'And Tiggie – after the audition, call me immediately.'

* * *

'Phone for you,' calls Dad. He hates it when the phone goes during 'Coronation Street'. 'Someone called Vita.'

'How did you get on?' says Vita's voice. 'When's your audition? Did you like her?'

'Fine, Monday afternoon and yes.'

'She gave you the script?'

'Yeah.'

'You're going to go?'

'Yeah.' But I don't know how, without telling Mum or taking a day off school.

'How you going to get there?'

'Bus.' I'll take a whole day off school.

'Hang on, just check. Somewhere here.' I can hear papers being shuffled. I think of that bedroom with the black satin sheets and the tray of pill bottles and the lipsticks lying in dust. 'Thought so. My call is for the afternoon. I'll come and pick you up.'

'No, I'll get a bus.'

'Tiggie, I'd *like* to take you, okay. If I didn't want to, I wouldn't have offered.'

'It doesn't feel . . .'

'What — right? Me a cover girl and all that crap,' she laughs. 'You'll get over it. Pick you up at 1 pm from — what's that horrible uniform you wear?'

'Eastern College.'

'One pm at the gate. What's the scene like?'

'My character is telling her trainer about the teasing she's been getting at school about winning this prize. But she won't tell the trainer why she's got these bruises on her face and arms.'

'Great. Use a tape recorder. I'm going away for the weekend otherwise I'd have offered to hear them. But I'll hear them in the car on the way over.'

'Vita, what do I wear? I forgot to ask Emily.'

'Not your school uniform, that's for sure. Just something you feel good in, not too dressy. Jeans, sweatshirt sort of thing. Don't wear black, or white, or tomato red or anything too patterned and busy. Keep it simple.'

'I don't wear make-up.'

'Well, it's about time you did. I'll do something subtle but gorgeous to you in the car. Must off, lines to learn. Glad you liked Emily, she's the best in the business, sharp as a tack. And she wouldn't have sent you for the audition if she didn't think you had a good chance. She never does. Oh, by the way, they might get you to do a bit of improv, talk about yourself and that. Cheers.'

Now I've got two sets of lines to learn. And lists of names and biogs to collect for the programme. And production meetings to go to, before school, during lunch breaks.

This busy life isn't quite what I anticipated at Eastern College.

Mum, trying to make up for being so nasty to me the other night, takes me shopping. The mother and daughter thing. She thinks I need some new clothes and for once she's not working this Saturday. I say yep, thinking of my audition, and steer her in the direction of some jeans shops in Newmarket where I hope they might have the odd size 16 and possibly even the black jeans which all actors seem to wear. They do, and they fit, with a bit of a squeeze. I won't let her in the changing room. I won't let her even peek her head in. I won't come out. But I've learnt to tell for myself whether something fits. These do, just, if I hold my breath and suck in the tum and stand up straight and lose a few pounds.

Then it's sweatshirts and some cotton knit tops, and a new jacket and even a pair of Doc Martens' and by that time Mum's gold credit card has been given a bit of a fright. I've got used to shop ladies fussing round Mum because they recognise her. She's quite surprised at my new interest in clothes and choice of jacket. I do let her see that on me, because I'm not quite sure and it's expensive, so fair enough. But she likes it. The shop girl says she loves it on me and remarks about the miraculous slimming effects of black. Next Monday I'll wear the black jeans and the emerald long-sleeved cotton knit jersey which wasn't exactly cheap either. I like green, it goes with my eyes.

Both Mum and Dad have gently prodded me about the flowers. 'An admirer,' I say grinning, enjoying the power this gives me. I can just about see them biting their tongues off in frustration. Mum doesn't like people withholding information. She prides herself on being able to prise anything out of anybody.

Just to make sure, I hide Vita's letter in my school backpack, down the very bottom. At my old school I was always hearing people complain about their mothers snooping round their bedrooms reading their diaries and stuff. On the other hand, I think some of them wanted this to happen, otherwise they wouldn't be stupid enough to leave their private diaries lying there. And probably it was the only way the mothers found out anything.

But Vita's letter I kept with me, safe. And Emily's fax. When – and if – I have to tell my parents what's going on, I want it to be a surprise.

It won't happen, Antigone. You're just going for an audition. If you have to do any improv it will be a total disaster. You won't get the part. Ask yourself if there's any point going on with Rowan's classes.

Nah.

But I spent most of the weekend learning the lines, with the cues coming through headphones on the tape recorder. Homework, I said to Mum.

TWELVE

At eight o'clock on Monday morning, Gareth is doing me a big favour. He once used me as unwilling target practice for his video camera; I am now perched on the same stool in the same drama suite, but at my request. Sitting bolt upright so that my stomach rolls don't show, with my head bravely up, I am trying to get used to that wide black lens pointing at me, and the tiny red light which tells me it's recording.

If he is mystified as he sets up the camera, starts it running and sits down to talk, he isn't showing it.

'Ready when you are. Action.'

'Give me a subject,' I say, my stomach churning. My theory is that if I put myself through this little ordeal now, it will pay off this afternoon. Vita has told me she never thinks about the cameras even when they're almost literally in her face, so it is possible.

'Well,' he says, thoughtfully, deadpan. 'What about the history, psychology and theory of bungey-jumping, from the Solomon Islanders to A.J. Hackett.'

'Ga-reth!'

'Life cycle of the Indian tree snake. Homer Simpson as American archetype. No? Well then, try acting lessons with Rowan Hughes, a new student's impressions.'

I collapse like he's stuck a pin in me.

'It's not fair. Oh *bugger*. How did you know?'

'Greg, one of the class. He's a Year Twelve here. He says you've made quite an impression on Rowan.'

'That's bullshit. They laugh at me.'

'Antigone.' He leans forward, suddenly serious, and puts his hands on my knees. 'Listen to me. That is not true. They respect you.'

I can't hold his gaze and his hands are making me feel uncomfortable, so I swing around and stare out at the empty courtyard instead. It's too early in the morning for bullies to have found their targets. Seagulls with red feet are pecking at some bit of attractive edible rubbish in a corner.

'I wanted to see what it was like without anyone knowing, or talking about me, or laughing.'

'If this is for an audition, Tiggie, you'd better get used to it. People do talk. They're *interested.* Is that such a bad thing? Do you want to run through the scene you're learning?'

'Learnt. It's this afternoon.'

'You don't waste any time!' he says. I feel myself blushing at the compliment as I dig the script out of my backpack and hand it over. 'What show's this for?' he asks.

'Don't laugh. "Shapers".'

'You're kidding! For real?' I can see his mind ticking over: where do I fit in? 'Good for you. What happens to the character?'

'I don't know. She comes to the gym, for obvious reasons. Well, she's won a year's free membership. The token fat girl. I've been told I can't lose weight during the shoot. *If* I get it.'

'So she must . . .' Like Emily, lifelong skinnies both, Gareth falters. 'Then she must be one of their . . .' He can't quite bring himself to say 'failures'.

'I don't know how it ends.'

'I think you should find out.'

'I will, don't worry.'

'Do you want to run through this scene? Just a line run?'

'Okay.' I'm suddenly aware again of the red light. 'You're the trainer.'

We rip through the scene. I can tell he's not much impressed with the writing, but he's too polite on this occasion to say so. By the third time, I've nearly forgotten the camera and I'm wondering if I'm getting the hots for this lanky guy with the black ponytail.

84

By the fifth run, I have forgotten the camera and I'm burning.

In the white Fiat, parked beside the beach a block away from the 'Shapers' studio, Vita has stubbed out her second of two cigarettes and is about to do something gorgeous and subtle to me. On the way over through the city and across the bridge and up the motorway she's already asked me to describe my character, state what's going on between the characters, asked me to think what Faith has been doing just prior to the scene, what sort of outer action she might be showing, what might be beyond the fourth wall. At what exact point in the scene does Faith make the decision not to be co-operative? When does the trainer decide to back off because she can see that Donna is becoming upset. Who 'wins'?

Now she has given me a speed run of the lines, and a 'shouting' run, and an ordinary run, and is doing something with an eyeliner. Apparently I'm so lucky with my dark hair; I don't need any eyebrow pencil or mascara.

'Look up,' she says.

'I don't want to look like an owl.'

'You won't. It's just to make your gorgeous green eyes look even more gorgeous to the camera. Touch of lip gloss. Okay.' She looks at me critically and hands me a mirror from her large make-up bag. 'So subtle you'd hardly notice. Agree?'

'Agree.' My eyes look bigger, darker, quite nice really.

'Happy?'

'Oh sure, ecstatic.'

With her face so close I can't help noticing she has a fuzz of fine hairs on her cheeks. She also looks exhausted. 'Did you go to the doc?' I say, opening up a Moro bar I've brought with me for comfort. I take a big bite and offer the other end to Vita.

'Why? No thanks, don't eat chocolate.'

'Well, you fainted and you still look a bit spaced out.'

'No worries. Just got up too quickly.'

'But you hadn't been sitting down.'

Her look tells me to back off.

'You gave me a hell of a fright,' I say.

'Yes, sorry. Won't happen again.' She looks at her watch. 'Do you want to run the lines one last time?'

'No thanks.'

'Nervous?'

'What do you think?'

She fires up the car and I finish off the Moro bar. 'Rather you than me today. I've just been to the gym. Real one. It's in town.'

'How long've you been going?'

'Since I was thirteen. Love it. And got to get rid of the bulges before shooting starts.'

'Who says?'

'They do. I do.'

'What bulges?'

'For starters, this one, down here.' Again, she has practically no clothes on, just shorts and boots and a crop top with a lot of bare flesh showing. With her little bony fingers she pulls at a flap of skin somewhere down near her tiny waist.

'You call that a bulge?'

'Sure it's a bulge. Got to go.'

I am speechless. But now we are in the parking lot and Vita is saying that she goes to that scruffy entrance through a café over there, and I go in through the main door and ask at reception for the casting director. The room where the auditions are held is up the stairs. I forget her bulge; my stomach is turning cartwheels now, independent of me.

'Good luck,' she says.

'So what happened?' asks Vita that night.

'Total disaster.'

'Why? Did you freak out? Run away screaming?'

'Nothing like that. She gave me that card with my name on, and made me say my name and address. I forgot it.'

'You forgot your *name*.' Down the phone line I could hear her smiling. I wasn't going to tell her about tripping over a wire as I went in, dropping the card because I was shaking so much, feeling like a total dork, fraud, wannabe. I know now, despite Gareth, that I am camera phobic.

I say, 'I had to turn around and show off my horrible profile. Then we did the scene.'

'Was another actor there? There is, sometimes.'

'No. She sat beside the camera and read them. I just mumbled through. Rowan would say, no energy, flat, dull and boring, darling.'

'How many takes?'

'Three times. She tried to make me get angry in one, and weepy in another. Then she asked me to tell her in my own words, but still being Faith, how I felt when I went shopping for clothes. Did I enjoy buying nice new clothes? Well, she couldn't stop me until I'd told her all about nothing nice above size 12 and what you see in mirrors, and stuck-up shop assistants who laughed at you and didn't care if you noticed, and then I got onto saying how Faith's great ambition was to be a photographer so she could always be *behind* a camera making the images and after about five minutes of that she stopped me and said sorry, this was absolutely fascinating but she had another actor waiting. She was laughing.'

'Edwina doesn't laugh at people. She's a pro.'

'She was smiling then.'

'Did she say anything good, like, encouraging?'

'Oh yes, everything was good, that's good, fine, well done. Stuff like that.'

'Perhaps you were good? Perhaps she was smiling because you were *good*.'

'Not after that. I wasted her time. Yours. Everyone's. Sorry. Bye.'

'Tiggie, I'll see you at class next Tues . . .'

'Doubt it.' I put the phone down and stare out at the Sky Tower. Flash. Flash. The phone goes again, and it's probably Vita, but I don't answer. Her flowers on the dresser are beginning to look a bit tired. Suddenly I can't stand them in my room any longer. I consider tossing them to the winds over the glass windbreaks out on the patio but end up putting them in the bathroom to smell nice with the aromatherapy oils, for Mum and Dad to enjoy while lying in the spa.

I looked again – bitterly this time – at the note with its tiny handwriting, so friendly and confident. The flowers weren't for helping her back on her feet, or to thank me for a miserable few photos. I was beginning to understand why she'd sent them.

It seemed sort of appropriate to flush the shredded pieces of the note down the loo. You learn to recognise the signs. It takes one to know one.

'But, Vita,' I say on the phone the next night. 'It's Tiggie, and I want to say sorry for being rude.'

'You weren't rude. I know how bad you can feel after one of those things, if you think you've blown it. You still don't know that you have.'

'Oh yes I do. Anyway, you did try, and I want to say thank you. After class next week if you're coming, can I buy you a hamburger? A pizza. Or McDonald's?'

'Sure, great.' Was I imagining the tiny pause before she answered? 'So you're coming back to class. I'm really glad.'

'How's rehearsals?'

'Shitty. We start proper shooting week after next and the scripts are running late and everyone's stressed out of their skulls. We're doing lots of improvs and workshoppy stuff with the characters to find out what all their relationships are. Have you rung Emily yet?'

'Yes. She said she'd let me know.'

'She will. And I've still got a good feeling about you.'

The week seems endless. For the first time in my life I find out about *waiting*. I don't like it. At home my heart leaps to my mouth every time the phone goes. I wait for Mum or Dad to call out, 'Tiggie – phone for you – someone called Emily!' It doesn't happen. I use the school callbox in breaks to monitor the call minder and rush home to check for messages. I consider ringing Emily and telling her to forget it.

I am desperate to catch even a glimpse of Gareth, but the days go by and no matter how often I go between classes and in breaks to the drama suite, concocting some excuse to talk to Sophia or Tara, he's not there. No one seems to know, when I ask ever so casually, where he's gone.

Everyone else seems to be coming and going to the drama suite – the writers, people from the production team, Sophia in her velvet culottes and so far about three changes of hair colour. She goes grey quickly at the roots. Tara hangs around looking busier and more harassed than anyone, of course; the actors make a lot of noise doing their improvs. If the writers have decided what they're writing, so that the actors can workshop it, then they're keeping it from everyone else.

I wander round the school between classes, tracking down the teachers and the student organisers of all these different groups, asking them for lists, names, biogs, pictures for the programme. They promise everything yesterday, but so far I've only got two lists of names, the choir and the Samoan group.

In every classroom, corridor, outdoor courtyard and pathway, I'm on red alert for a tall guy with a black ponytail.

Perhaps he's left school to go and help his mother fight for her money? Perhaps he's had to get a job because she hasn't any? Sophia eventually tells me that he's away on some film course, back next Tuesday after the long break for Easter. That's fine, except that if I had meant anything to him at all – even as a Year Nine nonentity he'd temporarily taken under his wing – he might just have rung home and found out how my audition had gone. There can't be many girls in this school auditioning for 'Shapers'. Any, except me! But he's on a film course, and everyone knows that film people are a race apart and think of nothing but film. I bet he's peering down his viewfinder at a whole succession of gorgeous girls, taking them for coffee and drinks.

Kissing them? Sleeping with them?

Everything stops over Easter. Four long days. Mum is working most of the time and Dad is away kayaking somewhere in the South Island.

Me, I'm fucking waiting.

On Tuesday night after class we end up, at Vita's suggestion, in a little Italian café. I'd forgotten about the disadvantages of places like McDonald's, thousands of people nudging each other and sidling up to ask for autographs. There are only about ten others around the tables, and a flirty waiter with gelled hair and a fake Italian accent.

The class, we agree, had been awful.

Vita reckons Rowan was being extra hard on her because she was a working pro and needed to remember certain basics, no matter how convincing she might be to others. My partner, another geeky male, wouldn't look me in the eye. It was a class about pace. None of us had any. We were all hopeless, too slow, self-indulgent, poor listeners. We didn't think ahead, we were not physically and mentally on our toes, we had not studied our scripts for new ideas or interrupted actions. We were, in a word, deadly dull and perhaps we were not as fully committed to our craft as we should be.

Our pizza arrives, to share. A marinara with lots of prawns and scallops and mussels on top. A big Caesar salad, ginger beer for me, iced water for Vita. She's not particularly hungry, she says. Work, the sort she's doing at the moment, always dulls her appetite. She gets so wound up and involved and focused, she forgets to eat.

How can you *forget to eat*?

With great enthusiasm, Vita starts telling me about rehearsals. Only a week to go before shooting. While she keeps me entertained, she scrapes most of the prawns off the top of the pizza. They're a bit tough for her; overcooked, she says. She drinks a lot of water, sucks a lot of ice, eats maybe the pointed non-crusty ends of two slices of pizza and about six lettuce leaves. You can't talk and eat at the same time. Because I'm hungry and the listener, I end up eating most of the pizza and I suppose nearly all the salad. She offers me her leftovers. I can't resist a pistachio gelato, which she refuses. I have a cappuccino. She sticks to her ice cubes and talks flat out, bright and funny.

She gets up as soon as we've finished and goes in search of a loo, comes back with brighter make-up and lots of perfume. But her hands are shivering slightly and she's already getting out her cigarettes and her gold lighter.

'Are you cold?' I say. As usual, she's got bare arms and nothing across her midriff, and as Mum says, the nights are drawing in.

'No, no. Well, yes, a bit. Perhaps you'll hear from Emily tomorrow. Do you want to check your call minder? What's the number?'

I give her the numbers reluctantly and take the tiny cellphone. There are messages for Mum and Dad, then a brisk voice saying, 'Emily Chatwin, calling 4.15 Tuesday, Tiggie, please ring me urgently. If not tonight, any time after 7.30 am tomorrow. Ciao.'

My heart leaps, but for some reason I don't want to share this with Vita, even if she was the brains behind it all. Not until I know for certain, one way or the other. I keep my face absolutely still, my eyes innocent.

'No message,' she asks.

'No.'

'Shit. *Shit*. Not looking good, Tiggie,' she says sadly, finishing off about her sixth glass of water. 'If you get a part you usually hear within a few days. But hey, there'll be others down the track. And why don't you think of coming to the real gym with me? An aerobics class. It's fun.'

'I don't do sport. Hate all that ra-ra team stuff, running round after balls.'

'This is not sport. It's keeping yourself healthy.'

She looks the picture of glowing health and girl power as she flirts with the waiter. Heads swivel and people stare at her while I fix up the bill with the woman behind the desk.

Keeping yourself healthy. Oh Vita!

Thirteen

I AM WANDERING INTO THE KITCHEN, STILL IN YELLOW PYJAMAS, PHONE in hand.

'Quarter to eight, Tiggie,' says Dad, already in his suit and shoving things in the dishwasher. This is obviously one of his days in town. He pours another cup of coffee from the machine. 'Isn't it time you got your skates on? Mum left the muesli out for you. And the iron on.'

'I'm not going to school this morning.'

'Why? Are you sick?'

'No. Dad, can I talk to you?' I'd hoped that after a long weekend away kayaking, this might be one of his home days. He's caught some sun. 'Like, now?'

'I've got to leave at eight. Meeting at nine and traffic to contend with. First day after the long weekend it'll be appalling. Major presentation to very demanding client. How important is it?'

'Very.'

He bangs the dishwasher door shut. Everything my father does creates noise. 'We can't leave this till tonight?'

'No.'

'What is it then? Unhappy at school? Teacher problems? Being bullied? Got a crush on someone? Homework?'

To each question fired bullet-like at me, true or untrue – and one at least is true – I shake my head. Reflected in the stainless steel fridge doors I look like a yellow tulip. Or whichever one of the Teletubbies is yellow.

'What, then?' he says impatiently. 'Do you mind if I keep on tidying up your mother's mess?'

I perch on one of the stools. Dad's where I get my tidiness from. Mum had not been in a state to tidy up anything when I came in last night. I always know: an empty Pernod bottle beside the rubbish, or mega drinks of iced water and cups of coffee and Panadol the next morning. Ashtrays of cigarette stubs and bowls with a few nuts and a layer of salt left in them. I don't think she's an alcoholic, she just has one too many sometimes. Like, most nights when she's home and every time she's out at a party. My mother is a party girl.

And I have no idea how she is going to react to my news. It has crossed my mind I might be invading her patch. After all, she is the television star. So I need to tell Dad first. I need to tell someone *now*.

'You remember,' I say, carefully pouring out some muesli, 'when Mum went to the launch of the new soap? "Shapers".'

'Sorry, I'm not with you.'

'It's the new big soap set in a gym. On tele? "Shapers"?'

'Oh, "Shapers". It's being very aggressively marketed. You can't open a paper or a magazine without being assaulted by some "Shapers" story or ad. Mum told me only the other day they've got funding for a creating of "Shapers" doco. She's in the running to front it.'

Something wicked in me wants to savour this coming moment. I want to see my father, who's usually described by journalists as 'Cassandra Tompson's partner', amazed and shocked. I want to see the person who has no idea what I do from week to week, stunned and perplexed. I want to see the man who speaks to me as though I'm some junior typist in his office, lost for words. Like, totally.

I am not disappointed.

'Well, they're starting shooting next week.'

'Yes. So?'

'And after that they have some storylines with guest actors. Like "Shortland Street".'

'Aha.' He's looking at his digital deep-sea diver's watch. 'I imagine they do.'

'Aaaaand.'

'Sorry, Tiggie, if this is all connected with some school assignment or softening Mum up for something, it'll have to wait.'

'I've just heard . . . by the way, I hate that tie.' It's buzzy bees on a gross bright blue. 'It's awful.'

'For Christ's sake, Tiggie, I haven't got time to spend listening to you rabbiting on about my tie! I like it. Where is all this leading?'

'"Shapers". I've just heard I've got a part in it.'

People's mouths do fall open at such times. And they do drop things. Dad drops the cellphone he is about to transfer from battery unit to briefcase. It bounces off the terracotta tiles.

'Oh s*hit!* You could have chosen your moment a bit better, Tiggie.'

'Excuse *me!* I say, as he hurriedly keys in some numbers and decides it still goes. 'Should I have told you to sit down first and made sure you had a cup of tea?'

I suspect this is a tactical error. I see his eyes flash angrily. He does not like to be reminded that he's rather older than most dads of a fourteen-year-old daughter, or that despite the trim action-man shape and dark hair he's on the wrong side of fifty-five. (Little secret: his hair's not really that colour.)

'Run that past me again,' he says.

'I've got a part in "Shapers". If I want it.'

'You've never done any acting, to the best of my knowledge,' he says, accusingly. 'I cannot begin to imagine how this happened.'

Then I can see his mind, recovering from shock, start to make connections.

'What's the part?'

'A girl who comes to the gym 'cause she's won a prize. A year's subscription.'

He needs a moment to take this in. 'Does your mother know about this?'

'You're the first. I've just heard from my agent.'

'Your *agent?*' He's torn between hearing the gruesome details, and his meeting in town. 'Jesus Christ.'

94

But he's a man of action. 'Throw your clothes on, Tiggie. You can tell me more in the car.'

'I don't want to go to town.'

'But you said you weren't going to school?'

'I'm not. I'm going round to see my agent.'

'You've got permission from school?'

'No.'

'Ye gods. Well. You can get a taxi back.'

Stunned, shocked, flabbergasted, blown away?

Yes!

Crawling along in the traffic past the Parnell Baths and the Coastguard building and the container wharves, he says that he thinks I should turn the part down.

I've told him some of the story. Like, someone at school heard that they were looking for a girl who wasn't a fishing rod to be in 'Shapers' and I went along to see this girl's agent just for a laugh, and the next thing I had an audition and this morning got the phone call. I left out Rowan, and Vita.

Even so, he declares, this is so out of character he's just – dumbfounded. *And hurt.* 'Why won't you tell us anything, Tiggie? We want to know! Be there for you!'

And protective of Mum. 'I don't know how she'll react, Tiggie. You know she's having a difficult time of it at work. Has to watch her back.'

'You mean she'll be jealous?'

'Oh no no *no*. She just might take a little while to get used to the idea.'

And protective of me. Had I thought, he says carefully as we inch towards Queen Street and his office building, had I considered I might be letting myself in for – well, it's going to be watched by hundreds of thousands of people. He wouldn't want me to get hurt.

And a coward. He can't bring himself to say straight out he's not too keen on the token fat girl in 'Shapers' being his daughter. I tell him that if it had been a glamorous bimbo part, and I looked like Ally McBeal, he'd have been proud as hell. No no *no*, he says again, don't put yourself down, Tiggie. I've got it all wrong. I'm just too young, untrained and there is my schooling to think of.

I bite my tongue, too scared to push him further into a corner.

'Will you come and see the agent with me?' I say, preparing to get out of the car just below the Sky Tower. 'It's got to be soon. This week.'

'I'll . . . think about it. Talk to Mum. Sleep on it.'

The walk to Emily's in Parnell takes me along some pretty streets lined with trees and villas with golden autumn gardens. The very thought of Dad's frowning face and the way he'd searched around for all the reasons *why not* rather than *yes* is making me feel sick. What if Mum . . .

I have to go past the cathedral. Getting out of a shiny white bus in the carpark is a whole bunch of girls in a uniform I know very well. Boaters, gloves, the lot – they're probably paying a visit to the bishop. The school choir holds its big annual carol service there.

You won't believe it, but they're my old class and right in the front is the friend who thought it would be great fun to make Tiggie Tompson walk naked down a bush track. Decision time. Options. Hide behind a tree. Walk on and ignore. Walk on and wave airily and keep on walking. Walk on and go and have a brief chat.

'How *are* you, Tiggie old thing?' they'll say. 'You absolute cow, not even telling us you were leaving. How's the new school? Do you like it? What's it like being with *boys*?'

Or they might wave once and/or just ignore me, which is the most likely scenario of all.

My footsteps slow. And then I think, bugger me, I'm going to see my agent. I've got a part, damn it. I've been chosen because I'm the *best*. The bosses want me, just me, and as I am, not someone who played Juliet's nurse at intermediate school or who's been learning speech and drama for a million years.

If I was still wearing that uniform I'd be safe and boring and certainly not about to act on national TV.

So I walk past the bus and when one of them spots me and I see them all looking over more curious than friendly, I just give a cheery wave, and call, 'Hi guys, have a nice day,' and keep right on going to where I'm going. Whether they are watching or not watching, curious about why I'm walking through Parnell in mufti on a school day or not curious, I couldn't give a stuff.

On an impulse, I whip out my camera and get just close enough to tell them to get in a group, and say sex for the camera. 'I'll send you a copy! Nice picture for the school magazine, Year Nine visit to St Mary's Cathedral, Parnell. Ciao for now!' On a second impulse, I cross the road and make for Mum's favourite Italian bread shop, where I buy two foccaccia sticks with pesto fillings. They're still warm and crunchy from the oven. They're for me to chew on now. At the florist's next door, I buy a bunch of red thank-you carnations to take to the agent who bent the rules.

Emily, agent to the stars, here I come.

That night, after I've talked to Emily, and (I think) Dad has rung Mum on her cellphone, and (I'm pretty sure) Emily has talked to Mum on her cellphone, and (I'm almost positive) Edwina, the casting director, has talked to Mum on her cellphone, and I've been to class and told Vita, there's to be a summit meeting at Emily's.

Mum and Dad pick me up from town and we drive up to Parnell with each of them telling the other what exhausting days they've had and carefully avoiding the reason for this little exercise. Clients have been difficult, Mum's new director is a shit, they're both exhausted. I don't think they mean to make me feel guilty for complicating their lives with agents and soap operas and keeping them from relaxing with their gins and dinner, but they do. I sit in the back, smelling the leather, thinking about the nice day I've had wagging school, talking to Emily, going to a movie, shouting myself a KFC Feast, going to class after school, almost enjoying being sternly told off by Rowan for lack of focus.

And after the class, on the footpath outside, telling Vita.

'You absolute bitch,' she had said after she'd stopped hugging me and dancing up and down. As usual, about the first thing she does coming out of Rowan's class is light a cigarette. 'How could you do a whole class and not tell me? How could you? How could you keep a straight face even?'

'Isn't that what actors are supposed to do?'

'Yes, but, every time I get offered a part I burst into tears and grin like I'm loony-tunes and go up to the ceiling.'

'That's 'cause you're Tinkerbell. Need a crane for me,' I said. 'I got you a present.' Now Vita must get lots of presents, but she seemed overcome with the silver photo frame I got her for her dressing room.

'Shouldn't have,' she said.

'You're the mastermind,' I said. 'Owe you heaps. Thanks. Gotta go.'

She gave me a last hug, taking care not to burn my ear with her cigarette. I could feel the ribs in her back.

Emily is just fantastic.

There sit Mum and Dad, side by side on the red couch. Mum looks a bit harassed and as though she needs a drink and Dad is doing his distinguished older husband act, his legs crossed. Emily has heard from me about Dad's cautious, negative reaction and is acting like it's quite normal for their daughter to be offered a part in a soap. So he doesn't get a word in and even Mum, a professional talker, is sitting quietly. I think they're still shellshocked.

Yes, God, it scares me to death but I want this so much!

Emily talks contracts and the huge (to me) amount of money that she is asking, and possible schedules within the given dates, and the fact that I'll have a minder and vocal coach who will be legally responsible for me while I'm on the premises. I'll be given the normal detailed call sheets. I'll be picked up each day I'm called, either by the coach or some designated driver. I'll be dropped home. The coach, a highly skilled woman called Lynda, will work on dialogue with me and be with me in the studio. I'll have a tutor to help me with prepared lessons, in cooperation with my school. I'm one of the first child actors they are using. The company wants to establish and maintain the highest standards where its child actors are concerned, from day one.

'Though I don't regard this young woman as a child,' she says, smiling at me. I'm sitting on a Turkish rug with Jessie in my lap. 'Except legally. You understand the reason for all this?' she asks me. 'It's important that your parents are happy right from the start.'

'Yes.'

'Are you happy?' she suddenly fires aggressively at the two on the red couch.

Dad uncrosses his legs and clears his throat but it's Mum who speaks first.

'We have one concern which we've not yet had time to discuss with Tiggie. This has all happened rather too quickly.'

'It usually does,' says Emily. 'They make up their mind and then, whammo, it's all go.'

'Even so,' says Mum, 'a third party does make it a little easier . . . from what you can tell us, within the overall concept of this particular show, the character is a . . . let's not beat around the bush here – a misfit. Square peg in round hole. We're concerned that she might get rather a hard time.'

'In what way?'

'She gets teased. Children can be cruel. The public can be very cruel, as I well know. About personal appearance, or age, weight, sexuality, supposed wealth or status. Some criticism can be truly, deeply and personally, vicious.'

'Would you like me to wait outside?' I ask.

'You're being prickly, Tiggie,' says Mum.

'Mum, I'm going to be *acting*,' I say. 'It's only a soap.'

'Watched by half a million people every night. A few of them will write in saying in no uncertain terms they don't want to see a . . . plumpish girl on their screens.'

'Fat, mum.'

'All right, fat – and probably a lot less polite than that.'

'Have you thought,' says Emily, 'that many more will write in and say, hallelujah, at *last*, someone on our screens who is not unnaturally thin? Someone real, warm, human and vulnerable?'

'Of course we have,' says Mum sharply. 'But the negativity is what hurts.'

'The humanity is what lasts,' shoots back Emily. 'Strike a blow for the real world, not the synthetic, false world that ratings-driven television has given us. Even — excuse me, Cassie — even your own programme is not the serious-minded examination of genuine public concerns it once was.'

Go, Emily!

'It's not for want of trying,' Mum says wearily, deflated. 'We do try.'

Emily says, 'You know what your mother is saying, Tiggie?'

'Yep.'

'How do you feel about it?'

'Okay.'

'Your mother is quite right to raise these concerns, now, before you sign anything. There could well be letters to newspapers and some of them may be extremely negative and hurtful. Do you want time to go home and think about it?'

'Last year,' I say, stroking Jessie's smooth warm coat, 'at camp, my friends stole all my clothes and my big towel from a shower about fifty metres away from the bunkhouse. They called me fatso, and podge, and Miss Piggy. You fat cow, and overweight bitch, and Teletubby, and watch out, the fat attack.'

'Dear God,' says Emily softly.

'You didn't tell us that,' explodes Dad. 'Why didn't you tell us? By Christ, if I'd known, I'd have been in that principal's office so fast . . .'

'That's why I didn't. Do you think I care about a few loony letters?'

Jessie breaks the tension by peeing in my lap. I feel this warm, wet feeling spread between my thighs. Emily produces towels and apologises for her elderly animal. She's on pills supposed to prevent these little accidents. I say don't worry, we're going home anyway, 'cause I don't think there's much more to discuss. Mum and Dad smile on, weakly, and agree that yes, Emily can ring Edwina in the morning and accept the offer.

It's only in the car going home, sitting on a towel so that the dampness doesn't get onto the blue leather, that I realise neither of them has actually said *congratulations, well done, fantastic.* Perhaps that will come later.

Gareth says the right things, though, when I bump into him walking into school the next morning. I don't recognise him. He's had the ponytail and most of his hair removed in what I think they call a number two haircut. Amazing – he looks mean and macho and like any other guy who's into film, but I get the smile and that hasn't altered.

'Antigone, my friend! How did you get on?'

'The audition was okay. Well, it wasn't, I hated it, but I must have done something right. I got the part.'

'Well done!' In the past I've only ever had a hand on my arm. Today I get the full squeezy hug and my heart goes into a cartwheel. He's wearing black, of course, and he smells of lemons. 'Can I take some credit for this?' he says, holding me at arm's length, pixie-smiling down into my face.

'Yep. Thanks.' We are getting some curious looks from several hundred people walking or riding their bikes past us. Everyone knows Gareth.

'Do you like the character?' he says. 'How many of the scripts have you seen?'

'None yet. And no, I don't know how the storyline ends. My agent couldn't tell me. She doesn't know either.'

'Agent now,' he mocks gently. 'Haven't we come a long way? Well, I have a price. Payback time.'

'What's that?'

'I'd be very interested to see those scripts.'

'Confidential, Emily said. I have to sign a confidentiality agreement.'

He just smiles at me. He knows that I'd trust him with my life.

'Maybe just one,' I say. 'And tell anyone, a living person, I'll kill you.'

'Any help you want with your character, hearing lines, even practice being in front of a camera, give me a yell.'

I can hardly believe my ears or my luck. Now I need no excuses.

'That'd be awesome. Thanks,' I say, trying to sound sensibly and professionally, rather than pathetically, grateful. Because for all my brave talk at Emily's last night, I don't know everything I'm going to be asked to do as Faith and that's scary.

Fourteen

April is when the year really starts in New Zealand. Before that, we've had Christmas and the summer holidays, Waitangi Day, Anzac Day, the long Easter break, one public holiday after another. Everyone goes back reluctantly to school and offices but stays in holiday mode, still cooking up barbies and spending hours at the beach. We've had the huge outdoor concerts in the Domain, and nothing but cricket on TV, and out on the harbour, all the challengers for the America's Cup — the Americans, the Italians, the Aussies and the rest — are training every day. My star sign which is Virgo said it was going to be a surprising and challenging year for me and so far it's not wrong.

End of April I have got a million names for Sophia's programme and had my first real fight with Tara. It was about whether or not I was prepared to take a whole lot of posters done by the graphic design students around all the local shopping areas and ask for them to be put prominently in shop windows.

I said sorry, I didn't have the time at present. She said this is what assistant producers do. I said this is what little Year Eights can be asked to do. She said find some. I said that's your job. She said most Year Eights didn't have the personal skills to talk nicely to shopkeepers, especially when lots of other people wanted their posters up too. I said thank you for thinking I talk nicely, but this was not my problem. She said she was disappointed in me. I said I was not the only person on the production team and anyway, I was doing the programme. She said she had a magazine to edit and half-year exams coming up and she was having tests for glandular fever. I said I was sorry to hear that and walked off.

I am still going to Rowan's classes and not getting quite so paranoid each Tuesday. I'm even sort of enjoying them, now that I can see what his technique exercises, which seemed so itsy-bitsy at first, are actually all about. And I now have a secret reason to be there other than some stupid, pathetic fantasy. I haven't told any of them about my 'Shapers' part, and don't intend to, but I sort of think Rowan knows. Probably Vita told him.

Vita comes to most classes. Rowan won't let us do exercises together all the time. Some of the others are really good. But we have a Diet Coke afterwards and sometimes we have a hamburger and she drops me home, and I'm more convinced than ever that even though she's a star and has started shooting on a show which is going to make her an even bigger star when it goes to air in ten weeks, she's got a *big* problem. I don't know whether to ask her if it's true because I don't know what she sees in me. Basically, I am scared to lose her friendship.

Mum and I have visited the producer at 'Shapers' and talked contracts and conditions and minders and schoolwork and stuff. She's happy enough. Dad's backed off, but he's not that happy. He's more interested in planning the guest list and menu for Mum's big Four-O surprise party which is going to be at a restaurant in Parnell with the rich and famous and me.

When I went out to the studio with Mum, I only saw the producer's office, nothing of the set, because there's strict security about all the storylines, deliberately (says Vita) fuelling media speculation.

What they *are* saying is that everyone is very excited about the scripts, and the directors, and the actors, and the absolutely *brilliant* sets which are going to blow people away when it goes to air. It's going to look wonderful. Yep, the sets are amazing, but they're talking up a storm, says Vita grimly. It's possible to hype things so much people get sick of them.

I'll be shown around the set when I go out to have measurements taken and for first rehearsals, but I've been sent most of my scripts and found out the beginning, the middle but not the end of what happens to Faith.

According to the character breakdown, which comes with the scene where she first appears, 'Faith Hopkins is a dumpy kid with low self-esteem. Her Mum left years ago and her solo parent father is a pathetic figure who can't hold down a job. Though he loves his daughter and tries to provide a home for her, he also hits her and calls her names.

'As well as jobs, he is always moving to new apartments, often leaving behind unpaid rent. Faith fuels her dreams of Mr Right, a secure home life, a career and travel through reading the women's magazines. She also dreams of one day being slim.'

As I read through the scripts, I find out that Faith wins a year's gym membership sponsored by one of her favourite magazines. She had sent off the entry form as a result of being bullied at school, for a joke. A condition of entry is that at the end of the year she will feature in a 'before and after' story. The staff and Rata, her personal trainer, see her as a real challenge. She develops a very close relationship, almost a dependency on Rata, so close that Rata starts to become uncomfortable and worried. Faith expects miracles which the trainer cannot deliver. She becomes surly and misses sessions. In an accidental meeting in a city McDonald's, the trainer finds Faith having a binge. She reveals that her happy home life is all lies. She promises to come back to the gym and try harder.

That's not the end of the story, 'cause I'm still waiting for the scripts for the last two weeks.

I like Faith. She's a victim, but in her own way she tries. I've got some good meaty scenes, nearly all with Rata. I don't get any scenes with Holly. I've met plenty of girls like Faith, all confused and aggressive because things are so horrible at home. They don't know who loves them or where their real home is any more. I mightn't like my highrise goldfish bowl as much as I liked the villa where I had a dog, but it's definitely home and Mum and Dad are okay.

One night, two weeks before my first day of rehearsals, as I sit on my bed gazing down at the harbour, I start thinking of Rowan's last class. He'd been talking about the relevance of research, what actors can do to prepare for a part.

I don't know why I didn't think of it before.

* * *

Well, actually I do know. I know *exactly* why when I walk in the door of the big gym in Newmarket, just a short bus ride away, and say I want to join.

I want to get a personal trainer and a figure.

Within half an hour I've been signed up by a girl who looks and talks like Rachel Hunter in a navy trouser suit with brass buttons. She thinks I'm very brave coming here without my Mum and all. This is my Dad's credit card, right? Would I like a bloke for a personal trainer or stick with the girls? I'll stick with the girls. It just happens, she smiles pityingly, that a really, really nice PT called Amy is up in the women's gym and may be able to take me now. But first she'll show me round.

It is absolutely as bad as I expected. I won't say that all the girls look like Ally McBeal or Xena. Some of them are actually quite hefty, or short, or nuggety – or even quite old. I won't say that all the blokes are spunks or hunks; a lot of them are also quite hefty, short, nuggety or old. But from all of them, as we go through huge rooms full of equipment being used, and crowded pump classes with instructors yelling numbers over funky music, I get the same looks.

Great research, Tiggie. Hang in there.

In the privacy of the tiny testing room, my PT, Amy, who's an aerobics champion and finishing off a course at polytech, takes my measurements and weight. She then takes an electronic body composition and then wires me up to a heart monitor while I pedal an exercycle. Neither of us expects these results to be any good; they are my baseline so that we can measure my progress. She's astonished that I've done little or no sport or real exercise, apart from walking, since I was about ten at primary school. She thinks it's just criminal that so little Phys. Ed. is taught compulsorily in schools these days. A whole generation is going down the tubes and more are following as the population turns into couch potatoes. I can tell she sees me as a bit of a challenge and *good on me*, for deciding to do this *for myself*.

For Faith, I'll remember this feeling of embarrassment, isolation, square peg in round hole – although I still think 'misfit' is a bit strong.

I promise to come three times a week after school to begin with –

what a busy little bee I've become!

Vita rings on Friday night. How am I going learning lines? Okay, I say. I've learnt eighteen scenes out of twenty-five and I meet the dialogue coach when I go for my first real day next week.

Picnic on Sunday, she says. She'll pick me up. Man, does she need her weekends to recover! She's exhausted. We'll go somewhere nice, get a pizza or fish and chips. If it's raining we'll go to a movie.

We've crossed the harbour bridge and driven half an hour up to Long Bay beach, but it's not until we've flopped onto the sand and she momentarily takes her sunglasses off to rub at her eyes, that I begin to think — something's majorly wrong here.

'Yeah, yeah,' she gets in first. 'I know I look like death. Got to give my skin a break, have *one* day a week without all that muck on my face. If it doesn't clear up soon, they're threatening me with a dermatologist.'

It's not only the zits and blotches around her chin, or the shadows under her eyes. She hadn't been at the last class, so it's ten days since I've seen her. How can anyone already so skinny lose even more weight in ten days? Well, she can and she has.

'Do you want to pig out first, or go for a walk?' she says.

'Um . . . walk.'

'Okay. I might have a wee run later, if you don't mind.'

'Sure.'

There are quite a few family groups splashing around in the water, playing ball. Mostly they're Maori, or Pacific Islanders wearing lava-lavas — kids, adults, even grandparents having fun together. I can't remember the last time Mum, Dad and I did something like this so that some stranger watching would have thought, here's a family having fun.

Fat white cumulus clouds come over occasionally, blocking off the sun and the warmth. I have to ask Vita to slow down a bit, mostly because I had my first real session with Amy doing weights at the gym yesterday and I'm sore. All the way to the far end she tells me about the show. How the bosses, as the first episodes get edited, are pleased with the product. How the publicity machine is winding up 'cause it's going to air in three weeks. How they expect bad reviews from certain critics who always give New Zealand shows a hard time.

I'm beginning to think this is to avoid talking about anything else. We do a U-turn by some rocks.

'Vita, tell me about your mum. Your family.'

She starts picking up tuatua shells, trying to get them to dance and bounce across the shallows. It's a while before she answers.

'Mum's an unreconstructed martyr. She works her butt off for a charity for next to nothing. You know the sort, the sucker who stays late to get five thousand appeal envelopes in the mail? Gives her last twenty dollars to someone collecting for crippled kids?'

'Sounds as though she cares.'

'Yeah, but she gets tired and between us, we don't have money to throw around. Fergus and Greg are both lazy sods and take her for granted.'

I remember the house, all those sneakers and dirty dishes. The rude note. 'I know who Fergus is. Your brother. Who's Greg?'

'Mum's partner. He's kind too, but hopeless. Dithers. My real dad left home when I was eleven. He was a lot older than Mum. Decided to trade her in for a new model.'

I shiver. 'So's my dad,' I say. 'Older, I mean. But they're okay. They are really.' Even if they never go playing beach ball together.

'Watch them. Watch them like fucking hawks.' She does three or four swift cartwheels on the hard damp sand, legs and arms flashing like bronze spokes. There's nothing to her. 'I thought Dad was okay too. Bastard. Greg tries, though. We get on all right, but he's always sniping at Fergus, and Mum's the meat in the sandwich.'

'What does he do, Greg?'

'Architectural draughtsman, but there's not been much work for ages. Architects are always the first to go. He's always moaning about his cash flow and proposals that would have come off, if only some bastard hadn't undercut him, but really, he's unemployed. Before I got my "Shortland Street" job we were just about broke. Mum swallowed all her pride and went to her grumpy old dad for a loan. He's got millions, literally, stashed away somewhere, but no way would he help. Short of the ready, he said. I hate him.'

'All my grandparents are overseas. If they remember, they send me birthday presents.'

'Mum's dad doesn't even do that. He's got emphysema. I hope he dies. Not that we'll get any of his pile. That's going to his new wife, as far as we know. I hate her too. I like having a good job so that even though I'm only sixteen I can say stuff them.'

She walks along the beach on her hands. I think she was once a dancer or one of those rhythmic gymnast people.

She says, upside down, 'What's it like having a celebrity for a mum? I'd like to meet her sometime.'

'You know what it's like,' I say surprised at the question. 'Same as you. Nudge nudge wink wink — all the time.'

'Be a celeb yourself soon.'

'I just want to do a good job.'

She laughs and does an agonisingly slow controlled back flip, one slim leg at a time. 'That's what we all say. People will like Faith, you'll see. She's a nice character. They'll feel sorry for her. You'll get fan mail.' She caught my look of disbelief. 'You will! By the sack. You'll have to employ a secretary to deal with it all.'

I laugh and laugh. I even try a couple of lumbering handstands. Vita laughs too, but with her I don't mind.

'Vita,' I say, rubbing the sand from my hands and clothes (because I'd toppled over). 'Why do you bother with me?'

'Why not? I like you. I like acting with you. You're non-threatening.'

'I'm not a rival, you mean?'

'No, I didn't mean that.'

'But I'm not, am I?'

'You don't push yourself forward or use people. You're generous. You don't play games.'

'But you must have heaps of friends. All those people you work with?'

'Excuse me!' she snorts. 'And before you ask, no I haven't got a bloke. After the last one, I gave them up. He was an actor who used me to be seen and be photographed in cafés around town, and as soon as he started getting parts dropped me like a stone. Could charm the birds off the trees, but an arsehole. Actually, there's more — I think he's gay and was using me as a beard.'

'A what?'

'A female cover to convince himself and everyone that he wasn't.'

'That's gross!'

'I've got a bet on with someone at work that he'll be out within a year. Prancing around in the Hero parade, wearing nothing but a G-string and wrap-around sunglasses.' She jumps up and down. 'I'm hungry. Starving. Race you back to the car.'

The surprising thing is that I gave it a go, and didn't mind rolling in a bad second. And even with the tide coming in and quite a few more people up this end of the beach, especially families, I went for a swim, too.

Vita had ordered the fish and chips. Carrying the package out to the car, I thought it seemed large for two people, but what she opened up on the beach was enough for six or even ten. 'We won't eat all that!' I said, looking at the parcel unwrapped on the grass. I could count at least five big pieces of fish poking out from a mind-blowing heap of golden chips. 'Can't possibly.'

'Yes we can. I've been told to put on some weight. I'm *starving*.'

She's away with the tomato sauce sachets, like a train. Any other meal we've had, pizzas, hamburgers, she's picked at. Now she's eating, gobbling, stuffing the slightly soggy chips in as though she can't stop.

'Good, eh?' She sees me looking at her. 'I have to watch what I eat most of the time, be a little bit careful. Good to have a blow-out occasionally, huh?'

This is no blow-out. This is another word beginning with B. I look around. Yes, she has parked quite close to a public loo. Funny that. And funny, that when the pile of soggy chips is gone and she's had a good swig at the Diet Coke bottle, she lies back sighing as if content for about three minutes, saying we should both just lie there and go to sleep in the sun, snuggling into the warm dry sand. The beach is so-o-o beautiful. She is so-o-o tired.

I pretend I'm asleep. I hear her get up and through slitted eyes I see her go into the loo. After ten minutes she's back. She's been to the car and put some more clothes on, as well as sunglasses and a straw hat, though there's not much heat left in the sun now and no danger of sunburn. Though the loos are quite busy with mothers and kids going in and out, I'd bet a hundred dollars that she went in there to throw up. Knew she was going to throw up. Put her fingers down her throat to throw up. Planned to do this throwing-up today, with me, 'cause I'm safe and non-threatening and won't hassle her.

Is she trying to tell me something?

I've asked myself that question before, and today I think the answer's yes.

Faith has a binge scene and in real life I know all about binges. I've always known about binges, though I'm not one of those – like quite a few I could name from my old school – who go off to the loo and stick a toothbrush down their throat. I've just got fatter.

Some little part of me is angry. I don't want to get sucked into this, girl, just as I'm about to walk into your fantasy world for the most terrifying thing I've ever done. I don't want to be reminded every time I look at you.

It's not my problem, Vita. It's yours and your mum's. Just like my problem is mine and would be my mother's if she thought enough about it. But I don't feel brave enough yet to say straight out, Vita, I think you're anorexic and bulimic both at once and I think you need some real serious help. Once you've said that, she could then say, well look who's talking about EDs, and everything would have changed.

Fifteen

'FROM THE TOP? SPEED RUN?'

'Yes please.'

Sitting on the carpet floor of the drama suite before school, we rattle through twenty-four scenes. After five of these sessions, Gareth now needs only to read the ends of the lines, the cues, highlighted in pink. I come back with my own lines, highlighted in blue. Except for two hesitations, I'm word-perfect.

'That's great,' he says. 'You've worked hard.'

'Yep. I haven't shown you the scripts, have I?'

'No you haven't. All set for tomorrow?'

'I've got an hour with the dialogue coach. I get to see the sets and watch some shooting. I have my measurements taken for wardrobe, which will give them a bit of a fright. Hope they've got a tape measure long enough.'

He laughs and looks at me critically. 'You've lost some weight recently, Tiggie.'

'No I haven't.' I don't want to discuss my weight with this guy, now or ever. 'Anyway, I'm not allowed to. It's in the contract. And thank you for all your help.'

'We won't see you for a month or so?'

'I have a few days off, here and there. Dad says school as usual. It'll be a bit of a waste of time. I do have the programme to finish, though.'

'You can get up Tara's nose. She's driving everyone up the wall. You're the only one who tells her to get lost.'

111

I look at him amazed. 'I just say no occasionally, too busy.'

'She's not used to that. I love watching her try to manipulate you and failing every time. It's very funny.' He gives me back the heavy pile of scripts. 'Good luck, Tiggie. Give me a ring at home. Tell me how you get on.'

Can it be that he possibly *likes* me, cares, actually *notices* I'm around or not around, just a little?

Dream on!

Dream I do, that night, muddled and confusing, in between long periods of staring at the ceiling. The same old dream about a thousand cameras, only this time I'm one of the photographers and the person in my viewfinder is a tiny girl doing cartwheels and getting smaller and smaller until she fizzes and whizzes away like a Catherine wheel. Then all the other cameras slowly train their lenses on me and I know that these are not cameras but guns and I watch with amazement as little pinpricks of blood spurt out all over my body – they must be bullets – but I don't feel a thing, and everyone is laughing and pointing.

At six o'clock sleep is impossible, so I do what I've never done before – get up and try some of the abdominal exercises Amy gave me. Press-ups. Lunges. Crunches. I even try one of Gareth's headstands against the wall and of course fall over. I try again and on the fifth go, though I'm wobbly and I hate the way my stomach hangs, I do manage a whole minute upside down. Hey, this rush of blood to the head feels quite good!

Dad is taking me out to the studio at eight. Leave at 7 am to beat the traffic. Then he's taking some guy to lunch, someone who he hopes will renew one of his contracts. He's been extra stressed lately.

He's knocking on my door. 'Tiggie?'

'I'm awake,' I call, crashing back to earth.

'What was that?' he asks, knowing he's not allowed in under pain of death.

'Nothing. Just me doing a headstand.'

'A *what*?'

'Just joking.'

* * *

Mum would have taken me for my first day – and of course being a television star she would have waltzed in and everyone would have known who she was and I would have trailed along behind. But she's off shooting down country, doing a story about some winemaker in the hills behind Tauranga, and so it's Dad who drops me down by the beach. I tell him I want a little bit of time to myself, some fresh air. I'll walk back. I'm okay on my own.

He asks me if I'm nervous. I say no, not really, which is true. Nervous is not the same as having a dead, cold weight in your stomach and wondering how you are going to remember your lines with three black probing eyes in your face and, maybe, a magician behind them.

If I have a thing about cameras, why the hell am I doing this?

Vita, driving home from the picnic, had warned me: your first day will be worse than any first day at school. Remember your first day at school and double it. Ten times it. Don't even *try* to remember everyone's names or who they are. Just go with the flow. Remember your lines and don't trip over the furniture.

So what's the first thing I do?

Start going through my scenes in a tiny office with Lynda, who's the dialogue coach, and find my mind a total blank, as though someone's pushed the delete button. Gradually, as I stop trembling and feeling stupid, they come back. Then I have to know that since my scenes are filmed out of order, I need to have an 'emotional diary'. This means I have to know in each scene where Faith's coming from, what's happened in the last scene and before that. And talking through each scene helps a lot, just as I do in Rowan's classes; finding out the beats, the new ideas and the interrupted thoughts and thinking exactly where in the scene my character backs off or digs her toes in and what exactly is it that she wants.

Lynda, who has a thick grey bob and wears big shirts and big earrings, is pleased with our first session. She used to be a famous actor but is now loving her crew job because she's had enough of stress. She is my coach, minder and surrogate mum, legally responsible for me while I'm here. If I want to go for a walk, even if I just go to the loo, I must let her (or one of the assistant directors) know. I'm glad I like her.

And what's the second thing? Get taken into Wardrobe where a huge woman in trackpants takes my measurements and because I loathe the very thought of a stranger writing down that I have a 94cm waist, I turn around too fast and accidentally sweep her desk clean. Clipboard, a large box of pins, a glass full of pencils, scissors and assorted mess crash to the ground. Everyone leaps up from their desks and from burrowing in racks of clothes to pick up pins. Up on a corner TV monitor I see Vita among other actors in brilliant colour and not much clothing. There's no sound, but a lot of activity on the set. I have my first glimpse of the Greek gym and as the images hop and sweep at random from one actor to another, a massive camera.

There are two million pins on the floor. I have made enemies already.

'Don't trip over the furniture, Tiggie.' Some miracle-worker produces a small magnet and load by load, up they come.

An hour earlier I had walked in through a foyer with lots of people drinking coffee. I later found out these were extras, called like me for 8 am and waiting to go to make-up. They were all wearing their own gym gear. They were mostly either size ten girls or tall skinny guys, with a few hunks, older slightly less skinny women and a couple of skinny grandfathers thrown in.

Apart from the fact that they're all skinny, it looks just like the café at my real gym.

Past them towards a bald teenager wearing headphones, battery unit, cellphone and black. Clipboard. He's Damien, third AD – that's assistant director – and I have to let him know where I'm going, every time I make a move. He had called up Lynda, who had taken me to Wardrobe, and left me there cause she had another guest actor to see.

Now back in Damien's care, I sit in a scruffy area outside the set with a silenced black and white monitor and four proper actors, as opposed to extras. I think they must be the personal trainers, judging from the bodies. Their make-up is heavier and perfect, their arms and legs smooth and brown, their hair sleek, and gym gear gorgeous. They are softly running the lines of the next scene, fast and offhandedly, not looking at each other, running on the spot, shaking their arms, rubbing their hands together, absorbed in themselves. Two of them are pedalling away on exercycles kept in the corridor, to get the circulation going.

I don't exist. They are twenty-something Famous Faces and in their wake I am about to get my first look at the studio where everything happens.

The red light goes off just as Lynda returns. She has to go with me onto the set.

'Scene 27 travelling in now,' announces Damien into a mike wrapped around his face. He swings open the heavy padded door with relish. 'Lambs to the slaughter. Tiggie, my friend, you too. Just lurk around the back, by the monitor. And sweetie, don't touch *anything.*'

Vita comes out.

If she used to look gorgeous just in a nurse's uniform, in gym gear she looks utterly stunning. Her complexion is flawless, her eyes wide, mouth glossy. I can tell just from the way she's breathing that she's hyped up to the max.

'Tiggie! Fantastic. This is Tiggie everyone, playing Faith,' she says to a general chorus of 'Hi, Tiggies'. Five or six keep walking, vanish into a corridor of dressing rooms nearby. 'Can't stop, Tiggie, have only one scene off, might have a change and I've got no idea which scene is next.'

'Want to run lines?'

'Would you? Got time?'

'Course. Today I'm just looking.'

'All strange and wonderful, huh?' She has led the way into her dressing room, which is almost as much a mess as her bedroom. 'Welcome to my hovel.'

There is a dark green suit, labelled and hanging neatly on a rack, with high heels underneath. 'Costume for next scene,' she says, lighting up a cigarette, stripping off her headband and yellow lycra bodysuit, spraying on deodorant, wiping herself down, swigging water, seemingly all at once. 'My receptionist's gear. Script's over there. Not much time. Not supposed to smoke in here.'

'There' means a long cluttered bench below an equally long mirror.

Lots of photos have been blue-tacked untidily to the mirror. The scripts, however, are neatly in a huge ring-binder, everything highlighted in yellow and open at the scene she's just done. I find Scene 45 as requested.

'Isn't that funny?' she says, casting a swift eye over the two pages as she zips her tiny skirt across her flat tummy. It's not a struggle. 'This scene's talking about Faith. They do that, pop in little signals to prepare for the arrival of a new character. Rip into it.'

From my own learning, I already know that she's Holly and that Ruth is the owner of the gym.

'Ruth's the tough bitch boss with heart,' adds Vita. 'Two scenes ago she bawled me out for being offhand with visitors. I was having PMT and a bad hair day.'

By the third time, Vita's word-perfect. Ruth is telling Holly that she should expect a representative from the magazine to call tomorrow afternoon, bringing with her the winner of the competition to sign up and have some photographs taken. She's an ordinary-sounding 15-year-old called Faith Hopkins. Holly will, of course, make sure she's properly looked after, delivered to Ruth's office.

'Subtext. Your job here is on the line, girl.' She suddenly slumps into a chair. Her thin face goes slack and she looks like a dressed-up child. 'Shit, I'm whacked and it's only ten o'clock.'

'How many scenes today?' At every mention of photographs being taken, the lump in my tum grows heavier.

'Fourteen. Some are only tiny, like this one. Three big emotional numbers this afternoon. I need a great big humungous coffee. Let's go.'

'What about food? Had breakfast?' I say, taking a big risk, sounding like someone's mum.

But she's up and stubbing her half-smoked cigarette out, pulling on her jacket, literally pulling herself together. If she heard me playing mum she's not replying and she's not playing the hostess any more. I trail her into a little room where she makes herself a strong black coffee at the sort of hissing espresso machine you see in cafés. She spends about two minutes in the make-up room getting her famous corn-coloured bob slicked, smoothed and hairsprayed back into place. Outside the padded door she runs the lines with Ruth, who's a thirtyish blonde power-dresser in dark grey and whose real name is Stephanie. Bald Damien tells them all to keep their voices down.

This is Vita the pro. The red light goes out. A bunch of actors appear. We all troop in for Scene 45. This is what I'll be doing in a few days. Someone else's clothes, a face that's not really mine, my heart thumping.

Help!

It's quiet in here. Parts of it are dark and hushed like being in church, but the end which is brilliantly lit is the reception area of a Greek temple, with pillars, tiled floors, nude statues and exotic palm trees. *But,* the difference between what's real and alive and happening in front of me and what I'm seeing on the big monitor in a dark corner is truly amazing.

Like everything else on television – well, except for the news when they show you ordinary people or some ghastly accident or African children crawling with flies – like nearly everything else, the gym image is bright, clean, fresh, new, and I now know, artificial. Unreal. It's all a big trick. Just like the difference between the real Mum and the '60 Minutes' Mum. The gorgeous together Holly and the hollow-eyed girl who never eats called Vita.

When this goes to air, everyone will think they've really built a whole Greek gymnasium on the North Shore, right? Wrong. It doesn't exist. There's only bits of it. Bits of the reception area and cafeteria. Corners of the gym floor and the staffroom. Okay, they have built a swimming pool and sauna in another building, because you can't have half a swimming pool, but everything else has only two or three walls. Just what you see through a very little window. What you don't see is what's going on outside the frame.

You don't see the hundreds of lights above and the cables connecting the cameras with a control room somewhere else. You don't see the fat microphone held out over the heads of the actors, just out of the frame. You don't see the unused sets with built-in windows and doors all piled around the studio walls, and the furniture and gym gear heaped up in corners, and the props in cardboard boxes, the extras waiting silently in a corridor, the crew who've already done five hours straight and it's not even lunchtime.

You don't see what looks on the screen like a huge gym with about a hundred bits of equipment is actually quite a small set. Those marble walls and archways are actually thin bits of wood on wheels. Offices and massage rooms get put up, taken down. *Nothing* is as permanent or as solid or even as clean and fresh as it eventually looks on the screen. And who's in charge here? Anyone?

Lurking in the shadows through that first day, I begin to get the hang of it. There's a director in charge and another guy, the First, who seems to give most of the orders. They bring the actors into the set, rehearse about three times. No joking, this is serious stuff to a strict schedule. The cameras glide silently around into new positions. People mutter into head mikes. The extras are brought on. All the crew do their final checks – actors get powdered, get given things to hold, and suddenly it all goes quiet, tense. Some guy calls, 'Standing by, extras,' then, 'Roll record, please.'

Vita says 'What's the first line again?' The First tells her and someone sniggers. Someone else then does actually snap the clapperboard in front of a camera, like in Hollywood.

'Scene 45. Standing by!' The man up on a little gantry thing working the boom says, 'Set.' The director, watching the monitor, says 'Action!'

Holly and Ruth have their conversation. They sparkle off each other, like someone has switched them on. The director says, 'Cut! Go again, please.' She talks quietly to the actors, then to one of the camera operators. The guy who's doing most of the talking to the crew says, 'Back to the top, extras, please.' They go through it all again, and again, and after the fourth time the director quietly says, 'Well done, I'm happy.'

She is already talking about the next scene as the actors scurry out and new ones arrive. That little scene which the script said took 95 seconds has taken about fifteen minutes to shoot and that, Vita has told me, is *fast*.

It goes on like that for ten hours a day. Each day they film about twenty-five scenes, about twenty-eight minutes of television time. On big feature films you're lucky to do three minutes.

The crew, she has said, love you for getting your bit right first time, doing it right or nearly right as often as it takes. They get very impatient, stern and finally angry with anyone – actors, crew, admin people, drivers – who stuffs up.

It rarely happens. They only hire people who don't stuff up.

As I watch Vita eat a single sandwich for lunch and then do her three big emotional scenes in the afternoon, dropping a couple of lines in rehearsal and causing the director to ask her if she wants a drink of water, I remember that.

When it comes to the takes, she's fantastic. The crew murmur their appreciation after the director calls, 'Cut!' but I still remember.

Sixteen

You might think I have enough going on for someone who's supposed to be a lazy nonentity who does nothing.

I'm going to the gym three times a week and have lost two pounds, nothing compared to what's falling off Vita.

I go to Rowan's class and occasionally to school.

There's a rumour flying around that I've got a part in some new TV show.

Mum's about to turn forty and is ripping into the Pernod big-time. There are the expected rude, hurtful and false comments at school about insider running 'cause *your Mum*'s that tough interviewer on telly nudge nudge, and you must be the token *fatty* wink wink, and let's hope they've got a wide-angle lens to get all of you in. These I ignore.

My first day at 'Shapers' is the rehearsal day, Monday. Artiste Antigone Tompson is required to be at the studio at 11.45 am, first to spend an hour with Lynda and then after lunch to rehearse seven scenes.

She has spent the entire weekend going over her lines of the seven scenes to be rehearsed, with her Walkman. She has done them standing up and sitting down, running on the spot and while doing crunches and stretches and headstands (without toppling over).

Her father will be driving her out to 'Shapers' today. Her father will be driving her out this week and maybe even the next and the week after that. Her father is almost, but not quite, unemployed.

It happened on Friday. When I came back from my watching day at

'Shapers', Dad was home. There's nothing unusual about that, half-past five on a Friday, nor Dad sitting in the living room, staring out at Rangitoto, having a drink. But the bottle in front of him on the table was whisky which he hardly ever drinks and it was nearly empty.

I decided he was pretty drunk. 'You work too hard, Dad.'

'We all work too hard, those of us who've got work in these ruthless, heartless times when the only measure of a man left is how much he earns. And what have you got to show for it, at the end of the day?' he peered mournfully into his glass.

'Well,' I said, sitting down with my orange juice, 'where do I start? This. Three cars. Overseas trips. Eight suits.'

'As Oscar would say, to lose one contract, Mr Tompson, may be regarded as a misfortune; to lose two, looks like carelessness. To lose three in as many weeks is someone sending you a very clear message.'

'What message?'

'I've put in bids to renew five contracts in the past few months. And lost out on all of them to whizz-kids in their thirties. The last kick in the guts was this afternoon.'

'There'll be others.'

'There won't. No. The message from the free market, Tiggie, is that I'm way, way past it. The message is go away, old man.'

I'd seen Dad a bit drunk before. But a happy drunk, not this bitter old person, slurring his words. He was sweaty, pale, shaking. When he began to cough and cough and cough, I started to get worried. I tried Mum's cellphone but all I got was that message telling me the Telecom mobile number I had called is either switched off or outside the coverage area.

Eventually he asked for a bucket and was sick. I took his tie off, put his feet up on the couch, put the whisky away and made him drink water. I got a cold facecloth for his forehead and a mohair rug because he was shivering. And then because I couldn't think of anything else to do, other than ring an ambulance – and to that he said, 'Absolutely no way' – I sat with him and we watched the news and 'Shortland Street' and the usual Friday night crappy programmes until finally just before midnight we heard the lift and Mum came in the door.

I learnt my lines and did homework during the weekend because it seemed like the best thing I could do was keep out of the way. Mum took over, and said I'd done a good job and Saturday morning they went to the doctor. He has to have all sorts of tests. It may be a heart condition, or simply stress. He's been ordered to take some time out.

I also heard him crying, and Mum saying, 'Well, if we have to move, Murray, we have to move.' And him saying, 'At least you still have your job,' and Mum saying, 'Yes, I still have my job and I'm good at it, damn it.'

And I'm thinking, Mum is turning forty soon and she has been heard to say that in this country you don't see many females doing her sort of work after they hit the big Four-O.

Rehearsals are held on the set, but without lights and with no cameras and only three or four crew, all wearing black. So it's even more like a church and I can see from the schedule that the director has pages and pages of scenes to get through. My seven are just seven of forty-two, would you believe, which get rehearsed today and then shot during the week.

'Tiggie, in you go,' says bald Damien cheerfully, and I am walking with Lynda through the padded door as a working rehearsing nervous actor, all the lines in my head and a deadweight in my stomach.

I have already been shown my very own little dressing room and told to watch my valuables because every now and then things get stolen by lightfingered kids who get ID cards from God knows where and wander through the place. I've been through the scenes yet again with Lynda, said hello to a pale depressed Vita who is taking it quietly today. I've not yet properly met the Maori girl playing Faith's personal trainer, Rata.

I am walking through this dark jumbled place towards the voices.

'G'day, Tiggie,' Rata says, waiting from the last scene. 'Kia ora. I'm Tania, playing Rata.'

'Yes, I know. I watched on Friday,' I say, adding, 'Um, kia ora.'

'Fighting fit? Ready to party?' she says, shadow-boxing at me.

'Yep.' Apart from looking gorgeous even in black tights and UCLA T-shirt, she has the most gorgeous chuckling voice, deep and fruity. She's a jazz singer as well as actor.

'I'm Eve.' The director I watched on Friday is wanting to shake hands. I bet she can feel me trembling. Behind those nerdy circle glasses, she's actually younger than I thought, maybe thirty. 'Lynda tells me you've been doing some good work with her.'

'Oh. Okay,' I say, with a stupid little laugh.

'Ready to go?'

'Yep.' This only a rehearsal, Tiggie, chill out.

'Got your script?'

'Um, no.'

'Better go and get it. Didn't Lynda tell you to bring it to rehearsals?'

'Um, yes, she did,' I lie. 'I just forgot. Sorry.'

She doesn't need to tell me to be quick, that I'm losing them a whole thirty or even sixty seconds, that I've stuffed up already without saying a single line. I flash past Damien, skid into my dressing room, and sprint back in through the padded door.

'Get your breath,' says Eve, quite kindly under the circumstances.

'Sorry. Sorry.' Oh fuck, now I'm all panting and hot and hassled, as well as nervous. While Eve is saying that this scene is all about Rata trying hard to establish a relationship with Faith, a crew member gets up from the small desk where she's writing things in a very large ring-binder and gives me a pencil.

'It's okay,' she whispers. 'You'll be fine.' Oh shit, I think, I don't want your pity. I want to be good and professional and not to stuff it up.

But the rehearsals have to be so quick that I've hardly begun to get used to Rata's voice or her brown eyes boring through me before we've actually done two scenes four times and it's all over. I have written on my script that I'm sitting on the floor here, get up here, move here, be very still here. Eve is saying, 'That's fine, Tiggie, see you tomorrow,' and I'm out the door and the next lot are coming in and I'm driving home with Dad almost before I know what's happened.

Seventeen

The script for my first scene looks so simple — only one and a half pages. I have a total of seven words. I've run it with Gareth, and discussed it with Lynda and rehearsed it with Eve.

Now, I'm sitting cross-legged on a gym mat under brilliant lights, thinking that if I get through this I can get through anything.

If they'd asked me which scene I'd like to do first, the very first, Scene 17 would have been bottom of the list. But you don't get asked. They don't know or want to know about my problems with cameras. If I've got any I shouldn't be here. It's my choice. Deal with it.

Two hours ago I arrived as ordinary old Tiggie. A pale blue T-shirt and black shorts were hanging on the rail in my dressing room, labelled Faith, Ep. 36, Scene 17. I promised to bring my own sneakers and white socks. I dressed slowly, feeling odd, knowing that they'd chosen clothes to make me look dumpy and plain. If they'd chosen stretch lycra in some fluorescent colour like all the cast instructors and most of the extras I'd seen the other day, what then?

I couldn't decide which would be worse. I left the T-shirt hanging out.

In the brightly lit and cosy make-up room I sat silent and rigid in a high revolving chair while some of the core cast chatted away with the make-up girls – gossip about this morning's headlines, politicians, celebrities. One of the make-up girls had just broken up with her boyfriend. High in one corner of the room, a monitor showed what was happening on the set. They were doing scenes in the gym this morning, reception scenes this afternoon. I wished Vita was here.

Faith's face gradually and carefully was painted on: skin sponged on, blusher dusted on with a fat brush, eyes and brows shaped with little soft brushes, and eyeliner so subtle you can't really see it. Not much powder because, my girl says, consulting a file where all this is written down, Faith's been working out, hasn't she? Later, on the set, someone will give me a healthy glow.

Then hair. They gathered it up into a ponytail, deliberately untidy for the same reason. Only a *little* untidy. 'This is not your gritty drama, darling,' said the make-up girl, aiming the hairspray at me. 'Soaps, everyone looks pretty all the time. Even the kid from New Lynn who wins a magazine contest.'

'Everyone's not pretty on "Coronation Street",' I said, immediately regretting it.

'That's true, they're not. We're more the American tradition, where everyone's over-the-top gorgeous. Now, darling, are you happy? Love those green Irish eyes. Just look straight at the camera.'

I was swung around in my chair to face another girl aiming a Polaroid camera at me. *Click.* 'That's for continuity,' she says. 'So as you have the same hair, or when we have to give you cuts and bruises. We use these a lot.'

I'd looked at this non-pretty person called Faith in her boring blue T-shirt and baggy shorts quite long enough. After all that, nearly half an hour, I just looked like me, only a bit more so. I slid off the chair, noting on the prominent clock on the wall that I still had an hour to go before my scene. Lynda would see me ten minutes before I went in.

The hour crept by. I watched some boys in the green room playing computer games, tried to read a book, wandered up and down the corridors, went to the loo about twenty times. Getting closer, Lynda took me back to my dressing room and we ran the lines of all nine scenes I'm to do this week.

Then I went to the area outside the padded door and got on one of those bikes which everyone doing a gym scene has to peddle for five minutes before going in, to get their heart-rate up and bodies alive and glowing. Bald Damien made sure Rata and I knew the lines.

Finally, the scene before mine is done. Seven minutes behind schedule and my heart-rate nicely speeded up, it is my turn under lights.

Faith is in the women's gym, sitting on a mat.

Rata is wearing a bright yellow tracksuit with *One on One* written on the back. She's got sleek hair and the same smooth, flawless, carefully painted face as me, except that being a stunning Maori she started with a big advantage. We're both ignoring the technical stuff going on around us, her because she's got most of the words and me because I'm now realising what I've done.

There are three cameras rolling towards me like tanks and a microphone is hanging about a metre above our heads. I feel like a possum caught in a car's headlights, trapped. I'm absolutely rigid with fear.

Can they all tell that I've never acted before? *Never* put on a costume and make-up and tried to be someone else? Remembered their lines?

Seven words, that's all.

Rata kneels behind me and pulls my arms up and back. We're rehearsing. She hurts me just a little, I have to act the rest. There are little silences before I say my first two words, then my second two. I'm pushed into position for the 'before' photo, I smile weakly and I don't have to act feeling sullen and unresponsive and unhappy cause I am, big-time. I just look at her, jollying me along.

'Okay,' says Eve. 'Go again.' She gives some directions to the photographer, who's a boy of about twenty with jet-black gelled hair. He must get us into exactly the right position against the mirrors, right on these marks. 'Okay, Tania, Tiggie? Your marks?'

I now know what *marks* are, but Tiggie, who's she?

It's back to the top and again my arms get wrenched out of their sockets and the flashbulbs go off and Rata's desperately trying to make contact with this sullen kid who's won a prize. I, Tiggie/Faith, can't think of anything else other than trying to sit and stand in a way that somehow, miraculously, to the cameras rolling video tape and the camera taking stills, makes me look less like Miss Piggy.

Lynda has listened to me and agreed that this is one of the reasons for

Faith's unhappiness. Lynda's a big lady too. 'So don't push it, Tiggie,' she said. 'Don't play the subtext. No face acting. Just let your mind focus on it. You won't have to do anything else. Trust me.'

Oh, I do, I do. I trust you, Lynda, and Vita and Eve and Rowan and Gareth because I have to, simple, and I sure as hell don't trust myself.

'Okay, let's go for a take!'

There is immediate activity, bustle, tension. The extras, wearing their slinky gymwear, are brought on and positioned on various bits of equipment.

A make-up girl is standing in front of me, painting my lips again with a little brush, primping my hair. She's brushing some sort of goo on my forehead and cheekbones. The healthy glow, I suppose. I *must not* ask for a mirror, to see what she's done to me. Another one is painting Rata's lips bright red and yet another is checking Rata is happy with the file she picks up off the carpet, the biro. The file's properly printed with '"Shapers", client Faith Hopkins, Personal Trainer Rata George'. The photographer is having his camera checked over, his face powdered.

Someone tells me to get into position, down on the mat. A water bottle is put down beside me. I see Lynda's face among all the people behind the cameras, giving me a thumbs up.

Vita darts into the light. 'Tiggie, I shouldn't be here but *had* to say, you look fabulous. Just made it, accident on the bridge.'

'Made what?' I mumble. 'Did you have an accident?'

'No, someone else. In time to see your first scene. You'll be great. Just relax. Forget the cameras and go with Rata. Break a leg.'

'What?'

'Actorspeak for good luck.'

She squeezes my shoulder and vanishes as quickly as she came. She came in early, specially? I can feel Rata's warm body up against my back as she gets into position, and after what seems like an eternity, gets a signal from the AD. She pulls my arms up into the stretch position. Funny, I hadn't thought: it's like a crucifixion.

My boobs are sticking out, pointing straight at the middle camera. Oh shit, should I have got a new bra? Did I use a deodorant this morning?

'Standing by extras. Roll record, please.'

The extras start working away at their butt blasters and rowing machines. Apart from this, it has gone incredibly quiet and the attention of three cameras, a microphone, about fifty people here and all sorts of bosses in the control room upstairs and the entire world out there is on me and Rata. They've all helped me get here; now the only person who can do it is me, alone and scared absolutely shitless.

I am fourteen and walking down a bush path naked.

Who's laughing now?

Although I am numb with terror for the first two takes and think that I'll never talk again, my mouth does open and words come out.

The reason we get to a third take is nothing to do with me. At least I assume that it's not, because it's Tania that Eve comes and talks to ('You're really working hard on this girl, Rata, your professional reputation is at stake'), and it's the photographer who forgets to say a line and the First has to call out, 'Cut, go again,' halfway through the scene.

Before the third take, Eve kneels down beside me and says, 'Tiggie, you're doing fine. Just give me a little more on Tania's last two lines. Think to yourself, a year of this! — I'm not going to cry, *I'm not going to cry.* I want a nice strong image to go out on.'

'Try,' I said, my mouth like sandpaper. I've seen enough of 'Shortland Street' to know that scenes often finish with a close-up of someone shocked, or surprised, or hurt, or scheming — or about to cry.

This third take is where I start to understand what Rowan's classes have been teaching me and why people put themselves through this agony. I am really feeling Rata's growing disappointment that she's not getting through to me. I'm *hating* being pressured, forced into photographs. But also knowing that by not responding I have a sort of power. I can control my voice.

So, as Faith gets more and more unhappy, and although I don't actually do anything consciously, I can feel my stomach tighten and my throat go taut and a prick of hot tears in my eyes. For a long moment the world stands quiet and still.

'Cut,' calls Eve decisively and everyone relaxes. 'Tiggie, you got it in one! And good work, Tania.'

A make-up girl is dabbing a tissue underneath my wet eyes. 'Not many people can cry on cue,' she murmurs. 'Was that really your first scene ever?'

'Yes.'

'Awesome.'

And here's Vita leading me by the hand, away from the lights, towards smiling Lynda. I was fantastic, it seems. I have fabulous eyes, a fabulous face for television. That third take had been amazing. They'd both had real lumps in their throats too.

And do you know, it might seem strange and incredible but as I stood there dazed, congratulating myself that I'd survived, I hadn't let anyone down and no one had laughed, I was starting to think, *hey, when's the next one!*

Eighteen

My real world and fantasy worlds are colliding, grinding together like icebergs.

I had to tell Dad about my gym in Newmarket, because with shooting nearly every day, I was only going to get there three times a week with his help. You'd have thought I'd won a medal, the way he went on about how delighted he was that I'd seen the light and made this decision. Perhaps, he said, changing to a new school had been a good move after all, though Mum and he both had had their doubts. Very considerable doubts, Tiggie.

Because he's not working so much in town, he's resigned from his own gym and joined mine. We go together, cosy father and daughter, sometimes before shooting, sometimes afterwards, depending on the schedule.

'Best thing that ever happened,' he says, loudly telling people that he's now semi-retired and taking on less work. 'Loving it. I'm going to the gym with Tiggie, and I'm going to do the round Taupo bike race next year. Started serious training already.'

He doesn't fool me. At the gym I see him reading the Executive Appointments in the *National Business Review* while he pedals the bike, and he never misses a chance to do a bit of 'networking' when he sees someone he knows. It's embarrassing, he's so hearty. 'Keep in touch,' I hear him saying, slapping some guy on the back.

Then he sees something on the noticeboard which gets him all excited. They want extras for 'Shapers'. Why didn't he think of that before? He's quite trim enough. Good use of time, since he was out there with me already. He didn't mind taking his work with him to do in the car and going for long walks on the beach, and he had his cellphone, and sometimes he got dressed up in his suit and came back into town for appointments, but this was too good an opportunity to . . .

'No way, Dad,' I say firmly.

'Oh come on, Tiggie,' he says. 'Give me a break.'

'No. You're too . . .' I hesitated, searching for the right word.

'Go on, say it.'

The show is going to air in two weeks so he hasn't yet seen the older guys pedalling their bikes as extras. But I can't bear the thought of Dad watching me acting. 'Shapers' is my scene.

'Old?' he growls.

'It's not that, Dad.' But already he's lent over and switched on the boring seventies tapes he keeps in the car. *Y-M-C-A, Y-M-C-A!* He's hurt, majorly, and stays hurt for the ride home.

Of course he could be an extra on 'Shapers'. But those two or three extras and Ruth, the tough bitch boss, are about the only people on 'Shapers' over thirty. Faith is the only one with anything less than a perfect figure.

So it's all make-believe, fantasy, all those Greek statues and white tiled floors and beautiful young people. I keep reading and hearing in the advance publicity that they researched real gyms before deciding on the design and the core cast, and they have gym consultants on the set all the time to ensure that routines and exercises are being done properly. But it's all fantasy land. At my real gym, not one of the instructors could get a job on 'Shapers', not even my trainer Amy, who's jollying me along in the same way Rata is jollying Faith.

The real gym bodies are all sizes and shapes, in all sorts of different gear and most are a long way from perfect. A lot of people have gorgeous bodies but haven't ever been told to hold their heads up and their backs straight, or if they've been told once a long time ago, they've forgotten. They slouch, limp, creep, shuffle around. I've become very body-conscious.

Besides, I read the small print of the notice, which Dad didn't, in his excitement. They only want trim, fit people under 25 who exercise regularly and can participate in aerobics classes.

Sorry, Dad.

I think Vita and I have some sort of pact going. Not that we've ever talked about it much. But I'm going out to 'Shapers' day after day, and working my way through scenes with Rata in the gym, and back to the first scene where I arrive with the magazine person, and forward to the scene where I turn up with a suspicious bruise on my forehead and Rata starts to get worried about what's going on at home. I work on the lines with Lynda, and I rehearse and film scenes with Rata, but even when I'm free, or it's lunchtime in the café with Lynda, I hardly ever see Vita. And when I do, it's never more than a few words.

In a way, I'm glad. On those few occasions I can't help checking her over, being reminded of the binge on the beach, wondering when she last ate. She seems to live on cigarettes, coffee, willpower and fresh air. And I don't want to be reminded more than I have to about eating disorders. Faith is doing this for me quite enough, thank you.

I know from the schedule that Vita is doing ten or more scenes a day. Fifty-seven in one week! Her make-up call is usually at 8 am, sometimes earlier. She has scenes in the reception area, and the gym, and the café. In and out through the padded door.

But it's not just that. The only clue I have is a brief conversation on the second day. Even this was just in passing, as she came out from shooting, and I was walking through on my way home. Holly as receptionist in her little bottle-green suit stood before me, all bubbly.

'Tiggie, you were great yesterday.'

'Thanks. Don't remember much, actually.'

'I knew you were a natural for this game.'

An echo: Gareth, once upon a time.

'How did it go today?' she asked.

'Okay. How are yours?'

'Well, you know.' She tossed it off. Subtext: I've been doing this for

132

years, and it's just a job. I think a lot about subtext these days and it's a worry.

'Good picture of you in the paper today,' I said. 'Nice story.'

'Was there? Haven't looked.' Her bubbles were evaporating fast.

'Don't you read it?'

'Don't usually bother. I just do what I'm asked to do. I have to do something at the Starship with sick children next week. The day after we go to air. Some stunt or other.'

I'd seen people come off the set still hyped up, eyes glowing, sometimes panting. A minute ago Vita was the efficient glamorous Holly with sparkling eyes. Now she looked like a Holly blow-up doll someone had pricked with a pin, with dead eyes and a cynical edge to her voice.

'Are you all right?' I ask.

'Why?' A defensive look came into her eyes and she suddenly darted into the little coffee room saying, her back to me, 'Need a coffee. Look, it's no big deal, Tiggie, but when I'm not on the set, I just have to have some space. That's why you see my dressing room door closed. I'm not being unfriendly. I just *have* to be quiet for a bit. Survival time.'

'Yeah,' I said from the doorway. 'I don't know how you do ten scenes a day. Four's enough for me.'

'You get used to it.' I watched her make a coffee, wondering if I was imagining things, like, was she propping herself up against the table the machine sat on? Another faint coming up? When she turned around, smiling and bright, I knew she was acting her socks off.

'And *everyone* says – you're going to be so great that when it goes to air, I shall quite rightly bask in a whole lot of humungous reflected glory.'

Yes, I thought, and you're also going to crack up. Humungously and quite soon.

Tonight 'Shapers' is going to air.

The publicity has been *huge*. The make-up room is where the latest newspaper cuttings get pinned up. Lots of faxes from other parts of the country. They are running out of wall space.

People swap stories about who said what on yesterday's radio interviews, and produce glossy magazines with long articles about the lives, loves and career ambitions of various members of the cast. The publicists have been busy, everyone agrees, but frankly, the media are a push-over for television stories about beautiful people in a beautiful show. Usually they have to write about 'Melrose Place' and 'Baywatch' and 'Friends', now they have a beautiful show which is entirely homegrown. No more nurses. *Bodies.*

Vita, as one of the most beautiful, stars in all of these. Popular former 'Shortland Street' actor furthers her career in new dramatic role. She's on the cover of the *NZ Woman's Weekly* in her gym gear, and in the *Listener* as Holly the receptionist. Various gym and fitness magazines think the whole idea is the greatest thing that's ever happened to them. They devote entire supplements to this new soap which is going to promote the virtues of exercise and good nutrition and have people running to gyms in droves.

Don't bet on it, I think rather sourly. It's all so glitzy and perfect it might put ordinary people off.

But it's impossible not to feel excited and a little apprehensive as I sit with Mum and Dad this Monday night, waiting for the programme to begin. For the last few days, everyone's been tense. Many of them have seen the first few episodes already. Though they all sound very positive, they sit in the make-up chairs trying to guess what the critics will say, making up silly bad reviews and roaring with laughter. The theory is that if/when these appear, they can be discounted and the writers dismissed as ignorant wannabees and be quickly forgotten until people settle down and begin to see 'Shapers' as the brilliant, innovative show it really is − a show that's here to stay and grow until it rates better than 'Shortland Street' ever did.

The trouble is, Mum had started drinking even before Dad and I came in, and is already being rude about the trailers that get shown with the ads at nine minutes to go.

'Have a baaaad feeling about this,' she says. 'Draw the curtains, darling, would you?'

'Why?' I say, pulling the heavy cord which swishes the curtains shut and blots out the twinkling harbour lights. 'That's only a trailer.'

'Whose job is to make me feel I want to see the show. Frankly, from that, I don't.'

'Give it a chance, Cassie,' says Dad.

'I said it was a vile idea, right from the start.'

'For Christ's sake, Cassie, be fair,' says Dad harshly. 'You of all people should . . .'

The doorbell goes.

'That'll be the pizza,' says Mum, pouring herself another Pernod from the bottle and the jug of water on the table in front of her. She holds up the large glass of milky white death. '*Skol!* No, wrong country. *Prosit?* Oh, bugger it, cheers. Large *quattro stagione* coming up the lift. Large *pasta marinara*. I ordered them while I was still sober. I know we can't afford Dial-A-Pizza any more, Murray, but I've had a hard day at the office. Cassie didn't feel like cooking.'

I see Dad's lips go tight as he gets up and opens the door to a delivery boy in a red uniform. To get away from Mum, I gather up plates, knives and forks, paper napkins from the kitchen.

'It's starting,' she calls. 'Ooooh, Grecian. I think they've strayed onto the wrong set. Would that be 'Hercules', or would it be 'Xena'? All those sickly pastels!'

'Shut up, Mum,' I say as pleasantly as I can.

'Excuse me?'

'I want to watch.'

'Well, of course, you want to watch, you're in it.'

'Later, yes.'

'How much later?'

'Six weeks later.' I thrust a plateful of pizza, dripping cheese, at her. She's all confused. 'Mine's not for six weeks. Now get eating and shush.'

It's a two-hour special, to introduce all the characters and get the audience on their side. I'd had that tiny glimpse into what the monitor was seeing the day I watched them filming. Now I see just how clever these magicians are. You could swear this was a whole gymnasium complex, with a tiled lobby and a gym floor, and a big café and an outdoor area where they hold debates and have music. Little rooms as offices and for testing and massage. There's a shot of what it looks like from the street, which is all glass and pink concrete. The actual building must be somewhere quite different, with false signs put up just for the shot — or a model.

'Shapers', the smart city gym in Auckland, lives.

'That's the girl who's my PT,' I point, when I first see Rata in her yellow tracksuit. 'She's great.'

'Something about Maori actors,' says Mum gloomily. 'They've got something, some *je ne sais quoi*.'

'Charisma?' suggests Dad.

'Poise,' says Mum. 'Smooth skins. And naturally beautiful voices.'

'There's my friend Vita,' I squeak. 'Her character's Holly.'

'I remember her from "Shortland Street",' says Mum. 'She's lost weight.'

'She's been at a real gym. And it's hard work, what she does. Fourteen scenes a day, sometimes.'

'She looks anorexic,' says Mum, accusingly. 'Is she?'

'I . . . don't know. I don't think so. She used to be a dancer.'

'Does she smoke?'

'Um, yes.'

'Thought so. Weight control.'

'Mum, I want to *watch* this.'

'Don't mind me,' she says. 'I shall just eat my pizza like the good little girl I am.'

I catch Dad's eye. We both hate it when she gets like this, soppy and girlish and pathetic. But with any luck, according to pattern, Dad will shortly swivel her legs up onto the couch and get her a rug and she'll drift off to sleep and snore.

So she doesn't see much of the very first two-hour episode of 'Shapers' after all.

Dad doesn't like the show, but decides to be loyal rather than honest. I don't know what I think, because I keep remembering the real people, the real sets, the real cameras. I honestly don't know, except it's better than 'Baywatch'.

The critics know what they think. In the paper the next morning, and on a radio review Dad and I hear driving over the bridge, they trash it. They trash the idea and the design and the acting and the direction. They fear that it will only fuel society's already unhealthy obsession with fitness and self. They predict that there was no way it would survive to take over from 'Shortland Street'. A waste of public funding, a waste of sponsor's money.

'That's just one person's opinion,' says Dad, staunchly. 'And critics have been wrong more than once.'

In the make-up room people are very angry and resentful, but they are also laughing and excited and joking and savagely pulling each critic and each critic's comments to pieces. Many of them say they expected nothing different from those jerks, because they always trashed New Zealand shows on principle. No one ever erected a statue to a critic, quotes someone.

Vita, on the other hand, is in her dressing room in tears.

'It's so unfair,' she howls, pacing up and down like a tiny animal in a cage. 'What right do these people have to set themselves up like that. Bastards. Don't they *know* how hard it is? Let them do better!'

'They couldn't, that's why they're critics,' says Lynda, trying to calm her down. 'Come in, Tiggie. Vita's got nine scenes to get through today and she's going to need a bit of help. You've got . . .?'

'Three.'

'Right. Well, I'm here for both of you today. Tiggie, you can set up camp in here.

'Vita says she likes to be on her own. I don't want to get in the way.'

'You're not,' sniffles Vita. 'I'd like you to stay.'

'There you go,' says Lynda. 'Party time.'

'And *stuff* the critics,' says Vita savagely. 'I bet the ratings will be okay. They'll be proved wrong. You see.'

'That's my girl,' says Lynda. ' Now, you'd better get off to make-up for some repair work.'

After she's gone, Lynda says, 'You and Vita see a bit of each other out of work hours, I gather?'

'Not much. Just at acting class. I've been to her house once.'

'Tiggie, I'll be honest with you. She's had bad reviews before without getting hysterical. She's becoming a bit of a worry.'

Lynda expects me to tell her why that is. I can't.

'There's something I can't quite put my finger on. I've talked to her parents. No worries that they can see.'

'I . . . don't think she eats properly. Perhaps she needs some vitamins and stuff.' Too late, I remember the tray of little bottles by her bed. Pills are what she eats. I add hastily, 'Bigger breakfasts!' Or any breakfast at all.

'There's nothing else . . .?'

I can tell you? No. *No.* It is not my business to dob Vita in to Lynda or anyone else. If they knew the truth, she'd lose her job and I'd lose a friend. Besides, it's survival time for me too. Tomorrow morning I have to do the binge scene. We are going on location to a fish and chip shop in the shopping centre nearby. They will close the shop to customers for two hours while they set up the cameras and the lights and we do the scene. Lynda has warned me, instead of the privacy of the studio, there will be public stopping to have a gawp and get in the way.

Faith, discovered by Rata having a binge, admits that her father is abusing her. She wants to stop her gym work.

I know what it's like, to order a huge pile of fish and chips, know it's *disgusting,* know I'm going to feel absolutely gross, know I'm going to regret it, but still sit down and eat the whole lot, every last one. So does Vita, as I saw that day at Long Bay beach.

Too much food, too little. What's wrong with us? Other people seem to know the secret.

Funny though, when I come to do the scene the next day, I have to force myself to eat the chips. The props guy puts them in front of me while we're rehearsing, a pile no bigger than some I've tackled, and it's all I can do to chew my way through about ten during the six takes we need. They're cold and foul and I have to force them down.

Is it because in this scene, Faith does most of the talking?

. . . I'm expecting a friend.

Faith, I'm not stupid. I know what an unhappy kid having a binge looks like.

I was hungry! I haven't eaten since last night.

Why not?

Nothing in the fridge at home. Dad gave me a ten dollar note and told me to get lost. So I did. He's gone to the pub.

And when he comes home he might push you around?

He might. He might stand in the kitchen and say fat cow, why haven't I cooked him a meal. I'm fifteen, and a girl, and girls cook. He might tell me to pack my bags 'cause he can't stand that bitch of a landlady and we're moving again. He's lost his job and he's back on the dole. He falls over, and when I try to help him up, he's so angry he takes a swipe at me.

(Rata looking at the bruises) *Is that what happened last night?*

The scene ends with Faith agreeing reluctantly to keep going to the gym, then offering to share her chips with Rata. We need six takes partly because on location you go straight in, Rehearse Record. No previous rehearsal, cold turkey. And partly because the pile of chips and this feeling of desperation are just too close to the bone, too real, too familiar. I have it every mealtime: I tell myself, go easy on the fattening stuff, no second helpings today, don't pick at those leftovers, *stop it!* – and then what happens? I *hate* myself for doing it, *loathe* myself, but I do it.

Lynda knows I'm going to have trouble with the scene. She's right by one of the cameras. 'I can't do this,' I say, tears any second now. 'Sorry, but I can't.'

When I stuffed up the scene for the third time, she takes me away into a back room, away from everyone. 'We'll just go through the scene quietly,' she says.

She sits me down and eyeballs me.

'Tiggie,' says Lynda, with that soothing voice doctors use when they're about to hurt you, 'we'll shoot it line by line if necessary. But you know as well as I do, that you must do it. Here and now, you must do it. You understand why, don't you?'

'Yes.'

'I want you just to take your time, say the words and don't panic about getting through to the end in one go. If you stuff up the long speech this time, that's fine, we'll do a pick-up. And another, if necessary, and another, until we get it.'

'Okay.' She walks me back into the lights.

The make-up girl blots me round the eyes while Lynda whispers, 'Tiggie, the best scenes are often those that have given the most trouble. That's because you're digging deep. You'll do it. You'll be fine!'

I get right through to . . . *he's back on the dole* . . . before my mind goes blank and I actually gag on one of the chips. I hear Eve say, 'Cut.' A sort of grim determination has settled on everyone.

'We'll pick it up from *He's lost his job again*,' says Eve. 'Tiggie, got that?'

'Yes. Tania, I'm *sorry*.'

'That's okay. We'll get there.'

Eve calls, 'Remember to give me those two seconds clear after I say *Action*.' Lynda has drilled me on this over and over again — count to two after *Action*, so they have a clear tape for editing.

'From line seven, pick-up, everyone.'

After the sixth take, the ninth pick-up, I don't remember, Eve calls 'Cut.' First says, 'That's a wrap.' I can feel the sudden release of tension, almost as though everyone's been holding their breath for half an hour. If Eve is happy with what she's got, then it's her responsibility and they can relax.

'That was great, Tiggie,' says Tania, leaning across the table to hug me. 'Well done.'

I just burst into tears. I can't help it, just like I can't help such a surge of anger at myself that I sweep the pile of chips off the plastic table onto the floor. Lynda, ignoring this, asks the real fish and chip shop owner, who was allowed to be an extra, to bring me a fresh Coke. The props one in front of me is flat.

'Stuffed it up,' I blubber, knowing how feeble and pathetic I must be appearing to everyone watching. 'Best scene, and I stuff it up.'

'Far from it,' Lynda says. 'Believe me.'

'I was just saying the words. *Pathetic*.'

'That was all you needed to do,' she says. 'You'll be surprised when you see the results. Surprised and pleased. Any more would have killed it.'

The little Chinese owner arrives with the Coke. 'You made me cry,' he says conspiratorially, from his accent obviously one of those Chinese born here. 'I get a lot of kids in here because they don't get meals at home, stuffing themselves with chips. It breaks my heart. When do I see this?'

'About two months,' says Lynda. 'The shop will look good.'

'No worries. I like the show. Watch it every night.' He grins as he begins to pick up the chips from the concrete floor, 'She's going to be a star, eh? Lots of fan mail?'

The star just looks at him stupidly, picking up the pieces of her tantrum, and bursts into a fresh torrent, crying for all the kids like her who have caring Mums and Dads and do get their meals at home and still have problems.

Nineteen

'Tiggie,' says Mum suddenly, 'tell me, is this girl Faith getting to you?'

'Why?'

'Because you're getting to me.'

'How?'

'Where do I start? You're uncommunicative, sullen and sometimes downright rude. I can't make any comment about your attitude problem or your increasingly scruffy clothes without you jumping down my throat.'

Today she's between assignments and is driving me over the harbour bridge. Dad has put on a suit and lots of Karl Lagerfeld and gone to a job interview. I don't like the way she drives – too fast, too close behind other people, and critical of them.

'Fuckwit,' she snarls, as someone who drives even faster whizzes up an inside lane and cuts in, right in front of us. She leans on the horn and gets a rude message from the man's raised left hand.

'So tell me,' she presses. 'Are you "identifying with the character", as actors are known to do? In which case, can I expect this phenomenon is merely a stage and will shortly pass? Or is it something else?'

'Nothing else,' I mumble.

'There? You see,' she says, triumphantly glancing my way, 'that's exactly what I mean. How? Why? Grunt. I had hoped that all this increased activity was going to give you a sense of purpose in your life. Bolster up your self-confidence. Do wonders for your self-esteem.'

'Don't you get tired of a TV camera in your face? Performing?'

'Of course I do,' she says dismissively. 'I'd even hoped that two months of filming might have done something for your waistline.'

'Not allowed to.'

'I beg your pardon?'

'I had a warning last week. All my horrible clothes are getting loose. Shouldn't you be in the other lane?'

'You don't look any different to me.' If she'd gone on to say, *more's the pity*, the message couldn't have been any clearer.

'I'm not. Anyway, I'm eating plenty. I don't want to talk about it. You need to get in the right-hand lane.'

We are whizzing up the Albany highway and today I have a nasty little scene, where Faith, with bruised face, trapped and torn between wanting to continue at the gym and hating every moment, semi-deliberately drops a weight on her foot. Like soldiers used to maim themselves so they'd be declared unfit for battle. Rata takes the blame, gets bawled out for unsafe use of equipment, making Faith feel terrible.

Besides, Mum's exactly right. I've noticed myself getting sullen and scruffy. They give me these horrible clothes to wear, they paint bruises on my face and arms, everyone in both gyms (real and fantasy) and at the studio (real life) looks sideways at me, this freak – so is it surprising?

I've had the last lot of scripts. In my final scenes, Rata sends Faith off determined to talk to a teacher at school, or a doctor, or a counsellor, someone. Faith reports a terrible scene with her father who's found out that she's talked to her teacher. Rata wrestles with her conscience – if she herself reports him to the police, Faith will see it as a betrayal. But the next time Faith comes she tells Rata it's goodbye – she's going to Australia. Living with her mum in Gisborne is not an option. She promises Faith that she will seek help for her eating disorder.

That's where I bow out. But there's the question of the magazine, which wants to sue Faith and her father for the success story that will now never be written. Rata persuades Ruth that this would destroy Faith's brittle relationship with her father and would be very bad publicity for the gym. Ruth decides to settle with the magazine out of court. Rata sadly realises that not all her clients will be success stories.

Not a great bundle of fun, Faith's story. I know that I'm going to begin and end up as a sullen frump. I *am* a sullen frump. If I played a bright, upbeat character like Holly, with gorgeous clothes and lots of guys chasing me both on the show and in real life, would I therefore become a bright upbeat character with gorgeous clothes and lots of guys chasing me?

Dream on, Tiggie. They don't write parts for glamorous size sixteens.

But something's not right here. I have some nice and expensive clothes, but they don't do much for me. And Vita wears gorgeous clothes and looks spectacular all the time, whether she's Holly or Vita, and they aren't doing much for her either . . .

'Muuuuum!' I screech as she realises she's in the wrong lane to turn right, tries to change lanes and a truck in her blind spot has to brake suddenly. She swerves violently. Now she's the one being loudly hooted at, by the truck and several others behind.

'Moron!' she bellows as she gets swept along in the middle lane, past the turn-off I've come to know so well. 'He sped up to cut me off, the bastard.'

'Your fault,' I say heartlessly. 'Now you've got to drive up to Albany before you can turn around and I'll be late.'

'No you won't.'

'That was nearly a major pile-up.'

'I was upset. Distracted.'

'My fault? *My* fault you drive like a maniac?'

'I'm a very good driver.'

'Mum, you're bloody awful. And you can't do a U-turn here!'

But she does, and we're whizzing back towards the turn-off, and down the main road towards the studio and I'm getting out of the wagon and I'm five minutes late and bald Damien will kill me.

'Thanks a bundle,' I hurl at her, slamming the door. 'Go and be famous. You're good at that.'

Five minutes later I'm sitting in the make-up chair in my ghastly dumpy black shorts having bruises painted onto my forehead when Lynda comes in and whispers to me that there's a four-wheel-drive sitting outside and

144

the person inside it having a little weep looks very like my mother. I say it will be my mother, 'cause we had a bit of a row.

'Do you want me to go and give her a message?'

'Like what?'

'What do people normally say to each other after rows?'

'Depends. Oh all *right*,' I say with bad grace, 'you can tell her I'm sorry for being rude but I still think she's a bloody awful driver.'

'That's it?'

'Word for word. And I was late.'

Lynda goes out to the street to relay the message that Tiggie's sort of sorry, but by then the wagon is gone.

That's my family pissed off with me. Who's next?

'Only a week to go,' says Lynda with irritating cheerfulness after a dressing room run-through of lines. 'Everyone's very pleased with your work, Tiggie.' *

'I bet.'

'Don't you believe me?'

'No.'

'Are you going to get involved in your school drama when you get back?'

'No. Why?'

'Because they offer a very good course and you have a lot of talent.'

'For playing a freak. Parts for people like me come along once every hundred years. So why bother to do drama or Rowan's classes or anything?'

'Tiggie, people are cast or not cast for all sorts of reasons. Ethnicity, age, physical type, emotional type, voice. You could get down to the last two contenders and miss out simply because the person you have to act opposite is two inches shorter. You don't match up. One of you has to go.'

'I don't match with anyone.'

'In the first instance, Emily will be a better judge of that. She'll send you for any audition where she thinks you've got a chance.'

'She's not going to be very busy then, is she?'

Bald Damien pokes his head into the dressing room. 'Tiggie, one away from your scene – running lines with Tania, please.'

Lynda follows me, looking thoughtful. No doubt she'll be pleased when I've finished and gone and she doesn't have to bother with me.

Tara rings that night to tell me that the deadline for the programme is next week and am I on schedule with it.

'It'll be done,' I say acidly.

'When are you back at school?'

'Next Monday.'

'That'll give you only two days. Are you sure that's enough?'

'If it isn't, it's my problem.'

'I'll have to answer to Sophia, who's nearly up the wall.'

'I said, it'll be done.'

'Tiggie, is it true that you're shooting some sort of guest part in "Shapers"?'

'It might be.'

'The critics hated it. And the ratings are lousy.'

'You enjoy saying that, don't you? Goodbye.'

I slam the phone down. Bitch!

I haven't spoken to Gareth for weeks. He's obviously been too busy with his precious production to ring and see how I'm getting on.

'Tiggie, how are you getting on?'

I nearly drop the phone.

'You were going to give me a ring,' he continues. 'How's it going?'

'Hard. Scary. Depressing.'

'Why depressing?'

'I'm playing a depressing character. It's catching.'

'When are you back at school?'

'What's it to you?'

Slight pause, while he decides how to deal with this person. 'We're missing you.'

'Yeah, yeah. Tell Tara I love her too. I suppose she told you to ring, check up on me.'

'She did not. I'm ringing because . . .'

I'll never know why he's ringing, because I've slammed the phone down on him too.

And with a sort of inevitability, Vita.

Three days left at the studio and I lose the friend who got me there in the first place. But that doesn't mean I have to feel obliged to her for the rest of my life. Or that I have to smile sweetly and say yes Vita, I think that's an *amazing* idea someone in the publicity department has had – no doubt to get a bit of free publicity and bolster the ratings – and of *course* you should trot off and do it, no worries.

For five weeks now she has been doing her eight or ten scenes a day and I've been doing my three or six or eight and I have no premonition that things are going to turn nasty. Lynda's worried, I know that, and I can't look at Vita without being reminded of why she worries me. So I've been avoiding her.

Until this morning, when I have an early call and find myself sitting next to her in the make-up room. She wasn't called early on the schedule – I checked. It turns out that this morning she's got a four-hour publicity call and she needs the works. She's having false eyelashes, a full shampoo and blow dry, everything.

She chats away with Tania in the next chair and the make-up girls who are working on each of us. The make-up room is the friendliest and most gossipy room in the building. Everyone has to go through there, go in pale and boring and spotty, come out like Cinderella, healthy looking and gorgeous – except of course if they need to have you dead, or dying, or injured in some way, like me. It never ceases to amaze me how long and much care it takes to make someone look just slightly better than 'normal' for television.

There are sofas and magazines for people waiting their turn. All the wall space that isn't mirrors has lists, letters, magazine articles, photos and clippings pinned up. So if you want to know what's going on, that's where you go.

First off, says Vita, she's got a session with yet another photographer for yet another glossy magazine. Then she's been asked to go to a school where they're having a health and fitness week and talk to the assembly. It's a private girls school.

The one where I spent seven years of my life.

'Yuk,' says Tania. 'I'd have said no way if they asked me.'

'Couldn't,' says Vita. 'Nice little arrangement got made while playing golf. One of their trustees and someone high up in Channel Three. Of course Vita will come. TV cameras will be there. I've been up half the night writing a speech.'

'What about?' I chip in.

'Oh, you know,' she says airily, evasively.

'No, I don't. You can hardly tell them about good nutrition.'

She doesn't answer that.

'Why not?' says her make-up girl, whose name I still don't know and am now too embarrassed to ask. 'I'm sure Vita knows all the right things to tell a hall full of girls. Plenty of veges and roughage and stuff. Keep off the chardonnay, girls, no flat whites and eight glasses of water a day. Just don't have a ciggie while you're there, darling. Do those eyelashes feel okay? Can't have them falling off in the middle of your speech.'

Vita bats her eyelids at her reflection.

'Lots of them are vegetarians,' I say. 'Or vegans. Won't eat red meat or dairy foods. First got pissed on chardonnay when they were fourteen. And they smoke.'

'How do you know that?' says Vita, looking everywhere in the mirror but at me as her make-up girl outlines her lips. Today she's not Holly the receptionist, she's Vita Rogers, star. Gloss and glamour, knock 'em dead.

'Friends,' I say quickly. 'Friends of friends.'

'I feel sorry for them,' says another make-up girl. 'Someone told me that a lot of them are anorexic, or that other thing, where you throw up all the time, you know . . .'

'Bulimia,' says Tania. 'Lady Di had it.'

'I do feel sorry for them,' the make-up girl insists. 'They get a lot of pressure. Parents who demand that they get three hours of homework a night. And their home lives don't come up smelling of roses.'

'They're pampered, selfish little snobs, eh, who don't have a bloody clue what's going on in the real world,' says Tania. 'How can they, rich Pakeha girls all cooped up together. Why didn't they ask me to go and talk to them? I'll tell you why.'

'You're twenty,' says Vita. 'Too old.'

'Too brown, more like. Well, good luck to you, girl. You fit the image, eh. They'll love you.'

'Feeling happy?' says the make-up girl to Vita, who has never looked more glamorous in her entire life, big hair, huge eyes. They both look at her image appraisingly. 'Go wow them, girl. When's your photo call?'

'Ten minutes. The studio upstairs.'

'Pop in if you need to.' She looks at me, friendly and innocent. 'Vita's an old hand at this. A trooper. She'll be just fine.'

'Thanks,' says Vita, sliding off the chair.

'Can't believe that girl's only sixteen,' says Tania when she's gone. 'A wise and sophisticated child. No man in her life?'

'Not currently that we know of,' says the make-up girl. 'She gave the last one the boot. He was a shit. Difficult, when you can't sit in a café without everyone staring.'

'Tell me about it,' says Tania, sighing. 'I used to read those pieces about "Shortland Street" people and think they were being paranoid. Do you want to run lines, Tiggie?'

'Sorry. Can I go to the loo?' I have to ask my make-up girl because she's only got as far as my eye sockets. 'Sort of urgent.'

I follow Vita into her messy dressing room.

'Will you do something for me?' I say, not bothering to check if I can come in.

'Sure,' she says airily.

'Just don't mention my name when you're at that school. I know you're going to talk about health and fitness and stuff and it's hardly likely – but someone just might ask you about the other stars of the show and guest actors and that, and you might say well not everyone in "Shapers" has an absolutely *perfect* body – there's this girl called Faith who's a real *dump* and we found a fat kid called Tiggie Tompson who's never done any acting

149

before and it might just pop out. So don't, that's all.'

'Why not?'

'Just *don't.*'

'But why?'

'I'm not telling you.'

She's looking at me, sly, smiling as she pulls up black pantyhose. 'You used to go there, didn't you? Before Eastern College.'

'Okay, I did. And everything's true about the pressure and the overachievers and the pushy parents and the anorexia. I left because if you don't get straight As or have the right figure you don't fit in. But *you'll* be all right. As Tania says, they'll *love* you. You're their absolute dream fantasy come true. And you'll get up on that stage in that great hall and tell them about eating three good meals a day and don't *ever* skip breakfast and I'm bloody glad I'm won't be there to hear them all being sucked in.'

'Why not?' she says, softly now.

'Why do *you* think?'

'I wouldn't have a clue. And I don't know why you're going off at me. What have *I* done?'

'You really don't know?'

'No. Haven't you got a scene to do?'

'I won't be acting any more than you will be on that stage. Less, actually. At least I'm sort of playing myself. Try-hard fat girl, wants to be something she isn't.'

'Oh Tiggie . . .' Quick as a flash, under the make-up, she's the old Vita, kind, concerned, everyone's friend, counsellor and helper. But I'm ready for her this time.

'I don't want your sympathy or help to find the next great part for Tiggie Tompson,' I say, 'because there won't be one.'

'Yes, there will . . .'

'No there *won't!*'

'Tiggie, now listen to me . . .'

Oh she's clever! This will become all about me, not her. 'How can you stand on that stage rabbiting on about nutrition and still have any . . .?'

'Any what?'

'You should have said no.'

'Why?' She's deliberately playing the bimbo, leading me to the brink. 'I couldn't say no, Tiggie. It's in my contract. *Such public appearances and other media opportunities as requested by the Producer,* something like that. There are things you'll have to do, when your eps go to air.'

'At least I won't be living a lie.'

'What lie's that?'

There is a long, dangerous silence. She puts on her jacket and some quite obscene black stilettos while I look at the pictures of Mariah Carey and herself on the walls and can't quite bring myself to jump.

'I'm due upstairs,' she says. 'And then a taxi to the school. I won't dob you in, trust me.'

'And I haven't either.'

'Haven't what? What are you *talking* about?'

This is where we jump, together. It's not the best timing, but nothing's ever perfect.

'You're . . . Vita, you get up after a meal and go to the loo, you binge, you eat one sandwich for lunch, you were doing all those sit-ups that day, you faint, you've got all those pills by your bed and any idiot can see you're losing weight.'

'You've lost some too, Tiggie. Looking good.'

If she thinks she's going to sidetrack me by flattery, she's mistaken.

'At the school you're going to, half the class was scared to eat. They're all on diets. They mightn't know much about the real world, but they know about EDs. I know *lots* about EDs.'

'You don't know *anything.* Tiggie. I've got a small frame and a naturally small appetite, I like to exercise, I take supplements because half the food we buy these days is full of chemicals and crap. That doesn't add up to . . .'

'You fainted. Healthy people don't faint.'

'I had PMT.'

'You have normal periods? Every four weeks?'

'Yes I do. Regular as clockwork. And I've got to go.' She consults her watch.

I know she's lying, about her periods, about everything.

'Tiggie, my friend,' she says, with a sort of icy control, 'you've got it all wrong. I'm not anorexic. I am not bulimic.'

'Good. Then you can stand up there and honestly talk into a mike and be on television telling people our age how to be healthy and feel perfectly okay about it? What you see is what you get? No lies? The perfect, honest role model?'

'If that's how other people want to see me, yes.'

'You haven't answered the question. How do you see yourself?'

Her eyes slip away from mine. She cannot, *cannot* look me in the face. Gotcha!

'It's a very beautiful school, on the outside,' I say. 'They love achievers. And they do try hard for the rest. Enjoy.'

Always the actor, she puts her hand on my arm, finds a glossy smile from somewhere. 'Thanks, Tiggie. You're a sweetie to worry about me, but I'm okay. Really, really okay. Might catch you later.'

I only have two more days here. I don't think she will.

TWENTY

I AM SITTING IN MY DRESSING ROOM, MY LAST DAY. IT'S NOT THE LAST scene for Faith – we did the scene where she says goodbye to Rata yesterday. I've taken down my photos of Mum and Dad and the dog I once had and a safe group from school which just happened to include Gareth. I've packed up the books which I've been reading between scenes, and the ring-binder files of schoolwork which have hardly been opened, and tomorrow some other guest actor will be shown this room and sit here working with Lynda and wait, their heart thumping, to be called by bald Damien.

Trouble is, they weren't to know that my last scene might also be my worst, worse even than the binge scene. Today they started shooting a whole heap of scenes in the indoor swimming pool, and ours is middle of the afternoon, 3.40 pm. Oh yes, Rata bullies Faith in for a swim. She hates it. She gets a mouthful. She has to be helped. End of scene.

I've only once seen the pool before, the day I was first shown around. It's surrounded by tiles and benches and palm trees in pots and statues of nearly nude men. I've seen hotel pools a bit like this when we went to California when I was eleven.

They have given me a *disgusting* pair of granny togs to wear – you know, with a little *skirt*? *Dark green*? Rata and the extras will be wearing bikinis, no doubt. I've had make-up as usual, which feels a bit strange when I have to dive in, and sitting here, with a rug Lynda has given me, it's bloody freezing.

I haven't seen Vita since she came back from the school. I know from the schedule she had eight scenes that afternoon, and then eleven yesterday when they were shooting mostly in the receptionist area. But our paths haven't crossed.

She's here on the set when Lynda leads me through another padded door, one that's not used so much, into the pool. She's also doing pool scenes today and her bikini, under the tartan dressing gown she's wearing, is white.

'Your last scene!' she calls brightly across the pool. 'Here to cheer you on, Tigs. The water's warm, you'll be pleased to know.'

Has she really no idea?

'Tiggie,' says Lynda beside me, quietly. 'You can ask for a closed set, if you want.'

'What does that mean?'

'No visitors, watchers. Only the essential crew.'

'Yes, please.' So Vita is asked to leave along with a whole lot of others. I watch her face drop, hear her say 'but I'm Tiggie's *friend*,' see her decide not to push her luck! I watch her go and I'm feeling smug and sorry at the same time. About fifteen people are left, that's all. Tania appears in a dressing gown, we run the lines and we rehearse the moves – without the dives 'cause for obvious reasons we can only do that once, and then for the last rehearsal I'm asked to throw away the rug.

It's the shower in the bush again, only this time it's not dusk. The lights, hung above and reflected off the water, are blinding.

'Lynda,' I say. 'I'm only going to do this once, like I said.'

'Fine,' she says. 'They're all ready for you.'

Tania's bikini is yellow and her Maori body gleaming bronze. Faith doesn't lie around on a sunbed, so I'm just my normal winter boring pudgy piggy white. The extras are already sitting with their legs dangling in the water or draped over the marble benches or swimming up and down. I grit my teeth and give Lynda the rug. Eve is quick with the commands. 'Roll it', through to 'Action!'

Rata urges the reluctant, shivering Faith towards the poolside. She tells her the water's warm, it's a reward for the great workout she's just done. Faith says she doesn't know how to dive, but standing on the poolside is agony. (Up to the dive, I have agreed I'll do two takes.) She flops in and comes up spluttering. Rata realises that she's not happy and dives in after her, superbly of course, and helps her to the side. Faith, coughing, says she's okay. Rata tells her she can put her feet down now. Faith realises to her surprise that she can stand up. She can even manage a little laugh at herself. She might even enjoy the swim, now she's in. Rata, her trainer and mentor, is pleased.

'Cut!' calls Eve. 'Thank you, Tiggie, I'll go with that. Good work, both.'

Tania hugs me in the water. We both look sleek as eels. And then the most amazing thing happens. I hear the sound of clapping.

Eve, the First, the ADs, all the camera operators, the sound guys, the props guys, the make-up girl, Lynda, the extras, they are all clapping. Cheering. I don't think I did the scene *that* well. But it's not for doing that scene, it's for me as guest actor. It's for all the scenes I've done.

They are clapping *me*! Eve is making a little speech, talking about what a pleasure I'd been to work with and how they'd admired me becoming so very professional in my approach so quickly. What a quick learner I was! And brave! And generous with other cast. ('I'll second that,' calls out Tania.) And good luck for the future, 'cause she was sure I had a future in television. Or film. Or stage. Good luck, Tiggie.

On with the next scene.

I'd be lying if I didn't say it was music to my ears. Sad but wonderful music, because I know that this might turn out to be the only chance I ever get.

'I've come to say goodbye,' I say to Vita. I've been sitting in her dressing room, reading, my bags packed beside me, waiting for her to finish. The way she walks in, I can tell she's whacked.

'Did the scene go well?' she asks, walking over to the basin and covering her face with thick white cleanser.

'Yes, it did. And I got a bit of a farewell.'

'They always do that. It's nice. When people have been here as core cast for years, it can get quite emotional sometimes. Will I see you at Rowan's class when he starts up again?'

'Might.'

There's an awkward pause while she swipes at her face with little pads of cotton, turning them brown.

'You got me this chance, Vita. I want to say thanks.'

'Any time.'

'How did the school go?'

'Fine.' Her real face is emerging, the black shadows around her eyes.

'You said all the right things, I'm sure.'

'Yep,' she says aggressively. 'I sure did.'

'And I'm sure they looked after you?'

'They did. It's a beautiful school, with a lovely caring atmosphere. Lucky girls who go there. Everyone's very polite.'

I notice she's reluctant to start changing, because it would mean dropping her dressing gown, letting me see her sticking-out ribs at close quarters. A cigarette is helpful on such occasions. She can't get the lighter to go.

'When's the TV stuff being used?'

'Oh, it was on the news but most of it's for that documentary – "The Making of 'Shapers'" on "60 Minutes". "A soap's impact on the community", that stuff.' She is flicking unsuccessfully at the lighter as though her life depended on it. Perhaps it does. 'Come *on.*'

I remember now, Mum had hoped she was going to front that documentary. Obviously she missed out. Maybe she missed out because I was in it.

'Well, cheers,' I say. I want to give her a hug, but I'm not sure where I stand.

'Give me a ring, Tiggie. We'll do coffee. Sorry, I'm just a bit whacked. Long day.'

'Yeah. Cheers.' She gets the lighter to go, takes a quick puff, and hugs me. We have become strangers. 'Cheers.'

Goodbye 'Shapers'. I walk past the padded door and the monitor showing the pool and Rata and Ruth having a go at each other, and through the empty café and out into the carpark and the real world to meet my unemployed – sorry, semi-retired – Dad.

'Your agent rang this morning,' says Dad as we turn onto the motorway. 'She wants you to call her over the weekend. Preferably Saturday morning, early.'

'What does she want?'

'Probably tax returns. Or just ask how you finished up. How did you finish up?'

'My last scene, I got a little clap.'

'Good for you!' As always, he's just a bit too enthusiastic when daughter's *done* something. 'I think the show's improving. Finding its feet.'

'The ratings are going up. They were all saying so today.'

'That's good.' We get down to the bridge before he says, 'Tig, I didn't get that job. Heard today. Went to a thirty-year-old. If things don't pick up, we might have to think about moving. We've got a lot of money tied up in the apartment. Money I should be putting into a retirement fund. How would you feel?'

'I don't mind moving. Can I have a dog?'

'If we find a suitable house, yes. I've an urge to grow vegetables again.'

Saturday morning I'm feeling flat as a pancake. No lines to learn, no Monday morning shooting to look forward to and dread, just the prospect of being back at school being bullied by Tara to produce all the copy for the programme and having to catch up with two months' work.

Gareth is the sole reason for feeling enthusiastic about Eastern College on Monday. But the production's in two weeks so he's probably too busy.

How I would love to have some lines to learn!

Emily wants me to go round. She won't say why. She's heard that Edwina was very pleased with my work on 'Shapers'. *Come on round, Tiggie.* She'll expect me in half an hour. Bring an umbrella if I'm walking, it might rain.

Well, I've got nothing else to do except homework, so I might as well enjoy a few warm fuzzies and Jessie sitting on my knees again. Though not being peed on.

'I've two things I want to discuss with you, Tiggie,' Emily says briskly, picking dog hairs off her navy trousers. 'The first concerns you and the second, Vita. We'll talk about you first.'

Jess has given me a noisy terrier's welcome, barking and jumping up my legs. Now we're all cosily settled in the office, with a gas heater glowing orange. It has rained, and the bottoms of my trackpants are damp. The room smells of coffee.

'I'm sending you for an audition next week. This is a big one, and I want you to think seriously right from the start that you have a very good chance.'

I can hear Vita's voice. *She doesn't send people for auditions unless she thinks they've got a good chance.*

'What's the part?'

'I can't tell you very much, but I do know the production company concerned. It's all still under wraps, more so than usual. I have a character breakdown, two scenes. They're auditioning in Australia and New Zealand, and filming the first three months of next year.'

'That's miles away. Six months away.'

'The final callbacks might not be until quite close to the end of the year. If you get that far, the waiting could be prolonged and difficult. Can you cope with that?'

'Yep.' I remember how she hated mentioning my weight last time so I'll get in first. 'They're after another big girl.'

'No, they're not. They're after a very good young actor.'

'That rules me out.'

'Why?'

'I haven't exactly got a size ten waist. First you have the size ten, then you have the talent.'

She stares at her coffee mug. She's thinking, how am I going to handle this?

'Tiggie, would you do something for me? Stand up.'

I put Jess onto the red couch and pull myself to my feet.

'Would you take all those dreadful baggy clothes off? At least the top layer. Yes,' she anticipates me, 'I want to see what's so artfully hidden underneath.'

158

I peel them off, the trackpants, the mammoth sweatshirt, until I'm in crew neck jumper and knickers.

'Thank you,' she says. 'I still want you to go for that audition.'

'Waste of time.'

'Excuse me, Tiggie, but that is my call. You can get dressed. How much weight have you lost since I saw you last?'

I know exactly. Without even trying too hard: 'Nine pounds.'

'Without even trying,' she echoes my thoughts. 'Or even being told you couldn't lose any more. You took that hard.'

'Of course I did. No one wants to stay . . . what I was.'

'Tiggie, has it ever occurred to you that you're not as big as you think you are.'

'The scales don't lie.'

'They are not the only measurement. You've been going to the gym. It's also had an effect, that and the stress of shooting. You're in better shape than you were. It wouldn't take much to put yourself into a normal range for your height.'

This is such a foreign thought to me that I'm silent. I pick Jess up off the couch and allow her to nuzzle at my hand. Her whiskers are going grey.

'Tiggie, I don't want to go any further down this track. I'm only concerned with your talent as an actor. Will you trust me and do the audition? Here's what I've got.' She hands over three pieces of paper from some production company, with *Confidential* stamped all over them in red.

CHARACTER BREAKDOWN. ELIZA MATTHEWS.

Eliza is a 15-year-old from an English aristocratic family. Made pregnant by her uncle, unable to face her parents, she has run away from her London home. At Portsmouth, desperate, penniless, and concealing her six-month pregnancy, she joins a group of single women emigrating to the colonies. On the voyage, she loses her baby and emerges as a leader of the younger women resisting

159

the sexual interest of the crew and the cruelty/incompetence of the matron in charge. She's physically attractive, strong, wilful, outspoken and stubborn, capable of great loyalty and deeply felt emotions.

I look up at Emily. It's fantastic. She's got to be joking.

'It's set on a ship,' I say stupidly.

'That much we know,' she smiles. 'You'll see from the two scenes that she's no shrinking violet. This is not a children's drama, or what some call by that appallingly clumsy word kiddult.'

I read them swiftly. In one, she's telling the captain that last night his first mate raped a 12-year-old girl and what is he going to do about it. In the second she's giving as good as she gets from the matron accusing her of being a foul-mouthed and provocative slut, far from the champion of the young she is making herself out to be.

My heart is pounding. I've got the actor's bug. It's strong, wonderful stuff and I'd give my right arm . . .

She gets in first this time.

'You have nothing to lose, Tiggie. Do it.'

'I . . . can I think about it?'

'Certainly. Ring me by tomorrow night at the latest.'

'Okay. If I get a callback, which I doubt, I'll tell my parents then.'

She weighs this one up, thinks of my audition for 'Shapers' and decides to let it pass. 'The audition will be sometime next week. After school sometime?'

'If I do it.' I can tell from her smile that she knows I'm going to.

'Now,' she says, getting up and pouring herself a coffee from the glass pot. 'The second thing is Vita. You know she's been my client for three years now. I want help. You've had quite a bit of contact with her over the past three months.'

'Off and on. I didn't see all that much of her. She had a lot of scenes.'

'She's causing concern. Yes or no, is she anorexic?'

I stare down at Jess's white and silky coat.

'Bulimic?' she fires again. 'Come on, Tiggie, this is not dobbing her in,

160

this is serious help time. You know they get letters and phone calls from the public. They take them very seriously. Her character Holly is getting way too thin for comfort. They're seriously considering they might have to write her out. My greater concern is that she might self-destruct before that. I need to know.'

'Shouldn't you be asking her mother?'

'I have. She swears there's no evidence. Her father's even more useless. I doubt they're ever very much in the house together, any of them. Have you seen any indications?'

'Of course I have,' I mumble treacherously. 'I've known for ages. She binges and throws up, she's got bad breath and those fine hairs on her face, she does a thousand sit-ups in her dressing room and eats a lettuce leaf for lunch. Sometimes I thought she wanted me to know. But it's none of my business.'

'It's mine, Tiggie. Have you ever spoken to her about it?'

'I tried, once. Last week, actually, 'cause I was so angry that she was going to my old school to talk about eating properly. How dishonest can you get? She froze me out, told me I'd got it all wrong. But I know. I went on camps with girls like her. I *know*. Just like she knows I've got the opposite sort of problem. We're both weirdos, really.'

I glance up from Jess to Emily's face. I am so ashamed and she looks so sad.

'Dear God,' she sighs. 'What are we doing to our young? Why?'

We sit in silence for a while.

'I can't talk to Vita,' I say, finally. Of course Emily would know how important her job is to her.

'No,' she agrees. 'It's gone beyond that. Thank you, Tiggie, for being straight with me.'

My head tells me that anorexics *die* and I've done the right thing; my heart, that I'm a traitor.

Twenty-one

I know I want to play Eliza Matthews more than anything in the entire world when I very nearly don't make it even to the first audition.

Why does this happen? What could possibly stop me, when I've coped with going back to school and a certain amount of curiosity? I've admitted that I'm in 'Shapers' and watched their faces go scornful and unbelieving. The girl's off her trolley, I see them thinking. She's one of those who makes up great fibs to get attention. She was just wagging.

About what's screened so far, comments range from gross, tragic, bullshit and bizarre to awesome, brilliant, glam and excellent. I don't want to even *think* about six weeks' time, when my eps will start. Most of them are watching it.

My teachers have made only passing comments about the work I haven't done. The programme has gone to the printer and I'm never talking to Tara again since she put her name first on the list of two people who compiled it: her and me. Thanks, Tara. Gareth, with dress rehearsals next week for the production, and the three performances following, has again vanished off the face of the earth. I'm back at the gym – having been, despite Dad's help, a bit slack during 'Shapers' – with the lovely Amy, who naturally thinks that 'Shapers' is the best thing since sliced bread and is pleased my latest test is a great improvement. My body fat has gone down a lot.

Rowan's classes start again in a month, possibly.

So having settled back into anonymity at Eastern College, at least until 'Shapers' hits the screen, what could possibly keep me from the audition for which I've worked for two weeks? I've read whole books about the single women and girls, around twelve thousand of them, who emigrated to New Zealand in the 1850s and 1860s.

It's not Vita, who according to Emily is still continuing to deny that she's got a problem. I want to ring her but I can't. Nor is it Dad, who has put the apartment on the market and is spending his days looking at houses with nice gardens where I can have a dog and he can grow vegetables.

No, my mistake was to come home first. I should have taken my decent clothes, changed at school and gone straight to the audition. But the audition wasn't till 5.30 and I thought no one would be at home. I could change in peace and put on a bit of make-up and shout my lines out to the winter northerly battering the twelfth floor. Wrong. Mum is home. She's sitting in front of her computer writing a furious e-mail to the bosses of '60 Minutes', the Pernod bottle beside her.

'Tiggie, whaddaya think of this? Read it, whaddaya think.'

Tom – I have instrcuted my lawyer to write to you in the strongest possible terms about the fact and manner of my dismissal today. It is insulting and inexcusable to read about one's sasking in a Welllington evening paper. I don't care how good or unprincipled the reporter was. You leaked it, you bastard.

That's what I hate about e-mails, all the mistakes.

And you know as well as I do that the reason has nothing whatsoever to do with restructuring or sinking lid policy or any other current euphenism for giving a loyal and experienced colleage the boot.

You have fired me, let's be honest about this Tom my ertswhile friend and colleague, simply because I'm 39, not 25. Your propensity for little girls is showing, disgusting in a man of 49. Now you can walk round with one on your arm and dye your hair blonde to look just like Robert Redford and feel just terrific, a regular little Peter Pan, but when you start throwing out experienced and established and well-liked reporters merely because they are females pushing forty, you are guilty of the most hypocritcal ageism and the most heinous, immoral, contemptible, offensive,

163

detestable, crass, despicable, treacherous, insulting, patronising and bigotted – words fail me – sjhocking double standards – a plague on you and your jumped-up hair-dyed mates and both your channels for the mixed, false messages you give to women on your scurrilous festering shallow pathetic increasingly dumbed-down banal programmes – are we surprised that today's young women are totally fucked up, can't eat a square meal, are terrified of turning 29 and think of nothing but themselves and their bodies –

'Not bad, eh Tiggly Winkle. How *dare* he?'

Normally I go totally spastic when I'm called that, and people regret it, but this is not a pleasant sight, neither Mum nor this e-mail she has drunkenly written and must not send.

'Where's Dad?' I say.

'House-hunting. Thrown on the scrap-heap. Moi, aussi.'

'Mum, you're good. You'll get another job. Tell them to stick it.'

'I'm forty next month!'

'So? You can't send that.'

'I can. Watch me.' Her hand moves to the mouse but I've still got time to bend over to the power point and pull the plug out.

'Power cut,' I say firmly. 'Oh dear. I'll make you a cup of coffee. Go and lie down.'

I am ready for violent anger – she might even hit me – but she's gone the other way, as though all her anger has been sucked into the monitor when the screen went black. She sits slumped at the computer desk.

'Come on. On your bed.' She allows me to prod and haul her on her feet, escort her into the bedroom. I get a bucket from the bathroom, tell her to use it if she must, then I ring Dad's cellphone.

'Dad? I'm at home. Mum's lost her job and she's drunk. Paralytic. Can you come home, *now*?'

'Oh Christ. I had a feeling . . .'

'Where are you?'

'In Epsom. I'm coming. I might hit the rush-hour traffic.'

'Yes, well. I've got to go out in half an hour, so make it quick.'

'Can't you stay until I get there?'

'No. She'll be all right. She's sleeping, sort of. I can stay until quarter to five if you shout me a taxi.'

He arrives with a minute to spare. Mum's been disgustingly sick, fortunately into the bucket, or most of it. I look at both my unemployed parents comforting each other and wonder why life has to be so complicated. If people are good at their jobs – and I know mine were – why can't they just keep them? What goes wrong? Why is everyone always 'restructuring'?

Dad's more worried about Mum than why I'm rushing out the door, to some secret destination. If I arrive on time it'll be a miracle. I've thrown on the first clothes that came to hand, and forgotten the one lipstick and brown eye-liner that I own. And I've forgotten my script.

No one's going to do something subtle and gorgeous to me this time. Goodbye, Eliza Matthews.

I am five minutes late and rush in the front door of the ordinary suburban house in Mt Eden to find a scruffy waiting room and a scrawny sour woman in black tights obviously packing up for the day.

'Traffic,' I gasp. 'Antigone Tompson, for Eliza Matthews. She told me to ask for Megan.'

'Who's "she"?' she says icily.

'Oh – Emily Chatwin Agency.'

'I'll ask Megan if she can take you. She was hoping to get away promptly today.'

'I'm sorry. Sorry.'

'Fill this in. She might want to make another time.'

'Could you – have you got a script for my scenes? I left it at home.'

'You should know them.' Late *and* scriptless.

'I do – oh, don't worry.' I'm a fool to have asked.

I'm also shocked by her rude indifference, nothing like Edwina at 'Shapers' who at least treated me like a human being. Doesn't she know my whole life's at stake here? Perhaps I would be better to come back another day, when my heart isn't thumping just from sitting in the taxi for three-quarters of an hour, and I haven't got on clothes which make me look the size of a house or got a mother who's just lost a high-profile job

– but I don't get that choice. Nor much time to fill in the form.

'Come through.'

It's another bare little room, with a video camera set up at one end.

'Stand there,' she says, adding before she leaves and after looking me up and down: 'I hope you're not going to be wasting our time.'

I'm standing there, so angry, exposed on a mountain-top, desperately trying to remember the lines on the script I've left at home, when Megan and a big man come in sharing a joke. They're both wearing black leather jackets.

'I'm sorry for being late,' I gabble before they have time to open their mouths, 'but anyone can get caught in a traffic jam. That very rude and unsympathetic woman said you wanted to get away and I'll try not to waste your time.'

'It's her that wants to get away, not me,' says Megan, laughing but obviously a bit startled. She's Maori, and younger than I expect, with hair so short she's almost bald and reminds me of some black American singer. She looks at the form I've filled in and starts fiddling with the video. 'Eliza Matthews? And you've just done quite a significant stint on "Shapers", I see. When does it go to air?'

'About six weeks. You can call me Tiggie.'

But I know, that as I get given my name on a piece of cardboard to hold, and get told to look at the camera (the red light is pin-pointing at me) and turn sideways and then around – I know that I've blown it. Auditioning in New Zealand and *Australia*? – Why don't I just leave now? She must have noticed I'm too big and fat for this part.

'I don't want to do this,' I say.

'Want to look over the lines?' says the man. He gives me his copy, a warm smile, a lifeline. He's youngish, losing his hair and he hasn't shaved for a week. He's not small. 'You know them?'

Oh God, I don't want to do this. But I do.

'Yes.'

'Let's run them.'

He's the captain and I'm Eliza, angrily trying to convince him that it's certainly possible that his first mate has raped a 12-year-old, and indeed that is exactly what happened last night. I know because I *believe* the child who staggered into the women's quarters distressed and bleeding, and I know the mate was on watch during the night, because I went up on deck straight away and saw him there in the moonlight. He probably didn't even know or care which female it was, or how young or old. He's a brutal pig and he must be charged.

The words come back. The righteous anger is wonderful. Because I instantly trust him as an actor, and because apart from Rowan's classes I've never acted with a man before, let alone in a scene which is angry, even quite violent, I let him have it.

'Very good,' says Megan, lifting her head up from the monitor. 'Now we'll go for a take.'

I get five takes before she's finished with me. I'm asked to be angrier, faster, softer, louder, then really OTT. She wonders if I can do an English accent and I say yes, if I work on it, but not today, 'cause I haven't and I'd rather not do it badly. She smiles a bit. The man represents all those up-themselves people who fired Mum, and let down Dad, who refuse to believe that a 12-year-old girl can be telling the truth, all those who have power to judge. I hate his brown, patronising, smirking eyes. I hate him.

'Thank you,' says Megan. 'Your agent'll be in touch.'

'Don't you want the other scene?'

'Not for the moment, thank you, Tiggie. Thank you for your time.'

I'm being politely dismissed. On an impulse, I peck the man, who's smiling at me normally again, on his stubbly cheek. Don't know why, maybe just to say thank you. At least I can tell Emily there was a nice actor there and I tried. I'm so embarrassed at myself that I turn tail and run.

Mum, Dad and me – all three of us jobless.

We've sold one of the cars and in September we are moving.

Because the challenge races for the America's Cup start in a couple of months, the apartment sold the first day Dad rang a land agent. It went to a rich Italian businessman who's going to be here for the whole six months of the racing, from October through to March. He's something to do with his country's challenge. He can watch all the Cup boats coming

167

and going and with a telescope, he can even watch the races further out in the gulf. According to the land agent, he thinks our apartment will be *magnifico*. He hasn't actually seen it; all this was done by e-mail, even sending pictures to Milan. *My* pictures, actually, because I heard Dad making arrangements for the land agent to come here with a camera and I said why bother, why doesn't he look at these first?

Funny, I haven't used my camera for a few months. I'd thought of taking it out to 'Shapers' with me, but somehow it didn't seem an appropriate thing to do, be taking pictures all over the place. I'd have looked like a geeky amateur.

The new owner wants the place free in September, so we have two months to find a house. Mum, after that awful day she heard about her job, has decided to give herself some time out from television work. Perhaps she'll get a job in production, or try directing, or write a book about women in the media? She even said one night, and I still don't know if she was joking, why not another baby? Lots of forty-year-olds are having babies these days! All the rage, to be a mum again. I don't think Dad was too impressed.

She and Dad are house-hunting together now, but they haven't seen quite the right place yet. I know exactly what sort of dog I want.

I am waiting for the phone to ring. Emily, Gareth, Vita?

Mum's sacking became public, of course, and she got lots of letters from the viewers commiserating with her and saying how good she'd been at her job as a reporter.

There were news stories quoting her bosses saying that her age had nothing to do with it; they were simply 'reviewing their staffing arrange-ments, both on and off screen' and 'wanting to give the programme a fresh look'. Of course they were sorry that Cassandra Tompson, a talented and popular broadcaster, didn't have a place in their plans but they had to look at the wider picture. They sincerely regretted that the decision had been unfortunately leaked before she had been advised.

Patronising *bullshit*, said Mum into her Pernod. Spin doctors! Jerks!

Eventually, after a few days and talking it over with some of her female friends in television, she went public too, saying that she believed that her age was a major factor in her dismissal. She made page three of the *Herald*, including a glamorous picture.

Life's really odd. If anyone had told me at the beginning of the year that by July, I was going to be moving house, have two unemployed parents, have done a big part on television, be auditioning for another, have an anorexic friend who haunts me and be ten pounds lighter without even trying, I'd have laughed in their face.

The unemployed parents are a bit of a worry, though. It's not that they're suddenly unable to pay the grocery bills and have their phones cut off, like a lot of people at school whose parents haven't got work. Even if they never worked again – but Mum will, I'm sure – they've got enough to be comfortable. Maybe a smaller house and only one trip overseas a year.

It's just – they're suddenly able to be model parents, the old-fashioned sort who are always home, cooking nutritious meals, baking bread, available as drivers any time and right up with school events to cheer their little darlings on.

The opening night of the production, for starters. I wasn't going to tell them about it, but of course Mum goes local shopping now and on the butcher shop's window she sees these ginormous posters. She's rung up and got tickets for three for the opening night.

'I could have got them at school,' I said glumly. All my efforts to locate Gareth in that teeming place called Eastern College have failed. He's never home, either. Perhaps he doesn't exist?

'You're so busy, darling,' she said, comfortingly. 'You've got a lot of work to catch up.' Yuk.

It's not schoolwork that's bugging me, and it's not even waiting to hear from Emily. What's getting to me now is that the first night of the production is a Thursday. The Monday before, my 'Shapers' goes to air. The date is written on my brain.

I could have seen my eps beforehand. Lynda offered to get me the tapes; lots of people like to see theirs before they go out. No thanks, I said. Not even Mum has quite made the horrendous connection yet: Faith on 'Shapers' and a Pie Girl at Eastern College. Should I take a few days off school, or leave the country?

But Mum clicks up on the Sunday and immediately gets the video ready and puts two bottles of expensive French champagne in the fridge to drink while we're watching. What the hell, she says, my daughter isn't a television star every day of the week. I'm surprised she didn't organise a dinner party for twenty people and ask me to set the table.

At twenty-nine minutes past seven, I chicken out. I ask Mum to make sure the video's on. I say I know I'm being stupid, but I just can't watch it. I will later, by myself.

Surprisingly, she doesn't tell me I'm being silly or precious, which I am. She just says, pouring the champers, well, fine, she realises it's a big thing for me. She'll keep a little glass of the Moët.

I can't go for a walk because it's dark and raining, so I try to do some homework. But I feel like those people in Tibet or wherever it is, who refuse to have their pictures taken – like some part of me has been hijacked, made into public property, stolen.

The half hour crawls by. I can hear the sound through my closed door. Then Mum in the doorway with my glass of champers. Dad is behind her. I can't look them in the eye, I am so embarrassed.

'Tiggie,' Mum says. 'You should be very proud of what you've done.'

'Absolutely,' says Dad. 'Very proud indeed.'

'It was just a part,' I say.

'That took an especial courage,' says Mum. 'We had no real idea what you were letting yourself in for.'

'Neither did I.'

'You know I'm not talking about Faith as the token chubby. I'm talking about you as an actor. I have to say, from what I've seen so far, I'm totally amazed. Why did you never get into acting at your old school?'

'They were all so . . .'

'So will you audition for more?'

Oh God, they don't know about Eliza Matthews yet. 'If I got the chance,' I say. 'Might. But there aren't many parts for chubbies, Mum.'

'Has it ever occurred to you, Tig, that you're not as big as you think you are?'

I look at her in amazement. Who . . . Emily! Word for word. Then I think of what she's just seen, dumpy me in frumpy black shorts and I know she's wrong too. They're both just being kind. I'm too big for Eliza Matthews like she's too old for '60 Minutes'.

I hold up the champers. 'Cheers, Mum. Young and skinny, that's what they want.'

The phone is going. It's Vita.

'Fantastic, Tigs. Are you pleased?'

'Haven't seen it yet.'

'Why not?'

'I'm scared.'

'You shouldn't be. You're real and people are going to love you.'

'Doubt it,' I say. 'How's Holly?'

Vita frowns ever so slightly. 'She's okay. She's having a bit of a break. They've written me out for two weeks. I'm off to Fiji, get some sun. Glad I saw your first ep tonight.'

It sounds very like she's been given a warning.

'Why have they written you out? The show's only . . .'

'Only for two weeks,' she says sharply. 'I'll send you a postcard. We'll do coffee when I get back.'

The phone rings again and I tell Mum to tell Gareth that I've gone to bed. It's only twenty past eight, but I've gone to bed. I'm asleep.

'He said, whoever he is, to tell you, bloody marvellous,' says Mum, genuinely surprised that I should have a boy ring me.

I creep out and watch it when I've done my homework and they're in the bathroom having a spa. They say they're going to miss the spa bath when we move downmarket.

There's some Moët left on the coffee table. My opening scene comes after the first ads. Compared with everyone else on the show, Faith is *fat*.

Fat and soft. It's not better than I secretly hoped it might be, it's actually much worse. As well as fat, even though she's won a prize worth hundreds of dollars, she's sullen and uncooperative with Rata and the gym owner Ruth, and her first session in the gym trying to do a clean-and-press with a nine-kilo weight would be funny if it wasn't so pathetic.

Sorry, Vita, but you're wrong. People are going to hate her. The ratings will plummet.

Except – there's one tiny voice in my head which is remembering Vita, that first class of Rowan's. 'You have fantastic eyes. They're a clear green and they're alive.' It's all that make-up – those lights, I say to the voice. 'But just look,' says the voice, 'they're beautiful. Faith is chubby and beautiful.'

I've had too much champagne. And I've got to go to school tomorrow.

Twenty-two

Later that night I dream that a million people are laughing their heads off. Mum shakes me awake.

'Only a nightmare,' she soothes me. 'You sounded like you were being throttled.'

'I can't go to school,' I sob. 'I can't. Ever, ever again! Now I'm that fat bitch on television. I wish I'd never done it. No matter how good I am, I'm still only a fat actor.'

She lets in the dawn, the *magnifico* view, and sits looking out for a while.

'All right,' she says. 'Let's go to a movie.'

'I can't even do that,' I howl. 'Everyone will recognise me. *And* you.'

'Tigs, listen to me. Today, even tomorrow, you can lie low. I'd love to take you to a movie. Better still, we've got a house to look at, one I rather like . . .'

'Yes please . . .' I sniffle.

'. . . but you know it can't go on much longer than that, don't you? At some point you've got to walk into school or into a shop and have people say "You're that girl on 'Shapers'!" and you've got to smile proudly and say yes. And even if they say, "You're that fat girl on 'Shapers'," which they will, you've still got to hold your head up and smile and say yes I am.'

'What's the time?'

'Twenty past six.'

'I want to die.'

'Can I show you something? Put your dressing gown on.'

173

Snivelling, I trail her into the living room and out onto the balcony. From there we have a seagull's view of the sunrise. Usually I have my back to it, eating breakfast, but today Mum indicates that we should sit together, do nothing else but watch. She puts her arm around my shoulders while we watch the clouds become rimmed with orange, gold, scarlet; the sky changes colour, from pale yellow to blue to a brilliant orange. The great ball of sun peeps over the black sloping shoulder of Rangitoto; as it does, a broad pathway across the sea, from the island to the rocky foreshore directly below us, slowly catches fire.

'Fair takes your breath away,' says Mum. 'I'm going to miss it, Tig, *desperately*. Like I'm missing my colleagues and my monthly salary. How do you think I felt, going in to clear my desk, hand over my car keys? With a monumental hangover, I might add.'

She let that one sink in.

'I've got my fortieth party coming up next month and Dad naturally asked all my colleagues, even those who subsequently fired me. Now I could cancel the party . . .'

'Don't do that!'

'Or I can shake their hands and look them in the eye and think, well, mate, you'll get yours one day. Those who live by the sword die by the sword, so to speak.' The red sun is clear of the island now. 'Isn't that the most beautiful thing you've ever seen? But,' she squeezes me hard, 'there's life after "60 Minutes" and there's life in another house, another job, when the time's right. Also, there's life after "Shapers".'

'Mum, it goes on for *weeks*.'

'The sun has been rising over Rangitoto for a thousand years, ever since it erupted out of the sea. A few uncomfortable weeks? Discomfort fades, you know. And people's memories are very short. Like their attention spans, they are growing shorter.'

'But they're going to hate me.'

'The jury's still out, Tigs. Now, here's my advice. Take a day off, two days, and the hurdle will still be there to jump. It might even appear to grow in size, become a mountain. Do it this morning and put it behind you.'

We watch a container ship creep down the channel towards the port.

174

'Oh, by the way, that person called Gareth rang again last night. Says he wants to meet you at lunchtime today. I wrote down the time and place somewhere.' My mother smiles knowingly at me. 'Will that make a difference?'

'Hello stranger,' he says. His hair's not quite so brutally short as the last time I saw him. 'What's it like being a celebrity?'

'Fucking awful.' And it has been, since walking in the school gate. 'They all think Faith is a woos and that I'm not acting, don't need to act at all. Stuff them, I say. How are you feeling about Thursday night?'

'Right at this moment, as though I've got a disaster on my hands. I can't believe it's all going to come together.'

'It will.'

'Tara walked out, which probably won't surprise you. Sophia's on another planet, the lighting rig isn't in yet, and the ticket sales aren't as good as we hoped. At least the programme is done, thanks to you.'

'No, no, *Tara* did all the work for that. The programme says so.'

'She's a wanker. I've got some house seats for you.'

'Mum got some already. Thanks.'

And like some ghostly rerun of the very first time I met him, this very drama suite in February, we're interrupted by some Year Eight boys in the courtyard outside, peering in, pointing and shouting.

'There's *Faith*! Hey, *Faith*, what's it like being so *fat*? Are you a lessie? Do you fall in love with *Rata*? Do we get to see you in your *togs*?'

As he did before, Gareth gets rid of them by opening the window and quietly telling them to mind their tongues and shove off. Amazingly, they do. 'Animals!' he says. 'I'm sorry. On behalf of all males . . .'

'That's okay. Well, no, it isn't okay. I could kill them with my bare hands.' My very limited supply of courage is almost used up; the last thing I want is Gareth to see how much it hurts, how close to tears I am, for about the hundredth time this day.

'Don't take this the wrong way, Tiggie – you've lost . . .'

'Don't say it! Just tell me if you think my acting was any good, that's all.'

He understands. 'You were very, very good. Also — oh Christ, don't take this the wrong way either — I know why they cast you. It's a show where everyone is handsome and even in unflattering clothes you're a very handsome woman.'

I'm neither handsome nor woman, but I know I am bright red. I don't know either the right way or the wrong way to take it, so I sneak a look at my watch, mumble, 'Golly, history class, good luck for Thursday,' and take myself swiftly to the door.

'Bring your parents to the first night party,' he calls.

It's only as I'm sitting in history class that I wonder if the offer of tickets and the invitation might be some sort of date.

'How was it, soldier?' says Mum as I emerge from the lift. She's sitting in the living room, reading, and I can see she's got an afternoon tea ready. 'Bad as expected?'

'Yep. Every bit.'

'But you did it! And you're alive to tell the tale.' She's offering me a cup of tea. 'That Vita wants you to ring her, urgently.'

'Did she say why?' I ask, my heart sinking.

'No. It's a cellphone number. She said if it's turned off, leave a message.'

But Vita answers. 'Where are you?' I ask.

'My dressing room. Only two more scenes, thank Christ. Lynda came in earlier. Apparently the phones have been ringing all day. People sending faxes, e-mails like you wouldn't *believe*.'

'What about?'

'You, stupid. I told you they'd love you. At last, they're all saying, a real person. Someone's who's vulnerable and real.'

'Don't they mean a fat person?'

'No, Tiggie Tompson, they do not.'

'I thought Faith came over as sullen and horrible.'

'So you watched it,' she teases. 'Well, you needn't worry. And they often bring a character back when the response is good. Think of that! Next time I won't be so distant, I promise. I didn't look after you as well as I should. I apologise.'

I'd rather think of Eliza Matthews than more Faith. 'If you see Lynda,' I ask, 'can you ask her to ring me?'

'Sure — I'll track her down. Was it horrible at school today?'

'Fairly.'

'Well, they'll put out a press release soon. Then you can tell them all to go take a running jump. Gotta go, Damien says.'

'Are you all right, Vita?' I know she's in the middle of filming and therefore fired up, but she sounds like she's on speed.

'Why shouldn't I be? she says gaily. 'I'm off on Saturday. Will send a postcard. Ciao for now.'

She's right, and Lynda's right when I talk to her, and Emily's right, when she also rings to congratulate me and to say she hasn't had any news about Eliza Matthews yet. It's too early for me to get despondent, she adds. Megan's casting agency always takes its time and the tapes have to be seen by the director and producers as well.

I suddenly feel a whole lot better about going to school and to the opening night of the production. I'm a success! Maybe a tubby success, but a success even so.

The first time I go back to the gym, people look at me very strangely. I think they're wondering which gym they're in and they half expect Rata to come round the corner. Amy is beside herself to be personal trainer for a celeb. She thinks I'm just wonderful! She wonders if she can get a job on 'Shapers'. Even as an extra, it would be such fun! Could I find out who to ask?

Things have changed at home, too. We haven't done much together, the three of us, ever. One or both of them was always too busy, working nights or whatever. Besides, at my old school I was never in anything much. Now here we are sitting in the gymnasium, with *my* beautifully printed programme in our hands, and I'm almost getting used to people nudging each other, turning round and staring. In the foyer there were compliments, plenty.

Gareth needn't have worried about his show. The house is full, and the three-hour programme, as a salute to the Millennium which is now only three months away, does everything I remember people wishing it would. I see now why I haven't been able to find him for weeks: it's a huge show in a huge space, with all the lights and gigantic TV screen and surround sound that he and Sophia wanted.

Mum and Dad, because they never saw anything like it at my old school, are absolutely bowled over. They can't believe that even a school of two thousand pupils can produce so many ethnic singing and dancing groups, so many orchestras and choirs, so much talent, or that the resources are found to mount it so professionally. Superb lighting! Wonderfully engineered sound! Marvellous multimedia *X-Files* style presentation by the drama students, quite spine-chilling! 'Makes me feel very much more optimistic about the future of the planet,' says Mum, when she gets to meet Sophia at the party afterwards.

I look around for Gareth. He's surrounded by all the grade one bimbo actorpersons of the drama class, both male and female.

I want to tell him about Faith and the viewers before the press release, which I've been asked to provide quotes for, hits the papers tomorrow. I want to convince myself that there was nothing significant about his offer of tickets. Just a friendly gesture to an insignificant Year Nine who has helped in a small way.

While Mum and Dad are talking to the senior management lady, the screen of bodies around Gareth clears momentarily. It's just enough for me to get a glimpse of the tiniest, most famous body from 'Shapers', with Gareth's arm around her.

Two stick insects together, how lovely. She can fit right under his armpit.

She's seen me, standing stupidly with my parents and senior management and Mrs Tariq, who had helped coach the Indian dancers. I'm listening to Mum and Dad rave on and I'm thinking how gorgeous Mrs Tariq's sari is: a stunning turquoise, with silver borders. Real silver thread, and heavy antique jewellery to match. She makes the rest of us in our winter black look so dowdy.

I hear a scream. 'There's Tigs!' And here comes Vita in a black leather jacket, dragging Gareth, also wearing black leather, by the hand. If this wasn't a school party where the most daring drink is Blue Jeans, I could swear she was drunk. She's playing the celeb, and she's certainly high on something.

'Tiggie, darling. Introduce me to your famous Mum, please? And this is Dad, and oops sorry, Gareth, I think I *might* be talking to your school principal.' She holds out her hand almost regally. 'I'm Vita Rogers. And that was a wonderful, *wonderful* show.'

'I didn't know you two knew each other,' I say flatly, after everyone has been introduced to everyone else in the circle.

'Met two weeks ago, at a party,' says Vita, bubbling. 'Sorry, Tigs, I should have told you I was coming tonight, your school and all. Too many scenes in my head, *you* know. Aren't you *proud* of your daughter, Mrs Tompson? And I have to tell you, she gets better and better. The scene where she goes for a swim, it's so moving and sweet and she does it so well.'

'You weren't there, Vita,' I say, embarrassed enough for both of us.

'The crew told me. They all wanted to mother you. And the ratings are going through the roof. Everyone's ecstatic.'

'Vita,' I say warningly. I can see the adults eyeing her and Gareth smiling down uneasily from his great height. He's clearly smitten, but I wonder if he's caught on yet. 'She's off to Fiji on Saturday,' I announce. 'Isn't she lucky? Real holiday. Two whole weeks.'

'Yes, you wouldn't believe how well it fitted in with Holly. That's my character. Holly's just been told to take two weeks off, 'cause she's been under a lot of stress.'

'Life imitating art?' says senior management who can probably sniff out an anorexic at a hundred paces. They do this, go OTT at the most embarrassing times and places, like now.

Vita laughs, innocent, transparent and brittle as a stick of glass. 'Oh no. Why should I have any stress? I've got one of the best acting jobs in town. Mind you, I've just done an audition for an amazing project for next year. Set on a sailing ship bringing single women to New Zealand, *lots* of marvellous female parts. Parts to die for.'

'I thought . . .'

Everyone is looking at me. It's supposed to be confidential, Vita, and if you're going for Eliza Matthews, why didn't Emily tell me and if you get it I'll kill you.

'Don't tell me you've done one too,' she says, smiling. 'You sly old thing. Don't tell me it's . . .'

'I'm not telling you anything, Vita,' I say as lightheartedly as I can with four adults listening to all this. 'You wouldn't believe how hard Vita works out at "Shapers". Fourteen scenes a day, sometimes. How many have you got tomorrow?'

'Tomorrow? Ummm, oh twelve, I think. Can't remember.' There's a flicker of the professional Vita, but even this she turns into a performance. 'Suppose I ought to be getting home. Lines to learn. Beauty sleep to get.' She smooths her lovely hair. 'God, it's nearly midnight. Gareth, I'll just slip away, into the night.'

'I'll see you to your car.'

'No, don't bother. Goodnight, everyone.'

Gareth is going with her nonetheless. Will he kiss her goodnight down in the carpark?

'Have you auditioned for something?' says Mum on the way home, the windscreen wipers on the wagon going flat out.

'No,' I say, feeling terrible, but since I blew it and I won't get a callback, why worry them? They just don't need to know what is, in fact, a non-event. 'Vita's mind works so fast, she gets it wrong sometimes.'

After a pause, she says, 'If I was Vita's mother, I'd be worried about that girl. She's manic. What do her folks do?'

'Father's a sort of architectural draughtsman. Mother works for a charity. She lives at home, but I don't think she ever sees them. It's like a motel.'

'Is she anorexic?'

'Yes, I think she is,' I hear myself saying. I'm sick of covering for her. 'Emily knows.'

And good luck Gareth, I hear myself thinking, nastily.

By lunchtime the next day I can't bear it any longer.

I ring Emily, which I'd sworn not to do. Still no news. It's looking less hopeful, she admits. Oh by the way, I ask, did Vita audition for a part too? I hadn't seen her much lately. There's a slight pause, and then she tells me kindly that she has to maintain a professional and quite separate discretion for each and every one of her actors. Vita would tell me if she so wished. But she knew I would understand why she herself could neither confirm nor deny.

'Is Vita all right,' I ask. She says investigations are proceeding as to the best course of action. 'That's good,' I say.

I can see her fingering her pearls as she reproves me for interfering.

Near the end of school there's something else I can't bear any more. I mumble something to Mrs Tariq about a dentist appointment, sorry I haven't brought a note, but I've had toothache all day and it was the only appointment Mum could get for me. She lets me go.

I'm in luck. I find Gareth alone in the big empty gymnasium, wearing black jeans and a cellphone, sweeping down the floor with a huge broom.

'Don't you get a slave or slaves to do that?' I say.

'I enjoy doing it. It's relaxing and gives me time to think. And I like to know my performers have a nice clean stage, nothing to slip or fall on.'

'I want to talk to you.'

'Okay. Just walk up and down. Better, get another broom. They're over there.'

Together we cut quite a swathe through the debris of last night's performance. There are empty balloons and tangled streamers, shells and pieces of straw and sequins that have dropped off costumes. Hats and necklaces that someone will want. It's amazing how much a high energy three-hour performance leaves behind on a stage.

It's a funny sort of togetherness, two brooms.

'Has Vita told you why she's going to Fiji?' I ask.

'Not really. Her Mum won a prize, or something.'

'She expects you to believe that? A holiday so soon after the show started?'

'I don't know her well enough to disbelieve her. We only met two weeks ago. I've been so busy, last night was the first . . .'

'Date?'

He laughs. 'I just asked her to come to my show. Actors do that.'

'Okay, try this for size. She's anorexic, and she's getting worse. Her agent, who's also mine, says that she's been given a warning. Writing her out for two weeks is the warning. Maybe she's not going to Fiji at all. Maybe she's being put into hospital. That's what they do, to stop them dying. Maybe she's being written out for good, but they're not telling her.'

His broom is stopped and he's staring at me.

'Are you sure?'

'No, I'm not *sure*. She got very shitty the only time I tried to talk about it with her. But I've been in a class with four bulimics and two anorexics and a whole bunch of others heading that way. Or the other.'

'What other?'

'Shit, Gareth, use your eyes. How do you think I got like this?'

I bend over the broom and start walking again, furiously pushing the shells and sequins before me. 'She's got one problem, I've got the other. You haven't got either, so you'll never understand.'

'You seem to be coping quite effectively with yours,' he says calmly.

'Bloody hell, Gareth,' I shout, standing upright again. 'Forget me. I'm a fat blob and later on I'll have heart problems and get diabetes, but Vita's fucking *dying*. Very publicly, right here and now, night after night on "Shapers", *dying*. Can you think of anything more ironic, in a soap set in a gym, all about fitness, that no one seems to have noticed?'

He catches up with me. 'I suppose we've all got used to the emaciated Miss Kate Moss. Those skinny wee arms . . .'

'I couldn't give a stuff about Kate Moss,' I shout. 'But I do care about Vita. If it wasn't for her, I'd never have got the chance . . .'

'She did tell me she'd met you at Rowan Hughes' acting classes.'

'She *knows* that I know,' I insist. 'She tried to buy me off with flowers when I noticed her scales under her bed. And all you can do is stand there and make *stupid* comments.'

He starts pushing his broom again. 'I'm just trying to get my head around it. I don't know much about anorexia. You say her agent knows. Surely they're talking to her parents?'

'I don't *know.*' I'm standing in the middle of this great gym, almost crying with frustration, my voice rising as the distance between us grows. 'And all right, it's probably none of our bloody business, except that I owe her something and she might be thinking of you as the promising new man in her life 'cause she got rid of the last one, an actor who took her for a ride and dumped her. Doesn't that count for *anything*?'

You wouldn't read about it in a book, but the cellphone hooked into his belt goes. The timing is spooky, although I do think some things don't just happen by accident.

'It's Vita,' he says. I drop the broom. The expression on his face spells out that we're too late. He mutters as he listens; she's obviously giving him a long and weepy monologue.

'I gave her this number last night,' he says when they have finished. 'She's being written out of the show for good. Fired. She fainted twice on the set this morning . . .'

'No food does that to you.'

'The second time onto a treadmill machine . . . it was a gym scene . . . her hair . . .'

'Oh *shit.*'

'. . . they called a doc, who sent her off to A & E for seven stiches in her leg and skin-grafting later and told them she's incapable of work and she's got to get serious about seeking counselling and medical help. The shit's hit the fan, big-time. They've got to rewrite all her scenes for the next seven weeks, bring in the writers over the weekend, create another character, redo all the schedules which she says is a major. She thinks they're going to sue her, something about concealing a known medical condition.'

He's dialling for a taxi. 'We've just got time to get out and back before the show. It's Mt Eden, isn't it?'

'Valley Road. How much hair did she lose?'

'She didn't say. I'd say that sounds ominous.' He stands there, thoughtful. 'Tiggie, I feel a bit of a fraud. There was nothing . . . happening.'

'None of my business . . .'

'It's you she wants to see. She asked me to track you down. Do you want me to come with you?'

Forgive me, Vita, but coming to see you gives me a chance to spend a little time in a taxi with him. I'm only human too.

Twenty-three

I EXPECTED TO FIND HER BETWEEN THE BLACK SATIN SHEETS, WITH HER mother playing nurse, but Vita's one tough cookie and she's sitting in the living room with her bandaged leg up on a stool, watching the children's programmes, and smoking. Gareth and I perch on the sofa and wonder what's under the dressing that covers most of her head.

'Which is your favourite, Tigs? Tinky Winky, Dipsy, La-la or Po? I fancy Po myself.'

'None of them. I'd send them all off on a one-way ticket to outer space, if it was me.'

She mutes the Teletubbies, but we all continue to watch.

'Do you know that tallest one is about two metres tall?' she says. 'They're actually huge. The actors can only spend about ten minutes inside before they're absolutely dripping with sweat and running out of air. They should get danger money. I suppose they'd rather be doing a Shakespeare, given the choice. Why do we do it, Tigs? Why does anyone do it?'

'I don't know. I have really no idea. Something to do with showing off, playing games, wanting to tell a story, enjoying the sound of your own voice? It's a great mystery. Vita, did you audition for Eliza Matthews?'

'Who's she?'

'One of the girls on that sailing ship. Supposed to be *confidential*? Eliza's the one that has the baby and then becomes the stroppy leader of the group. Well,' I say, watching her face and relaxing, 'if you don't know, it wasn't her.'

'God no. Doesn't sound like me. I get the bubbly roles, the space cadets. No, they wanted *me* to audition for some 12-year-old that gets raped. It's a pretty rugged scene, not much left to the imagination, and they didn't want to put a real 12-year-old through it. So they went for the midgets. The nearly-women in the little girls' bodies.'

'Have you heard?'

'No. And I'm not holding my breath. Did you audition for Eliza what's-her-name?'

'Matthews. Yes, I did.'

'I'm glad. Well, we're both waiting. Actors have to get good at waiting.' She finds a new position for her bandaged leg. 'Sorry I'm such a bore, I'm full of painkillers . . .'

This is where it gets difficult, because I'm thinking she might never work as an actor again. It's a worst-case scenario I don't even want to think about. She points the remote and the screen goes black.

'Tigs, I can read you like a book,' she says sadly. 'I know I've become a bit of a bad risk. I won't get soap work again, but Emily says I might on feature films, where you're only in for a few weeks. Do some modelling, later, when . . . And I'd *love* to do stage.'

'You've got to let people help you get better,' I hear myself say. 'Stop trying to save the world, get people like me jobs, please everyone.'

'I don't do that,' she says indignantly.

'Yes you do. Remember that first class at Rowan's, you were running round getting me a chair to sit on? I was so *embarrassed* I wanted to kill you. People out at "Shapers" thought you were marvellous, always trying to be helpful.'

'Did they?' She seems genuinely surprised. 'I was just being me.'

'You made a special point of coming in early, being there for my first scene. I'll never forget that. Please do *everything* the doctors and counsellors ask you to.'

She stubs out her cigarette in an ashtray full of butts. 'It's funny, to think I haven't got a job, can't go back to school, haven't got the bursaries and stuff to go to university. Pretty useless, really. Go on the dole. Do some sort of a course. Computers. Everyone's into computers.'

'I'm going to be making short films next year, at varsity,' says Gareth, finding his voice and no doubt trying to be helpful. 'I'll . . .'

'Don't say, I'll keep you in mind,' she says acidly. 'If all the wannabee directors I've ever heard say that had kept their word, I might be New Zealand's answer to Winona Ryder by now . . .'

She closes her eyes, which seems like a signal that she's had enough and we should go.

'There's no need to hang about,' she says, her voice slowing. 'Mum'll be back any minute. She just nipped out to buy food. They had to drag her away from work. Don't worry, I'll be fine. And in case you're wondering, I lost about a third of my hair on that fucking machine before someone hit the stop button. It'll grow back.'

Gareth and I look at each other. I think he's got tears in his eyes. I know I have.

'Haven't you got a show to do, Gareth?' she says. 'God, it was wonderful . . . And good luck with Eliza what's-her-name . . . Just a pretty face, at the end of the day . . .'

She seems to drift off to sleep. Without even discussing it, Gareth and I look at our watches, calculate how long we've got and sit with her until we hear a car in the driveway. We slip out the front door as her mother comes in the back. I can hear the rustle of supermarket bags.

I don't want to meet her, because I don't know or understand how she could live in the same house as her daughter and not do something.

In the taxi Gareth holds my hand. Maybe it's because he's as shook up as I am and just wants any old comforting hand to hold, but he's holding it, nonetheless, all the way through the Friday traffic and right back to school for the second show.

It's all too much for one day.

When I get back home, there's a note on the kitchen bench to say that Mum and Dad have gone to have another look at a really promising house, also shopping for her fortieth birthday present, may not be back until late – and a message on the answerphone from Emily. Ring her a.s.a.p. Interesting developments. If I can't get her tonight, because she may go to the movies, come round first thing in the morning after 8 am.

It's not *sorry, you missed out, no callback, end of sailing ship dream.* Interesting developments and she is *out?*

I have to wait a whole night? A whole fourteen *hours?* What am I going to do for fourteen hours? Catch a bus to do forty minutes cardio at the gym, watch another of my episodes on 'Shapers', walk round to school to catch the second half of the second show (and possibly see Gareth at the same time), clean my room, which has got a bit out of control lately? It's amazing what you'll do to pass the time when you're on tenterhooks – I did them all, in that order, collapsing into bed only shortly before Mum and Dad got home.

They came in to say goodnight. 'Give me a big hug,' says Mum dramatically, smelling of her new perfume and restaurants. 'My last night, my last few minutes of being 39. I will *never* be 39 again!'

'What did Dad buy you?'

'A new house, I think. It's in Mission Bay. You won't have to move school.'

'Good. I meant a present for just *you.*'

'This.' On her right hand is a beautiful greenstone ring. 'Isn't that fabulous? And we've made a time to show you the house in the morning. We want you to say you like it before we put in an offer.'

'What time?'

'Eight-thirty.'

'Could it be a bit later?'

'The land agent says he's got someone else sniffing around. I know it's probably bullshit, but we really like this house. All right? And then Dad wants to take us to brunch afterwards.'

It's her fortieth. Birthday girl makes the rules. Aaaaargh.

I take most of the night to go to sleep. I have this nice mental picture of Sophia and Gareth and all five hundred performers getting a standing ovation at the show, though I didn't see him afterwards. I hug to myself the satisfaction of watching 'Shapers' earlier – it was the binge scene, and yes, Lynda had been right, I hadn't stuffed it up at all. All the problems I'd had with just getting through the scene had translated into Faith's unhappiness, into her finally coming clean about her father's treatment of her. Faith almost had *me* in tears! Not bad at all. Yes, I can watch myself quite critically now. It's an interesting development.

I really like the house. It's not a wooden villa, because Dad says he doesn't want to go back to continual painting and upkeep, but a five-year-old low-maintenance townhouse down a right-of-way, built mostly around a small swimming pool. 'Fabulous indoor-outdoor living,' gushes the agent in her houndstooth check suit. There's a garden area behind for Dad to grow veges, and absolutely no problem about me having a dog. Upstairs are three bedrooms and an extra lounge which the agent sees as my very own space for entertaining my friends and playing my CDs without disturbing my parents below too much. Absolutely essential for today's teens to have their very *own* space.

'Take it,' I say, thinking of Emily. 'Love it, Mum. I'd rather have a pool than a view any day. Happy birthday!'

At brunch, over hash browns and eggs Benedict, I use Dad's cellphone to tell Emily I'll be around just after lunch. Been buying a house and detained at Mother's birthday brunch party. She's forty and *hating* it. Emily tells me it was her fiftieth that got to her. She'll expect me around 1 pm.

By the time I'm sitting on the red couch looking expectantly at Emily I'm nearly screaming. It's been eighteen hours! I know it's something good because of her body language, her welcoming smile and Jessie's especially enthusiastic welcome. Dogs always know the vibes.

'I had a ring from Vita's mother this morning,' she starts off. 'She's coming round to accepting that Vita may have to go into hospital, to stabilise her condition and give her a chance at recovery. It seems that she's been battling it for at least two years, poor child. I really had no idea.'

'People don't,' I say. 'What will the papers say about her?'

''Shapers' want it hushed up, which is hardly surprising, but Vita says that's dishonest and impossible, and her mother says she's rather keen for me to put out a brief press statement. Just that she's been diagnosed as anorexic and is undergoing treatment and counselling. Later, she wants to get some public debate going, to raise public awareness and help others.'

'Sounds like Vita.'

'I'm going round this afternoon to talk to them both. Now, what about the surprising Miss Antigone Tompson? What are we going to do with her?'

'Why surprising?'

'Well, you're in a bit of a fix, my dear. You've got a callback for Eliza Matthews and "Shapers" wants you too. For six months.'

I stare at her, my mind leaping and racing. Can I do both? Or either? Are my parents going to start talking about putting my schooling first, which means neither but just boring old School Certificate? Doing Faith was a brief interlude, but any more would . . .

'It's an uncommon dilemma, in my experience,' says Emily, 'complicated by the unusual conditions of the "Shapers" offer. The Eliza callback is quite straightforward − another audition, doing both scenes this time, and maybe some improvs. Whatever you decide, I think you should do this one, if only for the practice. You'll remember that shooting isn't until next year, so you've time in hand.'

She picks up some reading glasses and scans a fax. It has the 'Shapers' letterhead.

'The offer from Edwina is certainly unusual. Your first contract stipulated that you should remain the same weight. You fulfilled that contract.' She looks at me over the top of her glasses. 'Only just, I have to say. Ten pounds? Fifteen?'

'Thirteen,' I say, my heart singing.

'The storyliners want to bring the original chubby Faith back from Australia, after the death of her father. She comes back to the gym of her own accord and is given work there. It's undecided yet, but possibly as a receptionist. Her storyline will run for maybe six months.'

'You are joking,' I say, thinking of the departed Holly.

'No, I'm not, and neither are they. The public loved Faith, Tiggie. The response to her has been almost unprecedented. As your own fan mail has no doubt reinforced.'

That's true. Large bundles have been sent to me regularly these past weeks, along with special postcards with my picture and a thank you message printed so that all I have to do is sign them.

'Do you have any problem with committing yourself to remaining the weight you are now? Or putting some on, if required. For a period?'

I think immediately of Hollywood stars who've gone up and down the scales for special parts. The implications of what she's saying are too much for me. 'I . . . I just . . . I can't answer that. Not straight off. I'm . . .'

'Overwhelmed,' she says kindly. 'Of course. It's a big ask, and you don't have to decide now. "Shapers" have given us a week to get back to them. The Eliza callback is the first priority. Can you manage that?'

'I'll need another script,' I say. 'I forgot to take it first time round, and I think I threw it away when I got back.'

'Because you imagined that would be the end of it?' she says shrewdly, getting up and opening one of the files. 'My dear Tiggie, you need to have more confidence in your ability.'

I take the script she offers. 'Emily, I know it's not . . . but please tell me . . . did Vita get a callback? She told me she auditioned . . .'

'Oh yes, she did,' Emily says without hesitating, 'but she very wisely withdrew as of this morning. I should never have sent her for that part.' Her voice, usually so calm and precise, cracks slightly. 'It was . . . a major error of judgement. As I understand it, and I understand very little, anorexia is about young people who don't know how to grow up, a loss of self. The last thing . . .'

I think we are both relieved when Jessie, spying a large white cat outside the French doors of the office, creates a helter-skelter diversion. Soon after I'm on my way home and she is getting in the car to go to Mt Eden. She hadn't mentioned my parents, and I don't want to involve them either, yet.

You have some hard thinking to do, Antigone Tompson.

Faith, Eliza — both or neither?

Something happened at Mum's fortieth party that sort of made up my mind for me, though I wasn't aware of it until later.

Dad had been determined to make it a fabulous party, even more after she lost her job. He'd arranged with the restaurant to have it decorated as a Third Millennium space-age theme, all gold and silver, and the guests had been asked to come in gold or silver or spacey costumes. Mum and Dad themselves had been to a fancy dress place and hired slinky silver suits and since they've both got pretty good figures for their age and they'd had a bit of fun with the silver eye-shadow and Dr Spock eyebrows, they looked fabulous. Mum had hired me a long gold dress with a gold and black figure-concealing cloak. Interestingly, it was rather looser now than when I tried it on a month ago. She helped me do my hair in Princess Leah buns.

We arrived before any of the guests. 'Dear God, Murray,' said Mum, when she saw the decorations. 'You'll be getting us in the gossip columns! Out-of-work television star spends up large.' But she was pleased, I could tell. The restaurant people were falling over themselves for this glamorous party with lots of television people coming – about ninety, actually. Soon the place was full and humming and Mum had a whole heap of presents on one table; lots of bottles of French champagne.

I knew some of the guests – people who'd come to dinner parties where I'd been introduced before I scuttled off to bed. Some of them were quite famous faces, or big executive names in the television world. I asked Dad to tell me which one was Tom, who'd fired Mum, so that I could ignore him. But Tom wasn't about to ignore me.

'My dear Cassie,' I heard a booming voice just behind me, over the noise. 'I do so want to meet your actor daughter. I thought she was just fabulous in "Shapers". My wife cried, and my daughters cried and even this hardened old body felt a twinge or two. Where is she?'

'Tiggie?' called Mum. I got introduced to a big man with a very tiny and very much younger wife, both in gold glittery suits and top hats. He didn't shake my hand, he lent forward and kissed it and I disliked him on sight.

'Cassie,' he drawled, his accent just ever so slightly fake American, 'you didn't tell me you'd bred a beauty. I see now how fine her acting was as Faith. Even though they did their best to make her plain, in those appalling clothes. The little storyline of young Faith and her struggles with her unseen father was most effective. Female viewers became indignant. Female viewers became more numerous. The ratings went up. We always cheer when the ratings go up, don't we, Cassie?'

'We do, Tom,' said my mother warmly. 'To the exclusion of all taste and decency, all minority interest groups, all self-respect and any remaining pretence at integrity. Let the ratings go up. Let the advertisers be happy. Let the country rot in hell. Murray, where are you?' she called out suddenly, extracting herself from Tom's grip. 'I think it's time to eat.'

Tom kept his hold on my arm. 'I hope we'll see more of Faith. I thought you exceptionally brave. Though you absolutely *must* not lose any more weight. A little bird has told me they want you back,' he breathed in my ear before Dad swooped in on the circle and escorted me and Mum off to the buffet.

'I'm glad you don't work for *him* any more,' I said.

But Big Tom did me a favour. I knew as soon as he started talking about 'Shapers' that there was no way I was going to be tempted, by money or great scenes or the promise of more instant fame, into going back.

Which leaves me with Eliza – or nothing.

Twenty-four

Since the last night of the production is Saturday, and my audition is after school Tuesday, on Monday I take up Gareth's long-standing offer of help.

After we've done my two Eliza scenes about every which way we can think of, looked for every possible new idea and interrupted thought, and analysed every action and every beat, I tell him about the 'Shapers' offer. Does he think I'm doing the right thing, turning it down? We could do with the money, I say, thinking I'm sounding awfully like Vita. It could be six months work; my parents are having cashflow problems as they're tying up the deal on the apartment and the new house. There won't be as much money as they thought to invest for their retirement nest-egg.

'Your Mum's only forty,' he protests. He's sitting in the lotus position, both feet tucked somewhere up against his navel, his bony knees sticking out. 'She'll get another job soon. She's too good not to.'

'Yes, but I heard from Emily today that I could start at "Shapers" in five weeks. I've got to let them know by Friday.'

What do *you* want, he asks.

To have you kiss me, I think. To play a role because I'm a good actor, not a good fat actor. To be allowed to continue to lose a bit of weight, without even trying, instead of having to keep it on or worse, go back up again. To play stroppy Eliza because I'm just stroppy me and I don't want anyone ever again telling me I'm 'exceptionally brave'.

'Get Eliza,' I say.

'If you want it badly enough, you will,' he says. The miracle of a kiss doesn't happen, and probably never will, but I do get the warmest possible bear hug between friends before we leave the drama suite where my acting career started by needing a pee.

I don't know what happens or goes wrong, but the audition feels like a disaster.

First off, there are two other girls in the scruffy waiting room, and though they're both stick insects in boots, it's quite clear they're possible Eliza types. We look each other up and down, and one of them says, 'You were Faith, have you been going to Weight Watchers or Jenny Craig's?' 'Neither,' I say, 'they padded me up for "Shapers", it was a body suit, so clever no one picked it. I had wads of cotton wool in my cheeks, too.' I think she even believes me. The other one sniggers. In an Australian accent she tells us she has flown in from Perth. The girl in there already and nearly finished is from Adelaide, no less!

Then I have to listen to both her and the other girl doing the scenes. You can't hear everything from the audition room, but you can hear enough through the walls to know that they're good, really, really good and they are being put through the hoops. These are the final callbacks and Emily has told me that she thinks there are five. Thank goodness I'm again last for the day and the sour lady in black tights has been replaced by a granny who fusses over the clipboard we have to fill in and tells us where to go for a pee and get a drink of water if we need it.

I hear someone singing. Don't ask me to sing. Perhaps they're auditioning for other parts, after all. They must be. No one has said anything about *singing*. If I have to sing, Emily, I'll *kill* you.

When my turn comes, I've been there an hour later than my call time and I'm exhausted with waiting and nerves. Nearly bald Megan and the big unshaven man take me through the scenes, the rape scene with the captain and the second scene where he's the matron accusing me of being a foul-mouthed slut.

Maybe he's tired after doing this five times over, but somehow there isn't the same spark as last time. Maybe I'm trying too hard. I'm tense, unfocused, not centred, all those things that worried Rowan. Maybe I'm

195

still really undecided deep down about 'Shapers', because let's face it, this is a long shot. Maybe I am still too big and they've already decided that they want their Eliza to have a waist no bigger than Kate Winslett in *Titanic*.

Then Megan throws me by insisting that I try the rape scene in an English accent. I'd done this with Gareth and felt bloody stupid, even when he got out some old tapes of Shakespeare by famous English actors. They sounded so pure, so perfect, but even if Eliza did come from an upper-crust home, she was never going to sound like that when she was having a go at the captain. So I stumble along, hearing these odd sounds come out of my mouth, knowing that I'm making a mighty fool of myself, even when Megan asks me to imitate her with three or four lines. 'You've got a good ear, which is the first requirement,' she says. 'It wouldn't be a problem for you.'

I have two more ordeals. For the first, Megan asks me to forget the script but imagine a scene in which Eliza is trying to tell her pompous and patronising father that she's been raped by her uncle and she's pregnant. Such a scene doesn't occur in the film, she says, but let's role-play one. Oh God, I think, theatresports – that is where I've seen this big guy's face. He does it on television. He's brilliant. He waits for me to start and I say the first thing which comes into my head which is, 'I need to talk to you.' From this rather feeble beginning, it gets very heated, as 'father' resists every argument, every shred of evidence about his older brother that I dream up. The uncle, in my mind, becomes Big Tom, breathing into my earhole; to my father, Uncle is a pillar of the church, beyond reproach. After several minutes of this, Father orders Eliza from the room, and she says that if he refuses to believe her, she'll leave the house and never come back. Father laughs and taunts her about her lack of money – 'Cut,' says Megan. 'Excellent, Tiggie.'

It wasn't excellent, it was crap.

The worst ordeal she keeps till last. I have to sing. *Sing*, I say stupidly, resisting an urge to run for the door. Anything you like, she says. Eliza has a couple of singing scenes, a lullaby over her dead baby and a rousing number leading a chorus a bit like Nancy in *Oliver*. I ask her why I wasn't told I'd have to sing, because I really didn't want to scupper my chances by doing it badly. She says all actors, even with untrained voices, should be able to sing on demand and please would I give her just a small sample.

It's the absolute original classic lose/lose situation. I can't think of a single thing to sing. I just stand there getting redder and redder. Eventually, the big man takes pity on me and starts suggesting songs I might know. I don't know the words of any of them. Nursery rhymes? Most of them were of eighteen or nineteenth century British origin. Well, yes, and in sheer desperation I pull one of nowhere and start singing, getting louder and louder as I get more and more embarrassed at my pathetic choice of song, and my pathetic honking voice. There's no music or musicians in *our* family!

London bridge is falling down,
Falling down, falling down,
London bridge is falling down
My fair lady.

I'm about through to the fourth verse when she stops me and asks me to sing it very quietly as for a lullaby. Then I sing it very raucously as if I was at a very noisy party and had had too much vodka. By this time I'm in tears. The party version has a brief angry life and then, like a firework, fizzles and fades out.

'Sorry,' I hear myself pleading, 'I've never sung solo to anyone before. I've never been in any choirs or anything.'

'You've got a good ear,' says Megan soothingly. 'You can hold a tune, that's what we wanted to know.'

I'm utterly exposed and have nowhere to go.

'Can I leave now?'

'Yes, thank you for your time, Tiggie. I'm sorry we kept you waiting so long out there.' Then, as before, 'Your agent will be in touch.'

On Thursday I tell Emily that I'm turning down 'Shapers'.

She asks if I've discussed it with my parents and I say no, I don't need to, this is my decision. She asks if I could be persuaded if they came back with an offer of more money. I say no again. She asks if she can talk to my parents and I say no, no point.

So how am I feeling about the Eliza audition? I say I blew it, stuffed it up. The scenes were awful, the improv was awful, my English accent was terrible and the singing was just the most horrendous thing I've done in my entire life.

A small disappointed sigh comes down the telephone. Maybe it wasn't so bad. Oh yes, it was. Am I absolutely sure about 'Shapers', she asks again. Such opportunities do not grow on trees. She would ask for more money. I'm mean enough to think that she's sighing for her lost commission, which for six months' work would have been something. She's just lost Vita's commission, which must have been quite nice for more than two years.

She tries again. You realise what you're doing. Eliza is a very long shot — I know that, I say. Work on 'Shapers' would have given me a very solid professional base, both in terms of profile and experience. I stand to lose everything.

I know.

It might be a while before a suitable part came along . . .

'Emily,' I cry down the phone. 'I know all that! I just . . . No one *wants* to *stay* fat if they've got the choice and what I've got now, what I've never had before, is the *choice*.'

A week later I've not heard back from Emily and I've given up hoping. It's a Saturday and my last day of being fourteen. We're moving in two weeks, and as soon as possible I'm getting Brunhilde Two. A Labrador cross, which is a nice way of saying a mongrel. She's golden brown, with floppy huge paws, currently one of a litter of six tiny bundles snuggling up to her mum's milkbar.

The city's in an uproar. We've just had every world leader you can think of here for a conference up at the Museum. The America's Cup races start next month. The harbour is full of boats practising and of visiting super yachts, moored in every nook and cranny and spare bit of water they can find. No one goes anywhere in the rush-hour traffic if they can avoid it. If they can't avoid it, they don't go anywhere either because they get gridlocked.

It's like a great big party and all I can think of are the two chances I had, the one I've thrown away and the other that's going to be given to some other girl. The one from Perth, from what I could hear through the wooden walls. She must have been good to have been flown that far just for an audition. They wouldn't have spent all that money unless she was very good and almost certain to get it. She was beautiful, too. And a size ten.

Because Mum and Dad are sorting things in preparation for the packers – I've done my stuff – I tell them I'm going to the gym and then for a bike ride. I've got a bike! It's second-hand and I adore it and I don't wobble any more. 'Off you go,' says Mum, harassed. 'Mind all that traffic.'

I ask Dad if I can borrow his cellphone, on the very slight chance that Emily will ring. If there's a call for me, would he to be *certain* to put it through. *Promise*! 'A boy?' he asks, slyly. 'Maybe,' I say, though I don't expect Gareth to ring. He's got bursary exams in a few weeks and he's gone into hiding. I know Dad would like it to be a boy.

Gym is just gym, rather crowded. I've decided I quite like being recognised.

Being a spring Saturday morning, the waterfront road from Mission Bay to the city is full of traffic and people out walking, riding, rollerblading. I have the whole day. What I love about my bike is how far you can get in quite a short space of time. Before I know where I am, I've passed the Coastguard and the red iron fences of the port area and the Ferry Building and am outside the Maritime Museum.

It reminds me of Eliza. I've been once before with my old school, to look at the photos and models of sailing ships and cargo ships. Then, along with all my classmates, I thought it was dead boring. Now, because I've read some books and some stories about the single women who were shipped out to New Zealand, I can start to think what it might have been like for her, in her long skirts, cooped up on a ship, pregnant, having her baby, seeing it slide overboard in a tiny sack, standing up to the officers, standing in the captain's cabin telling him the first mate was a pig.

I wander past the Polynesian canoes, the famous racing dinghies, the vintage boats moored in the basin outside, the histories of the America's Cup.

In the section about the sailing ships and the people and cargo they brought to New Zealand a hundred years ago, there's a little room which is set up like the gloomy interior of a sailing ship and rocks to and fro. It's dark and stuffy, full of primary school boys being stupid. I'm feeling instantly seasick and at the same time my cellphone goes off.

I push my way through to the exit, trying to get it out of my jeans back pocket, cursing the safety helmet I'm carrying and the people who won't get out of my road, and the man who is burbling something about the midday gun over the loudspeaker. Then I can't remember which button to push and I press the wrong one and it stops.

I need some fresh air and I need this person to ring again. Dad wouldn't have put them through, if it wasn't for me. I can't remember Emily's number. Should I ring 018 and ask for Emily Chatwin Agency?

It goes again. I'm ready for it this time, leaning over the rail above the water looking down at the cannon and not registering anything at all. The answer will be sorry, no, got to the last two, the girl from Perth . . .

'Hullo?'

'Emily here, Tiggie.'

The gun goes off. Midday. I swear I leap a mile into the air. The bang echoes around the basin and all the seagulls rise squawking, flapping their wings in protest.

People do drop things in astonishment and shock. My safety helmet, hoisted onto my shoulder, slides down my arm and in scrabbling around to keep myself together I drop the cellphone into the water. It sinks like a stone, without trace. Gone.

'Can you tell me where there's a callbox?'

'Over there. You need a card.'

I haven't got a card. I buy one. There's a young guy with dreadlocks talking on the phone. He talks and talks and talks, even though he can see me standing there. If I go away, looking for another, he'll stop, just like buses come as soon as you've decided to walk and you're halfway between stops.

'Excuse me,' I say eventually, politely. 'You've had ten minutes.'

He ignores me. His whole body language is hostile, telling me to piss off. Eventually I ask the girl at the desk for a piece of paper and a pencil and am just writing him a rude note when he puts the phone down and slouches off.

'Sure you're finished?' I hear myself saying. 'Don't want to ring Alaska?'

I can't see the number in the phone book because my hands are trembling so much, from the shock of the gun as much as anything else. Dad will kill me for drowning his cellphone.

'Emily Chatwin.'

'It's me, Tiggie.'

'Dear God, child! It sounded like someone had shot you at close quarters! Then your phone went dead. I've been trying to get the police. And your parents aren't answering the phone either.'

'It was the cannon.'

'What cannon? Where are you? Just a minute, they're on the other line, I'll get rid of them. Don't go away.'

Don't go away! Some tinkling piano comes over the phone. The numbers in the display box tick downwards as my credit disappears.

Centuries pass.

'Tiggie. Sorry about that. Where are you?'

'At the Maritime Museum. I dropped the cellphone in the water.'

'You're at the Museum?'

'Yes.'

'Looking at the sailing ships? The models? The photos?'

'Yes.'

'Well, that's good, because I have some rather nice nautical news to give you.'

I pedal slowly home, trying to decide who I shall tell first. Maybe Vita, who's in a special ward in Auckland Hospital, but still has her cellphone. We've talked occasionally. Maybe drag Gareth away from his books?

Sorry, girls from Perth and Adelaide. It's me who's going to be Eliza.

Emily is talking to Mum and Dad first, before I get home. Easing the slips, she says.

The harbour has never looked more beautiful. My bike wheels are not touching the ground. All the children are angels. Everyone is smiling. People don't recognise me at a quick glance, because while Faith might still be seen on Channel Three some nights, the real Faith has gone forever.

Before I pedal back up the hill, I stop and buy a chocolate gelato. Old habits die hard. Gelato is full of sugar and fattening! And then I think, I've done an hour's cardio and I've biked for about five ks, I deserve a treat. Move over, guilts, and don't come back. It's the best chocolate gelato I've ever tasted, without a doubt.

Two sailing ships are leaving the harbour. One is black, with three masts and the other pure white, with two. All their sails are set and they are so beautiful and life is so beautiful that I'm in tears as I watch them come close enough to see the people on board. I'll sail on one of those, in real life, play at life for real. Watch me.

I decide not to take the lift up to the apartment. I walk these days, and enjoy the puffing. Enjoy too not puffing so much as I did even a month ago.

Mum and Dad are sitting out on the patio, eating lunch in the sunshine and watching the ships go out. There's an unopened bottle of champagne on the table. They turn around and look at me and Dad picks up the champagne and I know they've heard about my early birthday present and it's going to be okay.

'Hi,' I say, feeling embarrassed, victorious, proud, shy, every cell of me alive.

Dad, who's an expert, eases open the champagne. Even so there's a big bang that reminds me of the cannon. He pours three frothing glasses.

'Well,' he says. 'Seems like your birthday has already started.'

'Down the hatch!' says Mum, holding up her glass. 'We salute you, Antigone. It sounds like a part to die for.'

'It is.'

'Happy birthday – to a daughter we are so *proud* of.'

'Love you too, Mum.'

'The people from the kennels rang,' says Dad. 'We can go and pick up Brunhilde later today, if we want? We're not supposed to have dogs here, but I'm sure we can smuggle her in. I suppose that's a silly question . . .?'